# RAVEN'S GOLD

Jane Ashby's pleasant life in the city comes to an abrupt end when her father and brother decide to take up gold prospecting and she is forced to relocate with them to a small, remote gold field. And when one of the settlers takes her off by force to save her from a night in the bush she resents being made prisoner on his farm. Can Jane come to terms with this uncivilised country and become a settler's wife?

# RAVEN'S GOLD

# RAVEN'S GOLD

*by*

Ann Cliff

**Magna Large Print Books**
Long Preston, North Yorkshire,
BD23 4ND, England.

British Library Cataloguing in Publication Data.

Cliff, Ann
 Raven's gold.

 A catalogue record of this book is
 available from the British Library

 ISBN 978-0-7505-3868-8

First published in Great Britain in 2013 by
Robert Hale Limited

Published in Large Print 2014 by arrangement with
Robert Hale Limited

Magna Large Print is an imprint of Library Magna Books Ltd.

Printed and bound in Great Britain by
T.J. (International) Ltd., Cornwall, PL28 8RW

# ONE

*Bendigo, Australia. 1887*

'Janey, do look at that tall man with the big black beard. Doesn't he make you shiver? Sinister, I would call him.' Susan Brown gave a small trill of laughter. 'He looks like – like a bushranger!'

Jane smiled, smoothing her blue dress. Susan was a good friend, but she did have a tendency to giggle at the wrong moment.

'He's a friend of my brother's ... he comes from Gippsland. Goodness, they're coming over, you're going to have to talk to him.' Susan was right, he looked odd, but they had to be sociable.

Her brother made the introductions and the sinister individual nodded distantly. You couldn't see his face for the beard and Jane thought that you probably wouldn't want to. He must have spots, or a weak chin, to wear so much hair on his face. Father's neat grey beard was totally different of course, quite civilised.

'Evening, Miss Ashby, Miss Brown.' The man stood there looking down from a great height at the girls. 'Garth showed me ... your drawings, Miss Ashby. You have ... talent.' He spoke hesitantly and said no more. Come to think of it, he would fit in very well with a posse of bushrangers, intent on robbery under arms. Ned Kelly had been hanged five years ago, but there were still a few roving criminals about and they probably all looked like this Angus Duncan and spoke in his deep voice.

Jane smiled her thanks. 'I enjoy drawing.'

After an awkward silence, Susan moved away. 'We must find our seats, the concert's due to start soon.

Jane had heard from her brother that Mr Duncan said very little, but she wasn't prepared to stand there like a dummy.

'Have you been here before, Mr Duncan? I don't suppose you will have an art gallery like this in Gippsland.'

The beard twitched – was he smiling or scowling?

'Not yet.'

Jane saw another hazard coming and tried to make herself invisible behind a potted fern, but it was too late to escape.

'Miss Ashby, may I speak to you?' A plump man came a little nearer and lowered his voice. 'What I am about to say is for your ears only.'

The bushranger evidently knew the intruder.

'Good evening, Charlesworth.' He took

the hint and withdrew.

Jane sighed, turned to the other man, held up her head and looked him in the eye. She knew what was coming and she was not going to let him spoil a lovely evening.

'Mr Charlesworth, last month I–'

'Last month I intimated that I would speak to you again, if you remember.' He spoke intensely, moving nearer so that Jane was blocked off from the rest of the room.

He had a round face, with pale hair and pale, watchful eyes.

Jane did remember, but her mind was made up. She took a deep breath and stood a little straighter.

'It's time for the music, I think we should...'

Mr Charlesworth was in a hurry. 'I am in need of a wife and I have spoken to your father, as you know, with a view to asking for your hand in marriage. We need to talk about it, and soon. No doubt you are aware of my standing in Bendigo.' He looked round with complacency at several paintings on the gallery walls, each with a neat plaque announcing B. Charlesworth, Esq. as the donor.

Bendigo was a gold town, said to be the richest town in the world. The magnificent art gallery they were visiting tonight had just been opened to celebrate Queen Victoria's Jubilee. This was an important outpost of Empire and Mr Charlesworth was a prosperous citizen who intended to get his own way. The man was self-important and boring. He certainly didn't waste any time on small talk and his precise manner made him sound even more brusque. Jane caught her father's eye across the room, hoping he would come to rescue her, but he stayed where he was and worse, he was smiling hopefully at his daughter. There was no help in that direction.

'Er ... thank you, Mr Charlesworth, but ... as I have told you, I have not thought of marriage.'

*Especially to a pompous young lawyer with a fat gold chain across his waistcoat.* Jane sighed, feeling suddenly lonely. Really, it was too much. Father was desperate to see her settled before he left Bendigo, but it was time he realized that she had just as strong a will as he did and she had many reservations about marriage.

The lawyer smiled, not at all put out. 'Your father said as much, but he was sure you could be persuaded. I have a large house with good servants and I can offer you an established place in society.' He paused and then seemed to make an effort. 'I admire you, Miss Ashby, as you must be aware.'

Jane looked across the room. 'I have other plans, Mr Charlesworth.' Did that sound too abrupt? She shook the dark ringlets away from her face. 'Have you seen my brother?'

she asked desperately. Garth would at least change the subject of conversation.

There was a general movement of people towards the chairs set out at one end of the room.

'The recital is about to begin ... I will speak to you again at supper so that we can come to some arrangement.' The man strode off confidently, secure in his culture and evidently certain he would get his own way.

*He doesn't know me at all if he thinks he can bully me,* Jane told herself.

Jane's brother, Garth had saved her a seat and he winked at her as the audience settled down.

'Pa thinks he's going to marry you off, does he? Don't fancy his chances! It didn't work last time, anyhow.' The bushranger sat at Garth's other side and Jane wondered what a man from the wilds of Gippsland was doing in Bendigo.

'Garth,' Jane whispered, 'I'm coming with you to the goldfield. Anything would be better than...' she stopped as the first chords rolled out. What a wonderful piano! The music of Chopin floated through the gallery's beautiful rooms, full of sad echoes and thoughts of what might have been. The polished wood floors and elaborate plaster arches and cornices had been modelled on London's Tate gallery. In this town, one could almost imagine oneself back in England. This was civilisation, an oasis in the vast untamed land of Australia.

If only she could play as well as this, Jane thought dreamily, she would be able to stay in Bendigo, give music lessons and play at concerts. Marriage was not a pleasant prospect; most men seemed to take complete charge of their wives. Several high-spirited young women she'd known had turned into complacent wives with no opinions of their own. Jane was in no hurry to get married and if she did, she wanted to choose the man herself.

Life in Bendigo was enjoyable, with all the amenities of civilised society, but for the Ashbys it couldn't last for much longer. Jane had known for some time that John Ashby and his son were planning to go elsewhere, prospecting for gold, but they had told her it would be no place for a lady.

'Goldfields are full of rough single men,' her father had said. 'The living conditions will be primitive – not like Bendigo, you know. No libraries! No art galleries, either. And no music.' Hence, the plan to have her safely married and settled before they left. It was too neat, too convenient.

Jane also knew she couldn't stay in Bendigo alone; there would be no money to pay the rent for their pleasant house in town and she would need a companion, for respectability if nothing else. Money was the pressing problem. It was ironic that in a place bursting with wealth, they were facing poverty.

At the interval, people drifted down the wide oak staircase to the supper room, while music could still be heard above the babble of talk.

'No, Father,' Jane said firmly, taking her parent by the arm and leading him into a quiet corner. 'I have made up my mind. Please explain to the gentleman that I won't marry him. Ever.'

John Ashby looked down at her with grey eyes like her own. 'It's you I'm thinking of, Jane. I want you to have a good life.' He looked round at the fashionable crowd, the women in ornate gowns. 'In surroundings like these, fit for a lady. He would be quite kind, I'm sure. He gives money to charity, that sort of thing. Charlesworth's taste in art is quite good, he would be able to help you to develop your own art. Isn't that what you want to do?'

Since she was a small girl, Jane had been drawing with her father's paper and pencils. He'd made her a drawing board and she loved to sketch houses, trees, people. Some of her drawings of the city had been sold to visitors, with the help of Garth. 'I can draw on a goldfield, I'm sure. I could make sketches of your rough miners in their working clothes, like Mr Gill's, the goldfields artist.'

'And then, you have friends here ... Susan and Ruby, several young ladies. Surely you don't want to leave them behind?' Papa was clutching at straws.

'We'll all miss our friends, Papa, we'll just have to make new ones. I'm ready for a change, an adventure!' She smiled at him, but he still had that worried frown.

Garth came to his sister's rescue. 'She's coming with us, you know. Jane has spoken! Come on, Pa, lets get some supper.'

Jane was given an ice and made herself as small as possible behind her father, but soon Charlesworth bore down upon them. Ashby looked apologetic.

'I'm afraid my daughter is not willing to consider marriage as yet. Perhaps we can talk about it later. She will need time to get used to the idea.'

'Modesty in a young woman is most becoming.' Charlesworth smiled, revealing a gold tooth. 'A modest woman will always show some reluctance to commit herself... I am quite sure that when Miss Ashby sees my house, she will consider the offer. It will be an arrangement to our mutual convenience.' He paused. 'Perhaps I made my intentions clear too soon. I will need to take more time, to visit your family and to make myself better known to you. I will start tomorrow.'

'Lord, Pa,' Garth groaned when the man

had gone, 'He's even worse than I thought, he's like a steam engine. We'll have to take her with us.'

Later, as the family sat at home before going to bed, John Ashby went over his old arguments. 'Gold prospecting is the quickest way to get back what we've lost. You know that our capital disappeared in the shipping investment last year,' he reminded his daughter. He had bought shares in a company importing goods into Australia, but their ship had sunk and the cargo was lost. It had not been insured. Several families had suffered, the Ashbys more than most. 'And then, I haven't done much work since.'

'Surely if we lived quietly, we could get back to where we were without leaving town?' Jane looked down at her pretty blue dress. She'd never had to worry about money before this year. 'You're a good architect, Father, everybody says so.'

'I'm ready for a change from architecture, I seem to have lost my inspiration. And Garth wants to be off. I would really like to go back home, even just for a visit, if we can recover our money.' He sounded wistful.

'Home means England to you, Father ... everybody here seems to talk about "home".'

Jane shook her curly head impatiently. 'All those paintings in the gallery harking back to the past, reminding people of where they came from, English and Scottish and European scenes – why don't we have more Australian artists and subjects in our new gallery? I would think there are plenty of them.'

Garth nodded. 'Your drawings would look good on those walls, Janey! And your water-colours, as well. Maybe you could make them bigger, to stand out at a distance?'

'It's natural to want to display scenes of home,' John Ashby said quietly. 'You were a small girl when we came out, so I suppose you see it differently.'

'Yes, Father, I do. To me, this is my home, and if we can't stay here I will make a home wherever you are. Australia is getting to be more civilised all the time – just look at Bendigo!'

Garth broke in eagerly, 'I've told you about this small goldfield where fortunes are being made. Angus Duncan lives over there ... it's a chance for us to get back what we've lost, perhaps in a few months, or a year or two. We can't go prospecting in Bendigo, we all know that. Gold mining is a big business here, it's expensive to dig deep shafts. The gold's in the quartz reefs, deep underground. But further south, in this place called Gippsland, Angus says things are different. He says gold is in the creeks and near the surface. We'll have to rough it for a time of course, it's a long way from a town ... but as you say, civilisation is coming.'

16

'I'm surprised to hear Mr Duncan talks to you, I thought he was silent. It's his fault, then, that we're haring off on a chase for gold.'

Ashby sighed and suddenly, Jane thought he looked old. He was still recovering from the influenza that had laid him low in the winter and stopped him working for several months.

'I hope we won't need to be there for too long. But that's why it's not suitable for a female, Jane. You're too pretty to live among miners in the bush.'

'Marriage is not the answer, Pa. I think it would be immoral to marry just for money, or convenience.' Jane felt her chin lift, and lowered it at once. It would not help to look rebellious.

With a tired smile John Ashby looked across the hearth at her. 'If you only knew how many women do marry men chosen by their families, and go on to live happy lives! This is how the world works, child. I think we are fortunate to know Mr Charlesworth – he's a very good match, you know.'

'I'd rather live in a tent than marry Basil Charlesworth.' Jane was beginning to feel desperate. 'I am coming with you, Father. Besides, how will the pair of you keep house? I've done your housekeeping since – since Mama died, and I can quite easily do the rough work as well.'

'You'd better get Mrs Moss to show you how to do the rough work, then. I can't see you scrubbing floors, Janey!' Garth laughed. 'It won't be a tent, as a matter of fact. Angus Duncan has a cottage to let and he said it's empty at the moment.'

'They said Duncan looks like a bush-ranger,' Jane told him brightly. 'Susan said so. Can you believe him?'

After the concert, the said Duncan walked back to his hotel thoughtfully. It was his last night in Bendigo and he would be glad to get out of town and back to his farms in the south of Victoria. His business here was done, the property agreement reached and he had instructed Charlesworth to draw up the legal documents. He'd been a student with Basil Charlesworth, and it seemed a long time ago...

The memory of a pretty girl in a blue dress kept coming back to him and he found it hard to shake off a feeling of melancholy. Garth Ashby's sister had been the most at-tractive girl in the gallery that evening, lively and intelligent ... and obviously bred for city life. Charlesworth had his beady eye on her, but would she be happy with him? The fellow hadn't an ounce of romance in him, although he could talk all day and all night and had a high opinion of his own worth.

Angus went up the wide hotel staircase to

his room and prepared for bed.

*If I'd stayed with the law, I could have courted a girl like that.* The thought came out of the blue and Angus took up a book to get his mind off the subject. But the image of Jane came between him and the page and the book seemed insipid.

Leaving the law, going back to farm the family property as he had, would limit anyone's choice of a wife; it was obvious. Settlers, however prosperous, needed a wife bred in the bush, one who could shoot a dingo, calve a cow and stand the monotony and the dangers of isolation. Angus knew one or two women like that – not many, women were still scarce in country areas of Australia. He liked them, but he couldn't think of living with any of them.

On the other hand, city girls would not cope with the life he led. A girl like Jane, just to take an example, would be lost and miserable in his part of the world, where isolated farms were surrounded by forest and there were few other women. The Duncans had servants, but everyone in the household had to work, and it was skilled work. There was less distinction of social class than in the town.

There was no solution; he would join the ranks of bachelor farmers, growing old and grumpy as the years went by. It would help if he could talk, of course, but Angus Duncan knew he wasn't a talker and also, his looks were against him. Blast Charlesworth! He didn't deserve a girl like Jane.

He drifted off to sleep with the haunting music of Chopin, full of regrets, echoing in his head.

The next morning, bright spring sunshine lifted Jane's spirits until she remembered that the lawyer was coming to visit. If he thought she would give in, he was due for a shock, but surely his feelings were not really involved? He seemed to see her as a piece of decoration for the grand new house, designed of course by John Ashby. The Ashbys were currently living on the proceeds of that commission.

In her plainest gown and her oldest boots, Jane went into the garden, so as not to sit in the drawing room waiting for the unwelcome visitor. She could always find something to do in the garden, especially now that they couldn't afford a gardener. Jane's little grey-blue cat, Lavender, followed her and soon found herself a place in the sun. That was another thing; Lavender would need a basket for travel to Gippsland. She couldn't leave the cat behind. Jane swept leaves from the garden path with energy.

Mr Charlesworth didn't wait in the draw-ing room either; he saw her over the garden fence and came charging down the flagged path to meet her.

'What a charming garden! Shall we sit on this seat, Miss Ashby? I hope you will forgive the informality.' He took her arm and led her firmly to the seat. 'We must sit in the shade, to protect your delicate complexion from the sun. You should really carry a sunshade.'

*How can I sweep leaves carrying a sunshade, you idiot?* Jane bit her lip and tried once more to work out the best approach. He was trying to take charge of her already. She wanted to get rid of the man, but without hurting his feelings – assuming he had feelings. He was so complacent that she couldn't be sure.

In the end she needed to say very little. Mr Charlesworth did the talking, mainly about himself. He told her the story of his life, his ambitions for the future and his view of how Bendigo would one day become the most important town in Victoria, if not Australia.

'We are close to the centre of the state, well placed...' he droned on for several minutes, while Jane worked out how she could draw a caricature of him. He was not all that old, she supposed, but forceful, self-absorbed and totally out of place in a garden. The cat jumped up onto Jane's knee and she stroked the soft little grey head.

The interview was trying, but Jane watched bees working in the apple blossom and she felt calmer. Eventually, Garth came back from town and took pity on her.

'I suppose my sister has told you we're packing at the moment, ready for removal to Gippsland? We leave very soon.' He smiled down at Charlesworth.

The lawyer looked startled. 'Dear me, this is very sudden – I had no idea. I was going to suggest that I call upon you each week... Miss Ashby and I are just getting to know each other.' He put an arm round her waist before she could dodge him, and gave her a squeeze. She felt intimidated by him and apparently, so did Lavender.

Jane's cat, suddenly a ball of fury, shot out a paw and lodged her claws deep in the back of Charlesworth's hand. He let out a yell and tried to swipe the cat, but Lavender was too quick for him. Dripping blood from four wounds on the back of his pale hand, he glared at Jane.

'Horrible cat! I hate animals, dirty things. I would not have an animal in my house or garden.'

# TWO

'I'm so sorry, Mr Charlesworth, she's never done that before!' Hiding a smile, Jane went to the house for salve and a wound dressing, taking Lavender with her, while Garth tried to help with a clean handkerchief.

'Perhaps you will call when we return,' Jane said demurely after Charlesworth had settled down again and to her relief, he agreed. Lavender might have put him off the idea of marriage to Miss Ashby. In any case, by the time they got back to Bendigo, if they did, surely the man would have found a wife. There would be several young women in the town who would be pleased to be asked. Jane's friend Susan might well be attracted by a grand house and plenty of servants.

The garden was much more restful when he had gone. Lavender looked up at Jane with saucer eyes that seemed to hold a hint of mischief.

'Have you been training her?' Garth suggested.

'No, but wasn't it funny!' Jane pulled on her gardening gloves. 'If I needed another reason not to marry that man, Lavender has given me one – he doesn't like animals. Now, Garth, I would like you to trim the hedge. We must leave the garden tidy at the end of the lease.'

They worked for a while and when Jane flopped down on the bench for a rest, Garth joined her.

'Now tell me,' she began, 'while Father's indoors, just why we have to go chasing after gold. He's not a greedy man. It means leaving all the people we know, not to mention a nice house and garden.' She picked up Lavender. 'There must be plenty of work for an architect, buildings are going up all the time. Look at the new Post Office, it's got a clock tower, they say it cost thousands.'

Garth hesitated. 'Well ... he didn't want to alarm you, but he's worried about his health. Can't work like he used to, he gets tired. So he wants to make sure that there's plenty of money for you to live on when he's ... gone. I don't think he's in danger,' her brother went on hurriedly, 'it might just be that he's getting older. But at the moment there's very little in the bank.'

'We needn't depend on Father all our lives! We can earn our own living, Garth.' Jane moved impatiently on the bench.

'Of course,' Garth said soothingly. 'I've been earning a living of sorts, but it's a form of slavery, working as a draughtsman. I'm planning to find enough gold to set us all up comfortably, while Pa can still enjoy it. His health might improve, if he doesn't have to worry about money. And then, for a woman it's difficult to earn a living, you'd have to teach music or go as a governess or something. That's why he's keen on Charlesworth, you see. If you found a husband you liked, he would rest easy.'

'And you're looking for adventure, so you persuaded him.' Jane looked at Garth accusingly. 'What is wrong with him, Garth? He never talks about his health, but he does cough a lot.'

Garth sighed. 'No, he never talks about it, but Mother told me once. You remember Uncle Bertram's farm? A nice little stretch of England, alongside a river. Part of that should have been Pa's farm, his father left it to him. The two brothers got a farm each. But one summer, the weather was wet and they made hay – it went mouldy. Pa helped the men to feed it to the cattle, clouds of mould flew up every day, and they reckon it got into his lungs ... the doctors told him not to go on farming, so he trained as an architect.'

'And Uncle Bertram took the farm, as well as his own?'

'Yes, he paid for it of course – the money went on Pa's training. I'd have liked to farm, but it wasn't to be.'

They sat in silence for a while, Jane thinking about how glad she was the Ashbys were not still farming among the dust and the dirt.

'I suppose, then, that was why Father came here to Australia. For his health, for a drier climate.'

'That's right, but he hates anyone to mention his health. Don't say anything, Jane. And now, he seems to think that the open-air life of a gold prospector will be better for him than a stuffy office in town.' Garth looked up as the gate clicked. 'Here's Miss Brown, I'll leave you young ladies together.'

The purpose of Susan's visit was a thorough review of the previous evening, with no stone unturned. She evaluated the gowns at some length, her eyes sparkling.

'Your blue dress was the prettiest there, I thought,' she said generously. 'Mr Charlesworth was talking to you very confidentially ... now there's a good marriage prospect, Jane. You should encourage him.'

'Unfortunately, we're leaving, as you know.' Jane cast down her eyes demurely. 'Mr Charlesworth would make you a wonderful husband. I hope to see the notice of his marriage to Miss Brown, one day!'

'What's his house like?' Susan was laughing, but she seemed interested. 'I believe your father designed it.'

'I'm sure it's quite beautiful,' Jane assured her. 'Marble floors, gold taps, that kind of thing. Now, what did you think of the music last night? Which piece did you like best?'

'I'll arrange for us to stay for two nights in Melbourne with Alison,' John Ashby announced before they left Bendigo. 'It's time we paid her a visit.'

Garth had already gone ahead to the gold-field to arrange their accommodation and most of their possessions had been sent on to Gippsland. Their furniture, including Jane's beloved piano, had been sold and when it was carried out of the house she realized that the life she had known was over for good.

A few tears were shed that night, but Jane was determined to enjoy her new life as much as she could, starting with the two days in Melbourne. Alison King had been a friend of the Ashbys since they met on the ship travelling to Australia, a happy soul who had survived the death of her beloved husband many years before.

Once they left Bendigo, Jane's spirits rose and her father seemed lighter in mood.

Mrs King gave them a warm welcome, and sitting on her veranda, sipping home-made wine and watching the sunset, Jane felt hopeful for the future.

'It's brave of you, this gold adventure, John. I hear Gippsland is rather – wild,' Mrs King told them. 'Of course, gold is beautiful, it would be exciting to discover a huge nugget like – the Welcome Stranger, wasn't it called?'

John Ashby nodded. 'Not many like that, I suppose. It was twelve inches across, I believe, and found at the foot of a tree.' He laughed. 'I hope there's plenty lying about in Gippsland. If we do strike it rich Alison, you shall have a gold necklace. I've already promised one to Jane.'

'I shall look forward to it! But do remember, if it gets too much you can come here.' Mrs King waved an arm, heavy with gold bracelets, across lawns and flowerbeds to a range of buildings in the distance. 'There's a good house for a coachman over there, next to the stables. It's not used and you'd be welcome to stay there as long as you like, either or both of you.' She smiled over at Jane. 'You could leave your son digging away to make you rich. He's young, he can stand it. Meanwhile, I could introduce you to some charming young men, Jane. I would enjoy helping you to find a good husband. It's about time you thought of marriage, my dear.'

Jane blushed, trying to hide her annoyance at the assumption that she must want to get married. 'That's kind of you, Mrs King,' she said lightly. How embarrassing to be exhibited as a marriageable spinster! At least Father had not done that.

'My little girl is growing up to be quite strong-minded,' Ashby said ruefully, but with an affectionate look at his daughter. 'She'll not take advice on marriage, Alison.'

Mrs King settled complacently in her chair. 'Girls are so independent, now! But the day will come, I'm sure.' She paused. 'I don't mean to be – ah – critical, the colonials are a good sort of people, but one is hardly likely to meet society of our kind in Gippsland,' she went on. 'Of course, they don't have the advantage we have of being brought up in England.'

Their friend obviously clung to her heritage; she had heavy English furniture, English china and English pictures on her walls. Jane thought she was looking back too much into the past. *If ever I have my own house, I'll have light cane furniture, no heavy curtains and carpets, Australian paintings and my own drawings on the walls. I'll have a garden with native flowers … and lemon and orange trees.*

'I think the country areas down that way are more civilised, now that trains are running through to Sale,' John Ashby said mildly. 'And the prospectors are apparently from very varied backgrounds.'

'They are men from all walks of life, certainly, but living in rough conditions, mainly without families, and labouring from dawn to sunset. It's bound to have a coarsening effect, over time. And the settlers!' She rolled her eyes. 'Now that the large runs are being broken up and sold for farming, the lower classes are coming in.'

'On the better type of land, surely the farmers will be quite respectable? Garth and I thought of buying a farm, one day. We've met one settler's son, Duncan, quite an educated fellow. Apparently his father selected a large acreage, many years ago.'

Their hostess shuddered. 'Never a good idea to buy farmland, I feel. Australian soil is poor and the climate is most unreliable. I heard all this from my dear late husband, of course.' She sighed. 'He took a great interest in agricultural affairs.'

'So you're not recommending life in Gippsland, Alison?' Ashby asked with a humorous lift of the eyebrows.

'I am not, John, I believe it is quite uncivilised. Some of the settlers are quite well educated I suppose, sometimes the children can be sent away to school. But my dear, their lives are so hard! Never marry a settler, I beg you, Jane. Their women are out in the summer sun and they look old at five-and-twenty, especially when they're burdened with babies, with blacks all around them and no servants to speak of.' Mrs King shook her head sadly. Her complexion was still pink and white. 'I go nowhere without a sunshade. The sun is so bad for one's skin.'

'We might have the place to ourselves,' John Ashby told her. 'They've found gold in the west now, over two thousand miles away at the other side of the continent. That's where the rush will be.'

'I hope you and Garth don't think of going to Western Australia, we'd never see you again!' Mrs King laughed. 'And Jane would have to stay here with me. But I have heard that gold aplenty has been found in Gippsland ... it's a matter of luck, I suppose. Once you find your gold, you can come to live in Melbourne, in comfort.'

John Ashby smiled at her. 'We'll see, Alison.'

Their hostess looked at Jane for a moment and then added, 'I don't want to frighten you, Jane, but I hear there are bushrangers about, over there to the east. They wait for the poor, hardworking prospectors to find the gold – and then they steal it! You may get to hear of stolen gold, when you live there. For some reason they call it raven's gold. I don't know why, it sounds most mysterious.' She laughed. 'A friend who is a magistrate told me about it.'

It would be exciting to find gold, gleaming in the ground. Jane wondered whether she would be able to find some herself.

The train from Melbourne steamed east, through market gardens and small towns, giving way to areas of swamp.

'This is not the wilds of Gippsland, surely?' Jane smiled. 'It looks fairly civilised to me.' Spring had turned into the Victorian summer in the last few weeks. Bendigo had been hot and dusty, but here the countryside was green.

'Wait and see,' John Ashby said cautiously. 'Garth said in his letter that the railways have changed the place.'

They were on the rails again to their new home, with cabin trunks gone on ahead, their few bags with them and a small wicker basket containing a surprised grey cat. Lavender sat quietly in the basket on Jane's knee for the moment. Garth was to meet them at Moe and Jane hoped he would not be late.

After a time, the farmed land was gradually left behind. The day seemed to grow darker. In a greenish gloom they entered a tunnel of trees, immense forest giants with giant ferns growing at their feet. Jane peered through the trees apprehensively.

'Will we be living in a forest like this?' Dangers came to mind, wild dogs and snakes among them.

A middle-aged passenger talked to John Ashby for a while about his farm.

'You'll be looking to buy land yourself?' he asked John.

'Er ... eventually, I hope so.' Ashby was

evidently not willing to admit he was going to look for gold. He'd told Jane that thirty years ago, everyone thought about gold, but now the settlers were dominant and only a trickle of prospectors were coming in. But it was true that he and Garth did plan to buy a farm, if they were successful.

'Farming's a gamble, always was. It's always either droughts or floods, and in summer there's a good chance of a bush fire ... but we're selling butter down the line to Melbourne, so we get by. I reckon a dairy farm's the best bet,' the farmer told him.

Garth was sure that gold prospecting was the way to go. But what if he was wrong?

For the next hour or so there were trees and more trees, with clearings here and there in the bush, small settlements with sawmills beside the railway. Then they came to a place of rolling green pastures, prosperous and settled.

'Passengers for Warragul!' They rattled into a railway station with a crowded platform. Doors clanged, steam hissed.

The people here were certainly not as well dressed as those in Bendigo, but they were neat and cheerful enough. The farmer who shared their carriage left at Warragul, wishing them good luck. Perhaps life in this place would be normal, after all.

The train went on, puffing its stately way into Gippsland through more bush and low lying pastures. For some passengers the journey would end at Sale, but the Ashbys were only going as far as Moe. Surely it wouldn't be much longer? Jane stretched her cramped limbs and looked across at her father, who had fallen asleep.

It seemed a long time since they'd left Bendigo.

Jane shook black particles of soot from her dress as a gust of wind blew smoke in through the window. She felt grimy and wondered why people loved to travel. It was a dirty and tiring trip. Friends had warned her to wear dark clothing for the journey, because of the coal dust. She would miss Susan and Ruby, young women of about her own age who had been their neighbours and good company for Jane.

Thank goodness, there was the familiar figure of Garth, waving as the train drew into Moe. He found a porter to help with the bags and then led them to a horse and trap outside the station. The roads here were rutted, with water standing in puddles, but there were shops of all kinds and a branch of the Bank of Australasia.

'This is where we do business,' Garth said as though he had lived here for years.

There wasn't a single big stone building in the place, Jane noted as she looked round at the street of weatherboard shop fronts. Banks in Bendigo had inspired confidence by their solid presence; you knew your money would be safe in an imposing building with enormous vaults for safe keeping. Nothing in Moe imposed at all, although the Moe Hotel was big enough. It was all a world away from the stately towns of Victoria's north.

To Jane's relief, Garth took them first to a small eating-house, where they were able to wash their hands and drink a cup of tea.

'You'd better eat something, it's another twenty miles to Tangil,' he urged, so Jane took a bun to please him and the elderly waitress smiled.

'Off up to Tangil, are you? Got to keep your strength up for them hills, I always say.'

'Now for the tent town,' Ashby joked when they finished the tea. 'I hope you have plenty of needles and thread and so on, Jane, the things you girls need. From now on, we're in the wilds, you know.' Perhaps he was reminding her that he hadn't wanted her to come.

'Well, Pa, it's not quite so bad as that.' Garth shook the reins and they ambled out of town. 'There's a mail coach to Tangil three times a week, with two horses. The mail man brings meat, and deliveries – he brought your trunks up last week.'

Jane kept quiet; she could not imagine what the place would be like and reminded herself once more to make the best of it. A mail coach sounded civilised; at least she could write to her friends.

They travelled uphill with the scent of gum trees in the cooler air, along rough tracks and past the occasional farm. Eventually the road went downhill again; Tangil was buried in a deep-sided valley with the river at the bottom. Houses were scattered about the sides of the valley and a road ran through it. Some houses were empty and neglected, but a dozen or more had signs of life. Most of the trees had gone and the earth looked raw.

The place was desolate; Jane looked about her in dismay. High above them, an eagle sailed in slow circles. The harsh light was merciless and there was no shade.

Garth pulled up in front of a small cottage built of timber planks and surrounded by a rickety veranda and then a paling fence. The windows were grimy and the net curtains dirty and torn: this was their new home. Jane held back tears.

'Room to grow a garden here,' Ashby said jovially. Jane gave him an uncertain smile and as she walked into the little kitchen, her dress picked up dust and dirt from the unswept floor. Inside, the rooms were hot and airless, with the endless hum of flies.

The house had basic furniture; it looked as though the previous occupants had walked off and left it. Perhaps they found so much gold that they didn't need their goods any more? It was a slightly cheering thought.

'You won't have to bake bread unless you want to,' Garth told her. 'The Tangil store bakes bread.' He saw Jane's dismay. 'I only got the key yesterday, no time to clean the place up... I've been staying with the Duncans and looking for the right equipment. I'll show you, later.'

Jane took a deep breath. She opened the door of the rusty wood stove and a mouse ran out. Lavender the cat would have work to do here, and so would she.

'We'll need to clean this up before I can make a meal, let alone bread. Can you get me some vinegar? It should get rid of the rust. And plenty of lime for whitewash ... oh, and some washing soda.' *Think of the jobs to do, one by one, don't panic. Don't let Father see you crying. Oh, why did we have to come here? It's horrible!*

On the kitchen table was a jar with a bunch of flowers in it.

'Garth, how nice!' Jane smiled at her brother, but he looked guilty.

'Should have thought of it, Janey, but the fact is, I didn't. Somebody else must have brought them – and left the fresh loaf here as well.'

It was a small thing, but the flowers and the fresh crusty bread lifted Jane from the depths of despair. Someone out there in this dusty valley had a kind heart.

'I can get most things we need. We're part way between Tangil and Haunted Creek,' Garth explained, 'and there's a butcher's shop down there, a general store and another hotel. Oh, and a post office, too. Angus Duncan's farm is near there.'

'What about police?' Ashby asked. He sat at the kitchen table, tired from the journey, not interested in touring the rooms. He was probably disappointed, too. They'd known the goldfield would be rough, but not this squalid...

'There's land reserved for a police house, but there hasn't seemed to be the need. There's fewer folks here now than there used to be, and more families. Some of the miners are married and that tends to keep them quiet. There's only three or four Chinamen left.' Garth looked at Jane and then said quietly, 'They'll be sending police in soon though, to deal with the ... larrikins in the area. Angus thinks that there might be trouble, this business of raven's gold, that's what they call gold stolen from the diggers.'

# THREE

'It's a good job I've read tales of the early explorers,' Jane told Ashby as she cut bread and cheese for their supper. 'Wading through swamps, cutting through forest and living on flour and tea. This is civilised, compared to fifty years ago!' Trying to keep her father cheerful, she somehow felt better herself. 'Thank goodness, it's not damp. People in Bendigo told me that it's always wet in Gippsland. They said it rains for nine months of the year and drips off the trees for the other three.'

John Ashby shook his head sadly. 'It's bad enough, Jane ... not damp, but it will be in the winter, it's true that the rainfall's high here. At the moment, it's dusty. The whole house is covered in dust, it's impossible to keep it clean. I never wanted to bring you here.'

'Talking of rain, our water supply comes from rainwater on the roof, into a tank ... I wonder how much we've got?' Garth went outside to investigate and Jane followed him. By tapping on the outside of the tank they worked out that it was nearly full, probably because the house had been empty for some time. 'Take care not to waste water, Jane. Some of the miners have to pay to have water carted up from the creek.'

'I'll need quite a lot of water to get this place clean, you know. It needs scrubbing from top to bottom.' She would be careful, but Jane was not going to skimp on the cleaning.

Later, Garth showed them the equipment he'd bought from a man who was leaving the goldfield. He had a tub which had once been a beer barrel, and a paddle. 'You put the dirt in here, break up the clods with the paddle, and mix it with water.'

'So we'll need to do this by a creek ... and close to where you think there will be gold.' John Ashby peered doubtfully at the apparatus.

'Why do it that way?' Jane wanted to know. 'It looks very messy to me.'

'Because gold is the heaviest thing in the mix, so it sinks to the bottom. You rinse away the wash dirt. Some people just use a shallow pan, shake the river gravel about and sluice it off with water. You can try that if you like, some women do it.' He showed her a pan.

For a few weeks, Jane was completely occupied with scrubbing and whitewashing until the little house was spotless. She stacked the wood pile neatly in the wash house and scrubbed the ancient mangle and the wash tub until they were fit for use. There were spiders everywhere, but she developed a method of attack involving a long-handled broom. It was satisfying to face up to the hardships and to overcome them.

The hard work tired her, but it took her mind off the sadness of leaving Bendigo, although she wondered what their friends would have thought. Mrs King would have reminded her to carry a sunshade and Susan in Bendigo would faint if she saw the conditions here.

Garth turned over the soil in the garden, but it was too dry to plant seeds. Their water supply was going down quickly and there was no water to spare for the garden.

The cottage was not isolated because it was beside the track that led through the Tangil goldfield. Neighbours passed by the house quite often and some of them stopped for a chat, happy to talk about anything except gold. Garth asked questions, but gold was a closely guarded secret. Instead, the neighbours talked about land and how and where to find it. The few women who passed asked Jane how she got the windows to shine. She was happy to tell them that she used vinegar and water, as Mrs Moss had done in Bendigo. But the windows in this dusty spot would need cleaning far more often.

'Tangil Hills was a big cattle run, but now

it's split and being sold to selectors,' the Ashbys were told. 'There's blocks of all sizes, some are steep but there's some good land too. Best blocks have a creek through them, or river frontage.'

Quite often, Jane was left alone when Garth and his father went off to try the art and science of gold prospecting.

'Don't expect results too soon,' Garth warned her. 'We have to find our feet, first.' When her housework was done, she got out the drawing materials and set to work sketching: the cat, a twisted tree, and their little home.

It was quiet in the cottage. At first, she wondered who the 'larrikins' were, presumably bushrangers, from whom Duncan expected trouble, but she saw no suspicious characters and soon forgot about them. A man like Duncan could hardly be afraid of bushrangers, or he wouldn't dare to look in the mirror.

The Tangil store was about a mile from the cottage and the Ellis family who owned the store were friendly.

'Fresh bread most days, and we have butter and eggs on Thursdays,' Jane was told and so she walked down the track every week to buy fresh eggs, butter and cheese. Megan Ellis, the daughter, worked in the shop, while her mother baked and Mr Ellis delivered stores to the miners.

'I do like your bread,' Jane told Megan one morning and the girl smiled. 'On our first day here, someone left a loaf and a bunch of flowers on the table for us. It was so kind!' She looked at the blushing girl. 'It was you, wasn't it?'

With her rosy cheeks even redder than usual, the girl nodded. 'I felt so sorry for you coming to that house, all dirty it was, and among strangers.' Megan had a musical Welsh voice and pronounced words carefully, enunciating every syllable. 'Mr Duncan said when you were coming, it was really his idea, wasn't it.'

'Well, thank you, Megan. It was hard at first, but I hope it's not for long, if my brother is lucky.'

Megan nodded wisely. 'Luck is everything. My Dad, now, he was a miner in Wales, he knows the rocks, but he was not lucky, no indeed. He got the dust in the lungs, so he decided to open the store and now we can make a living.'

That was not encouraging, but Jane decided to hope for the best.

If Jane took the track for a mile in the other direction, there was a clump of trees half hidden by a little hill. One afternoon, she felt like looking for a new subject to draw. She took a walk up the track, but the trees were dying and would have made a bleak composition. Sometimes gold mining killed the vegetation and Jane wondered how long the land would take to recover.

Sad for the trees, Jane walked past them and the rough track took her over a ridge to a place where the bush was overgrown and more healthy-looking. Half hidden in the shade was a small, rather ramshackle cottage with a line of washing pegged out to dry.

A woman was leaning on the gate, watching her. What a drawing she would make! Bundled in black, wearing a man's felt hat and with a clay pipe in her mouth, she could have been a witch. She scowled as Jane assessed her with an artist's eye.

'And what might you be wantin', then? A widow's life is hard enough, without bein' spied on.' She scratched her head under the black hat. 'You'll know me again, that's for sure.'

It was bad to be caught staring and Jane felt embarrassed.

'Good day... I'm Jane Ashby ... just walking by. I live over there, down the track.' Jane turned to continue her walk.

That must have been the right thing to say; the woman visibly relented. 'Well now, and I was after thinkin' you was comin' to spy on poor honest folks. You might've been a copper's wife, easy.' She opened the garden gate, beaming. 'Come in, acushla, and take a drop to drink.' And that was how Jane came to spend most of an afternoon in Ma Dooley's sly grog shop, an illegal establishment of doubtful cleanliness and bad reputation.

Under a veranda at the back of the premises was a shelf of bottles and several barrels. A rough trestle table was obviously a bar and stools were set round upturned barrels, at one of which two miners were playing cards. Were they 'larrikins'? Jane thought they looked like solid, middle-aged men, too slow to engage in hit and run, too old to be larrikins.

Having declined the home-brewed beer and various types of spirits, Jane felt that she had to accept a cup of strong black tea. When it was poured, with a tot of rum in the hostess's mug, they settled down for a talk.

'Me name's Mary, but the lads call me Ma Dooley. And you'll be one of them English folks – not that I hold anything against the English, mind, even though they did kick the Dooleys off their land. Michael tells me your Da's a good man. You'll know me boy Michael,' she went on, 'he's been to see your Da a few times, but mebbe not Roy, he's been up country for a month or two. He'll be back next week ... if he did as I told him, he'd keep clear of the trouble. Dear knows what'll become of my boys, now they've got together with that dark one. Raven's gold will be the death of 'em. Getting the gold without the sweat and toil's fine, but then the trouble begins.' She stopped as though she had said too much.

'What does raven's gold mean?' Jane asked, but there was no answer.

Mrs Dooley got up to pour more beer for the card players and Jane had a moment to look round at the interesting choice of ornaments on the grimy walls and the drawings they would make: old shotguns, several cudgels of the Irish type, wood axes, picks and a crosscut saw or two. If the clients ever got to fighting, there could be a bloodbath in moments. A dusty pair of handcuffs hung in a dark corner, trophy of some long-ago scuffle. Michael Dooley had looked innocent enough when he visited, but he had dubious connections. This must be the home of the larrikins, but there was no evidence of gold.

Back in her chair, Ma Dooley relit her pipe and blew a cloud of smoke to the grimy rafters.

'As one woman to another, I should give you some good advice. I've done it hard Jane, I don't mind telling you, I've had a sight of trouble.' Jane looked at her enquiringly. 'Well, laws are made to be broken. What's the harm if a poor old woman sells a few glasses of beer?' Ma Dooley poured another measure of rum into her tea. 'A fat publican in the town, he's legal, he can make a good living, but a little grog shop out here's closed down. Regular. Sly grog, they call it. I reckon they've shut me down ... oh, about ten times now.' She took a swig of tea and wiped her mouth with the back of her hand. 'It's hard, I can tell you.'

'How do you manage to live?' This was a way of life that Jane had never encountered before. She had heard that liquor was not supposed to be sold on the goldfields, but no doubt it would be in demand.

'It's thirsty work out there in the sun, the lads are ready for a beer at the end of the day. They're ready for a smoke and a yarn, and a game of cards or dominoes. Sometimes they sing. If they're looking for tucker, I gives 'em bacon and eggs. There's no shortage of customers.' Ma Dooley smiled, revealing blackened teeth.

'Until you get closed down, I suppose.' Jane could see a painting here, the men at their cards, strong shadows on the craggy faces under the lamp, oils, in dark, sombre tones. One day, she would get some oils and canvas ... and be a proper artist.

Ma waved a hand at the bar furnishings, the trestle and the barrels. 'It's easy cleared, o'course. Five minutes and this is just a poor old widow's shanty. "Liquor? We got no liquor, officer. We's teetotal here, to be sure!"' She cackled.

Jane laughed. 'So what then? Your customers will be disappointed.'

'Not for long. Then I waits a while, I says a

prayer or two, I brews another lot of beer, digs up me bottles in the garden and off we go again.' She paused to light her pipe. 'I should be able to give yer some good advice.'

Jane wasn't sure she needed advice on evading the law, but one thing stuck in her mind afterwards; Ma Dooley said she should pan for gold in the Haunted Creek.

'I'm tellin' you as one woman to another, acushla. And lock yer doors at night, for all love,' were her parting words. It had been an interesting afternoon; not a bit like after-noon tea in Bendigo, with its china cups and lace doilies.

Panning for gold was worth a try. Wearing an old black dress, Jane walked down the track with Garth one day to try gold pan-ning for herself. In a secluded stretch of the Haunted Creek she scooped up gravel from the creek bed in the pan, swirled it around with water and then drained it slowly so that the sediment was left in the bottom.

'The gold's the heaviest,' Garth told her, 'so it should stay in the pan when the sand and gravel slip out.'

Jane looked eagerly for her first piece of gold, but after a while she found that the metal pan was heavy. Her back ached from stooping over the water. She was just about to give up when she saw a gleam, a speck of brightness in the bottom of the pan.

'Look!'

'That's it!' Garth was as excited as Jane. 'It's only a speck, but it shows that there's gold here.' He carefully transferred the tiny piece to a small bottle. After that, they found a few more specks. At end of an hour they stopped and straightened up painfully.

Jane looked round, breathing in the scent of the eucalyptus. At Tangil, the sun was beating down mercilessly on the scarred earth, but here beside the creek, all was cool and green. This was a land of contrasts and extremes.

'I wanted to find something worth taking home to show Father,' she lamented. 'We'd have to look for a hundred years before we could find enough to pay the grocer. Surely you didn't come all the way from Bendigo for this?'

'Of course not, Janey. Pa and I will be striking gold soon, you just wait and see. The creek's been worked over too many times, but where we're digging now, it's quite promising...' Garth broke off as kookaburras high above them suddenly broke into their manic laughter.

Jane thought the birds were ridiculing Garth, but it was an alarm call. A horseman was riding down the track. There were many bearded men on the goldfield, but only one so sinister; it must be Duncan.

The 'bushranger' raised a battered hat in Jane's direction.

'Good day.' He looked rougher than Jane remembered him in Bendigo, in riding boots and heavy working clothes. 'Any luck?'

'Not so you'd notice,' Garth said ruefully, rubbing his aching back.

'Women never do. It's too hard for them.' Duncan shook his reins and the big chestnut horse moved on.

Garth looked after Duncan as he rode away. 'He told me that he thought you should have stayed in Bendigo,' he said. 'He feels the house isn't good enough ... should have been improved and cleaned up before you came.'

'What on earth has it got to do with Mr Duncan? And how does he know what the cottage is like, anyway?' Jane picked up her pan angrily. 'He may be your friend, but I don't like the man. He seems to think it's my fault that we haven't found much gold.'

'Remember I told you, the cottage belongs to Angus,' Garth said mildly. 'I rented it from him on very good terms, he said I could pay the rent when we found gold. He would probably have given it a coat of paint if he'd known you were coming.'

Unreasonably, this made Jane dislike Duncan even more. 'He looks like a bushranger, he hardly speaks and now, I find he's our landlord and we're obliged to him. What an uncouth country this is!' The kookaburras cackled as though they agreed.

'Father likes him, you know,' Garth said quietly. 'I wonder why Angus hasn't married? You would think that a settler needs a wife.'

'It is quite obvious why he hasn't married, Garth. He would repel any woman – just look at him!' She glared at her brother. 'Father's no judge, he likes Mr Charlesworth. I don't happen to agree–'

'Charlesworth! I nearly forgot, there's a letter for you. It came to the post office in Moe and they must know we're at Tangil. Here, take it.' Garth held out an expensive-looking envelope. 'Sorry, Janey, it came a couple of days ago... Don't you want to read it?'

'I hoped he'd forgotten about me. No, I'll read it at home.'

That evening, Jane took out Charlesworth's letter.

*My Dear Miss Ashby,*
*I must commence with an apology. When we last met at your residence in Bendigo, I omitted to request your permission and that of your father to enter into correspondence with you. It was remiss of me.*

*Since your departure it has become evident to me that I am imperfectly acquainted with your character and disposition and that this should be rectified without delay.*

*Your refusal to consider my offer to you, in spite of your father's wishes, was regarded by me*

51

*as modesty in the first instance. Subsequently, and on further reflection, it occurs to me that you may have been exhibiting an independent spirit. I am aware that your parent did not wish you to accompany him, but that you disregarded his wishes.*

*Independence of mind is not becoming in a young woman. I believe that women should be willing to submit to the wishes of their parents and also, that a wife should obey her husband in all things. The male intellect is superior, as I am sure you are aware.*

*Of later years there has been a deplorable tendency for women to assume that they should be allowed opinions, strong opinions. Some even believe that they should have the right to vote in an election. Some of the women I have met in the course of my work as a lawyer have been strident in their demands. To my mind it is dangerous when women demand to be heard, especially the lower orders in our colony.*

*Perhaps you will do me the honour of replying to this letter in due course. I am confident that you will be able to put my mind at rest as to your modest temperament. When I saw you at church one Sunday, I was certain that you were a dutiful daughter and would make a good wife.*

*Yours truly,*
*Basil Charlesworth.*

Garth looked up from reading the news-paper.

'What does the old boy say? "I miss you, my darling?"'

Jane was so indignant that she spluttered a little. 'The – the man's impossible! He thinks I may not be dutiful enough... I'll have to write back and agree with him.' She glared at Garth. 'I suppose you believe that the male intellect is superior?'

'Of course!' Garth grinned and his sister hit him with the newspaper.

John Ashby looked at them both across the table.

'Charlesworth is quite a kind man, you know, does a lot for charity. He may be a little pompous, but that's just his manner. He's a lawyer, they are used to knowing better and talking for longer than the rest of us.'

'What's good about him, Pa?' Garth asked. He went to a cupboard and took out his concertina.

'Oh, when we built the hospital, he looked after the transfer of land and so on, and even collected donations. He was most efficient and didn't charge a fee.' Her father paused. 'Don't underestimate the man, Jane. He would make a fine husband.'

Garth started to play some of the English folk songs and ballads that their father liked. He was a good musician and Jane was thankful that they had at least one form of music in this barren place. While he played, she composed a reply to the letter in her head, a reply that would never be sent.

'*Thank you for your honesty in explaining your bigoted view of women. You've been born too late Basil, women today prefer to think for themselves. But I'm sure that you'll find a woman soon who loves the idea of marriage with marble floors and gold taps and is prepared to hide her own opinions, when she is with you. If she's clever, she'll make you think that her ideas are originally yours. Women are good at that.*'

Susan Brown, her Bendigo friend would be perfect for Basil, she was a clever woman. Poor Basil! Jane could almost feel sorry for him.

## FOUR

'Garth! Come here!' It lay heavily in his hand, almost covering his palm. Alluvial gold, washed out by the creek in flood, waiting to be found, just as they'd hoped. It had taken weeks of effort, but here it was. John Ashby stood holding it, grinning like a boy. It was his best find so far.

'Now you know how it feels, you'll want to go on!' Garth was ecstatic. 'Wait till Janey sees this!'

It was early evening. Father and son were walking along the bed of a dried-up creek about two miles from the cottage. Garth strode ahead but Ashby walked with his head down, putting one foot in front of the other with difficulty. He was trying not to stumble, longing to go home. The sun was setting, it would soon be dark.

Pausing for a rest, Ashby had seen a gleam of gold in the bank beside him, lit by the sun just before it sank out of sight; a chance in a million. Fool's gold, probably. They'd seen a lot of that, gleaming in the quartz. It was iron pyrite, a brassy yellow ... he had bent and pulled out the loose pebbles around the gleam, and there it lay. He had found a sizeable piece of true gold.

The Ashbys worked on the goldfield as summer turned to autumn, slowly, so slowly adding to their little store of gold. Gradually, John Ashby's health worsened.

He laboured in the heat and dust, trying to keep up with Garth, but it was a losing battle. Sometimes they worked through piles of dirt with a 'cradle' they'd added to their equipment. The cradle, a wooden box, was rocked to shake up the dirt. This was easier than the barrel and paddle, but the dirt still had to be shovelled in by hand. At other times, they looked for gold in the creeks, which was easier.

Whenever they did find gold, there was

jubilation in the little cottage and a realisation that their dreams might come true.

'How soon before we have enough?' John Ashby asked his son. 'Let's have it valued, then we'll know ... when we can leave.'

'Don't talk of leaving now, Pa! We've got to go on, our luck has changed.' Garth was picking up the miners' superstitions.

Jane looked at her father. 'Don't work so hard ... let Garth do the heavy work.'

John Ashby went on for a month or so longer, but his health was worsening and he was always short of breath. Garth brought barrow loads of dirt to the cradle and Ashby poured in water from the creek. Although they were in shade by the water, it was hot work and they were troubled by flies.

The buckets of water grew heavier as time went on, until the day came when Ashby could no longer work. He sat on the veranda of the cottage, reading and every day, his cough was worse.

'Have a drink of water, Father,' Jane urged one evening as the sunset gilded the cottage windows. She waited for the coughing to stop and held the drink out to him. 'There's a drop of whisky in it, don't tell these lads or they'll all want a glass.'

Several visitors lounged on the veranda, calling in on their way home as usual on fine evenings. Ashby's cottage had become a sort of gathering place.

'Thanks, love. Where's Garth?' The man could only croak. 'Nearly sundown, he should be home by now.' He had gone off looking in the dry creek bed again.

'Here I am, Pa.' A cheerful lad, Garth, these days. 'Found a bit today down in you know where...' He looked round the faces on the veranda, all filled with hope that he would name the gully. If they worked out where Garth had found his gold, the other miners would scratch about there too. Most of them were still looking for surface gold, the elusive gleam in creek banks and out-crops of quartz.

Absalom, a Ganai man, was standing on one leg, watching the others. He knew the country better than anyone. Absalom had caught fish for them and sometimes speared game. He was indifferent to gold and didn't understand what all the excitement was about.

'No good for tucker, no good for humpy,' he told Garth, meaning food and shelter. Aboriginal people were amazed by the feverish activity of the 'diggers.'

The prospectors on the Tangil goldfield visited out of sympathy, these days. In front of John Ashby they were cheerful, but when they spoke to Jane it was different.

'Poor old John ... he's dusted,' a short Cornishman had told Jane the week before. This man breathed heavily himself, he knew all about diseases of the lungs. 'Done and dusted. Know what that means? You'm a good maid, but you won't have him much longer. He'll never see England again.'

Jane could guess what he meant. The dust in the diggings had got into his lungs during the dry, windy summer and now, he could hardly breathe. It was not a healthy environment, especially for a man with damaged lungs; they knew that now, when it was too late.

Jane had always looked on the bright side, smiling like Garth, hoping for the best.

They'd both hoped that their father had something like bronchitis and would recover quickly. Now, she could see for herself that he was gravely ill. Would they ever be able to get him back to England? He couldn't die yet, not at the age of 48, just because he had given up architecture and turned gold prospector. Meanwhile, she must look bright and cheerful. A long face wouldn't cure him, that was certain.

One day, the Cornishman, Penrose, sat on a cane chair next to her father, breathing hoarsely and talking in short bursts about opals and where they could be found; at least it made a change from gold. On John's other side was the black-bearded, grim Duncan the landlord, standing with his arms folded. Why did he come? It wasn't for the conversation, he rarely seemed to speak. Two other men sat on the wooden veranda steps, smoking.

A fair young man leaned on the wall, Ma Dooley's younger boy.

'It's hard for you, Miss,' he said in a soft voice as she passed him with the empty glass. His blue eyes were sympathetic. 'This is no place for a lady. A rough place surely, and your Da taken badly...'

'Yes, Michael.' *It's hard for everyone out here. I wish we'd never seen the place.* To the lad she said cheerfully, 'But I'm lucky, we have a house, we've plenty to eat. And one day, we might buy some land and start a farm, somewhere shady with some trees. But what about you? Have you got plans for the future?'

Michael Dooley shook his head. 'If I strike lucky, I'm away out of here,' he told her. 'They've taken against us. Got into trouble with the law, because of Ma and our name ... but she has to make a living.'

'Well, if you keep quiet for a while, they might forget about you,' Jane suggested.

They both looked out over the desolate landscape. Tangil was a collection of bark huts and wooden houses, the deep valley now in shadow. Most of the trees had gone and the river wound its muddy way through piles of stones. Jane had come here hoping it was 'just for a short time'. And now her father needed care and they were far from medical help.

Tangil had changed however, since the

early days of the gold rush, from a cluster of tents into a little town. Some of the men now had families here and there was a small school. In the many creeks and gullies there was still the possibility of finding gold, although the heady days of the rush were long over. Mines had been started, then abandoned and the machinery left to rust. Most of the men with the capital to undertake deep mining had gone.

Jane had continued to sketch some of the scenes in Tangil and her father had pinned the sketches on the wall; drawings of the cottages and the odd twisted tree. She'd drawn her cat Lavender, stretched out on a rug.

'Keep it up, Jane,' her father had wheezed. She saw Duncan inspecting them carefully one day and wondered why he bothered.

'You should draw something every day,' her father told her. So to please him and because she enjoyed it, she kept at her drawing. Small sketches she sent to her friends in Bendigo, to give them some idea of the raw landscape. She had tried to draw Ma Dooley, but kept that one hidden away.

In the tiny kitchen, Jane started on the evening meal. She was peeling potatoes when Garth came in.

'Wish they'd go away, Sis. Pa's getting tired now. He needs to eat and go to bed. But I can't say anything, they mean well and he likes the company.'

Angus Duncan stood up straight; he was taller than any of them. 'Away home, the lot of ye,' he growled. 'Can you not see the man's worn out?'

There was a shocked silence; Black Beard hardly ever spoke.

'So you're a Jock, then? I never knew it,' one man ventured.

Apologetically, the men melted away with a last glance into the kitchen.

Duncan turned back when the others had gone. Leaning on the doorpost, he looked at John Ashby. 'Time you saw a doctor, John.'

John smiled in a tired way. 'No doctors here, you know that, Angus,' he wheezed. 'How's your farm going? They tell me you've got a big mob of cattle over there.'

If John was trying to change the subject, it didn't work. Duncan moved impatiently. Jane glanced through the door at him as he said, 'I'll telegraph for my brother from Moe tomorrow.' He turned abruptly to Jane. 'I saw you talking to young Dooley. I should warn you, that family makes bad company.' Then he was gone.

'Do you think he'll be a real doctor?' Jane asked doubtfully, tying her unruly hair back. Any help they could get would be welcome, anything to ease her father's suffering. 'Let's hope the brother is a bit more – civilised... I suppose the men come to visit in the hope of a meal.' She sometimes invited one or two miners to have supper or a cup of tea with them, but never Duncan. He seemed somehow isolated in his silence. You never knew what he was thinking.

Garth laughed. 'I think every man on the diggings fancies you, lass,' he told her.

'Rubbish, Garth. It's just that it's a man's world, some of the ones who come here have nobody to cook their suppers.' Jane drew the pan of potatoes from the fire. 'You've had another good day. Have we got enough gold now? You don't want to struggle on until you're old and grey, surely. Maybe we could get Father away, he really needs to get out of here.'

Garth sat at the table, considering. 'The plan is to find a lot of gold and then either buy a farm, or go back to England – that's Pa's plan, of course. We're nearly there ... I just need a few more weeks...' He looked at his sister. 'It's hard to stop, you know, once you get the fever. Once you've made some good finds.' He looked over his shoulder and then drew a nugget from his pocket, a piece of gold with a dull gleam. 'Here's today's find. I've paid Angus the rent for a year, we're doing quite well.'

A year! It sounded a long time.

'Do you really want to live in England, Garth? We were small when we left, I don't remember much. It might be better to stay in Australia, now we're here. There were pretty girls in Bendigo, remember!'

Bendigo ... a civilised city, with an art gallery, wide clean streets and elegant buildings. It was the place where her father had made his name as an architect – but where Garth had developed a passion for gold.

'Well, you know why we came to Tangil, Jane. I was keen to try gold mining, but at Bendigo the diggings were all taken over by big companies with machinery. Small men had no chance, so we came here...' he broke off. After a silence he said, 'At least we've done well here, Pa's pleased that we came.'

Jane stirred the stew in the pan. *It was the worst thing we ever did, if it kills him.* Aloud she said quietly, 'It's high time you put most of the gold in the bank. Just keep enough to buy food.' At Tangil and Haunted Creek, raw gold was the currency used to buy the necessities of life and the shopkeepers knew its value precisely.

'All in good time, my girl. When you're on a good lead you have to stick to it, or somebody else will take it. And nobody knows where ours is, anyway.' Garth stretched and yawned. 'I'd better wash before supper.'

About noon two days later, a big man rode up to the cottage and announced that he was Dr Duncan. He was dark like his brother, but clean-shaven and neatly dressed.

'My brother asked me to see John Ashby,

is this his house?' He smiled at Jane.

The doctor listened to John's breathing with a stethoscope and talked to him for a while. He produced a bottle from his bag, which he gave to Jane.

'Give him this to help him to sleep at night.'

John Ashby insisted on paying him on the spot.

'Not much we can do,' Dr Duncan told her gently, as she walked with him back to his horse. The doctor looked down at her and Jane thought the dark eyes were kind.

'Once the lungs are badly affected ... he should leave the diggings, go somewhere with less dust. Keep him quiet, and cheerful if you can ... you're doing a good job, but it's no life for a lassie, out here in the wilds.' He stood there for a long moment, then moved to throw up his bag.

'Thank you so much for coming to see us, doctor.' Jane was blinking back tears. 'I didn't think a doctor would venture so far from town.'

One foot in the stirrup, the man turned to look at her again. 'I've several patients here, I'll see them today, broken limbs and heads – it's a dangerous job, mining, as I'm sure you know, even without the fights. But compared to goldfields in America, this one is fairly peaceful!' He hesitated. 'If you ever decide to come to town, my wife Isabel might be able to help you to find work. Sewing perhaps, or looking after children.' Jane wondered whether he meant his own children. With a wave, Dr Duncan cantered off to the next patient.

When Jane went back to her father, he seemed quite cheerful. 'Good man, Dr Duncan. Told me I have the prettiest daughter for miles around. Of course I know that!'

His daughter laughed. Then she tried not to shudder as coughs racked his poor body again.

The next funeral at Tangil came sooner than expected. Jane thought the silence was the worst thing to bear; no birds sang. The only sounds were the sigh of the wind in a few straggly wattles along the path and the occasional creak of dusty boots as four miners carried the coffin slowly down, dipping at the front, to the little cemetery by the creek.

The goldfield was bleak, the sadness seeping into Jane's bones as she followed the coffin to the grave. She walked alone because her brother was one of the bearers.

There were no relatives to follow, or to mourn for him. The other three bearers were young men like Garth; she had fed them before they set out, as well as several other mourners.

The man had been honest and kind. He deserved a more dignified end, a better funeral. There should have been soft organ music and dim light filtering through stained glass windows. A more respectable parson too, than the dubious Irishman who said he'd been a priest and asked for a bottle of whisky for his fee. There should have been friends and relations from his previous life; none of them knew of his death as yet, and when they heard it would be too late. Burials were speedy affairs here.

About a dozen men had assembled in the graveyard, hats off as the coffin came slowly down. By contrast with the raw earth of the diggings this was a pleasant spot, a grassy bank where the creek changed course, fringed by tall trees, far enough from the goldfield to be free of dust. There was greenish light, filtered by the gum trees and it felt like a place of rest.

Jim Penrose, the Cornish miner with the bad lungs, had been a friend to all the little community and there was genuine sadness in their faces. Black Beard silently passed Jane a spray of blossom from a gum tree and she placed it on the coffin as it was lowered into the grave. The Irishman read the burial service quite soberly. He had done it at this place several times before.

When it was over, Jane watched through tears as the men quickly filled in the grave and Garth put an arm round her shoulders.

'Now, Sis, remember he's better off – he's

not suffering any more.' He paused. 'I have to go down to the pub with these blokes, to the All Nations. They want to drink a glass in Jim's memory ... now, I think you'd better come with us. You can always sit in the landlady's parlour, you know. Mrs Malone is a kind woman, she'll look after you.'

The All Nations was not far off, in the little hamlet of Haunted Creek and it was the miners' home from home. Jane had met Maeve Malone and liked the big woman, but the thought of going there today repelled her.

'I'll go home Garth, thank you, light the fire and make some supper. But I'll just stay here for a while, and rest.' The men turned and made for the pub. Jane watched them go, then sank down on the bank. The autumn day was cool, a relief from the heat of summer and new growing tips tinged the trees with light green.

Thinking of her father, Jane realized that a man with damaged lungs should never have come here, to work in the dust and heat. The hard physical work of digging, even pushing the barrow with their implements in it, must have been a trial to him. He could go the same way as Jim Penrose.

Two magpies looked down at her from a high branch and warbled as if they sang for her. The notes were beautiful. Jane sighed and dried her eyes, feeling a little calmer.

Thank goodness, Father had been spared this funeral. A week before Penrose died, Garth had taken John Ashby to the Melbourne train.

'I'll stay with Alison until I improve, she'll be glad of the company,' he agreed, once they had talked him into it.

'But you should come too, Jane. We have money now, to pay our way.'

Jane didn't want to go to Melbourne, to be introduced to handsome young men.

Garth would want her to stay with him and keep house, as she'd done ever since their mother died. But Jane was beginning to hate the diggings, to hate the lure of gold that brought men here from all over the world. It was no life for her – surely Garth would see that?

One day, her brother would surely get married and his sister would not be needed. But if she could persuade him to go back to Bendigo, they would both have a better life.

In a day or two, she would talk to Garth and see how much money they had. Some of the gold was to be given to her, it might be enough to get her away from Tangil. She remembered Dr Duncan's offer of his wife's help. She would have to earn a living somehow, but in Bendigo it would be much easier.

The sun was sinking as Jane took the path back to the little weatherboard house on the track. The evening was hazy, with a smoky

68

tinge. She rounded a large pile of earth and could hardly breathe for the smoke. There was a fire somewhere ... it was here, right in front of her. She stared in disbelief.

Their neat little house was alight, burning fiercely. Timber walls, dried out by the summer sun were glowing red hot and there was a roaring sound.

Jane ran forward, but the heat forced her back. She was too late, nothing could be recovered; as she watched, the roof fell in with a crash and sparks flew high into the air.

She looked round, but she was alone. Those who had not gone to the funeral or were working on the ceaseless hunt for gold would be at home now, cooking their suppers.

Her mind numb, Jane watched the flames leaping and dying again, as their few possessions were turned into ash. Beyond tears, she stood and gazed at the ruin of their home. She had no idea of what to do next. They had lost everything, even their little cat Lavender could not have survived this inferno.

# FIVE

There had been no fire on the hearth when they left, nothing to cause this. Who would burn down a house on the day of a funeral ... and why? Someone who had known that the house would be empty for the afternoon?

Jane took a deep breath and tried to be rational. Their gold was the most valuable thing in the house and it should not be affected by fire. It would be there in the tin box, under the floor and underneath whatever was left of Garth's bed. If that was what the arsonists wanted, they would have failed.

There was nothing she could do. Jane sat on a tree stump and waited for Garth to come home; her mind was a blank. Too much had happened and she felt powerless to do anything at all. She had no clothes apart from the black dress she wore; no possessions, no money. And no little cat. Where was Lavender? She'd been left in the house. Jane frantically tried to remember whether she'd left a window open. The poor cat, trapped in a burning house... 'Lavender!' she called out, but without much hope.

Her little cat appeared, sat down beside

Jane and washed her paws. The lavender fur was singed in places, but the cat was quite composed.

'Clever girl! You're here after all!' The sight of her calmed Jane a little. She would do her best to look after the cat in future.

The frenzy of the blaze gradually died to a glow. It was over; their lives had changed in a few minutes. When Garth came, what would they do then? It was too late get to Moe. Perhaps Garth would have an idea of where they could go for the night. Hurry up Garth, come home...

The shadows of evening were lengthening when Jane heard a deliberate footfall on the track and jumped up. But it was not Garth, it was Angus Duncan. The tall man stood beside her and looked at the blaze in his usual silence for a while.

'Despicable,' he said. 'When I catch whoever did this...' He looked capable of murder at that moment. 'Garth is ... still at the All Nations.' The deep voice was unfamiliar; he so seldom spoke – and where was the Scottish accent? Only a trace remained. Duncan spoke like an educated man, but with a slight hesitation at times.

'I saw the smoke, so I came over.'

'It's your property... We didn't leave a fire burning, it must be deliberate.'

Another silence and then the man sighed. 'You must come with me.' It was an order,

71

very abrupt. 'Straight away.'

Jane rebelled. Why should he speak to her like this?

'No, I will look for my brother. I must see Garth, so we can decide what to do.' She was not going to be taken over by Duncan, of all people. She picked up the little cat and held it protectively.

The sun had gone and it was getting dark. Duncan took her by the arm, not roughly but very firmly. 'You will come with me, Jane. It's not safe here.' She struggled a little, but he held her with one arm.

'Garth, where are you?' Jane shouted, but there was no answer from the shadows. 'I want to stay here, my brother will come, you can't force me to go with you...' What was his motive? She tried to fight the rising hysteria. How could it be unsafe?

'I'm not afraid of the dark, Mr Duncan, even if you are!'

Duncan said nothing, but his grip on her tightened. There was no help for it. Jane and Lavender were marched away from the cottage down a long track, under the trees by the creek and over a small wooden bridge.

The moon was rising and by its light they could see the track more clearly. In the distance Jane heard dingoes howling, one at first and then many others joining in. Wild dogs, shy as a rule but likely to attack if they were hungry... Then she heard another sound, the raucous singing of drunken men. She had never been out after dark in Tangil before and the only night sound at the cottage had been the hoot of an owl.

The howls were closer now and she could imagine the creatures slinking through the trees... Suddenly the deep voice spoke again, quietly in her ear. 'Don't worry, I have a pistol in my belt.'

This was far from reassuring. 'What sort of a man carried a pistol about with him? No one Jane knew did such as thing. She would ask Garth whether Duncan was deranged ... if and when she got to see Garth again.

'Where are we going? You could tell me that, at least. Tell me what right you have to drag me off against my will,' Jane raged. It made no difference. 'Tell me where you're taking me.'

'Home,' Duncan said briefly. Occasionally he stopped, as if to give her a rest and Lavender snuggled deeper into Jane's arms as though afraid of the big man, as well she might be. 'Watch where you tread, tiger snakes are about at night.'

'I'm not afraid of a snake!' Jane told him fiercely. She hadn't seen a snake since they came to live at Tangil.

'Half the people who are bitten, die. The other half are so sick, they wish they could.'

At one point Jane saw a bent stick dimly and thought it was a snake. She jumped and

73

the cat scratched her face, as she put out her claws in fright.

Jane wiped her face where the cat had scratched it. Her other arm was still held by Duncan and it felt bruised. When was this nightmare going to end? In spite of her defiance, tears welled up in Jane's eyes and ran down her face.

It seemed an age of stumbling through the bush before Duncan stopped by a high fence and let her go, to unlock a heavy wooden door.

'In here.'

She thought of trying to get away at this point, but where would she go? She was lost, with no idea how to find Garth.

Duncan dragged her through the doorway, the door banged shut and he turned a key in the lock. They were in some sort of compound. She was a prisoner now.

Ready to faint from fear, Jane looked round at lighted windows edging the yard.

Duncan led her to a door in one of the buildings and pushed her through it.

Jane stumbled and nearly fell and such was her rage that she turned on him.

'This is ridiculous, you can't treat me like this! It's illegal! I want to go to my brother! Do you hear?'

Duncan turned his back on his prisoner. He struck a match, a spurt of light in the gloom, and lit a candle standing on a table, before turning round and looking at her.

'Your face is scratched.' Gently, he took out a clean handkerchief and wiped the blood away. Then he left her without a word. She was in a place of shadows, in one corner a high wooden bed. Was she here to become this man's mistress?

Seen by candlelight, Jane's dress was dusty and torn. She stroked the cat and listened, but there was no sound. She remembered Garth said he'd stayed with Duncan when he first came to Tangil, but he'd told her nothing about the man or where he lived. She didn't think Garth was a very good judge of character. Her father had talked to Duncan about cattle, so she'd supposed he was a settler. She had never trusted the man; there was something sinister about him. If he'd wanted to help her, he could have taken her to Garth.

The normal Duncan brother, the pleasant and talkative doctor, had made Jane wonder more than ever what was wrong with Angus Duncan and whether he was dangerous. She was in a very tight corner, with no idea how to get out of it.

The wind began to rise and it moaned round the building, rattling shutters and bringing with it the faint howling she'd heard on the track. The sounds grew nearer ... had the dingoes followed them? A sudden shot rang out, then silence. The candle guttered in the draught.

Jane sat on the side of the bed for a long time, nerves quivering, her mind going in circles. Surely, Garth would come to look for her? But nobody came.

Eventually, she climbed into the bed and, worn out, Jane and her cat both slept.

Morning came, with magpies singing as if the world outside was normal. The funeral ... and then the fire, the horror came flooding back as she woke. And the black Scotsman had brought her here by force ... she was a prisoner. She must find Garth. Everything was gone; she had nothing, they had nothing. Jane gulped back tears and resolved to be strong.

Garth had let her down, but he would need her support; as a younger brother he had relied on her when they were children. Together they would start again. Make new lives. But how to get out of this prison?

Jane sat up in bed and looked round. With the shadows of night gone, the place looked cleaner and more normal. The bed itself had a patchwork quilt in bright colours, matched by the colours in the curtains. The walls were wood planks, overlapping and the floor was polished boards. There was a marble topped wash stand with ewer and basin, and cupboards. There was even a wardrobe, a bookcase in the room and a writing desk. The books were a mixture of farming textbooks, history and some classics. On one wall were several oil paintings depicting scenes on the diggings, with craggy prospectors toiling in the dirt.

The door opened and a woman with a forbidding expression came in with a tray. Jane stood up as straight as she could and faced her.

'I want to see my brother,' she said firmly. 'That man had no right to lock me up like this.'

Slowly the woman smiled. 'Angus has gone to fetch your brother,' she said quietly in a light Scottish accent. Her white hair was tied back in a bun and her neatness made Jane conscious of her own dishevelled state.

There was tea and toast on the tray and Jane found that she was hungry. She decided to be honest.

'I was so afraid last night, being dragged here in the dark,' she confessed. 'Where is this, and who are you?'

The woman shook her head. 'This is one of Angus Duncan's farms, Jane – you see I know your name – and I am his mother, Elspeth Duncan. I was sorry to hear that you've lost your possessions in a fire.'

'Thank you. I should sympathise with you, having such a son,' Jane said acidly.

It was good to be angry; it stopped her from crying. 'He behaved like a criminal. But why the high fences, the locks? It looks just like a prison, especially in the dark.' She looked at the woman critically. 'I must say you don't look ill-treated, but does he lock you up too?'

'Eat your toast, bairn.' Giving instructions seemed to run in the family. 'Angus says very little of course, but I expect he locked you in for your own good. It can be dangerous out there in the bush at night, especially since the bushranger gang came round here. He must have thought you would run away.'

'That was true. I would have walked out, to get away from him. Did it never occur to him to explain anything? He refused to let me wait for my brother and I had no idea where we were going.' Jane realized she was supposed to be grateful that he'd rescued her, but was it true that she'd been in danger? She doubted it.

Mrs Duncan shrugged. 'You may come to trust Angus in time. Or, of course, you may not. Most women dislike him, but I'm his mother, so I see his good side.'

'But surely you don't need to live in a fort? Your son must have a strange attitude to life.' Jane took a bite of toast. *I don't want to know Angus over time, so I'm sure I'll never trust the man.* She hated him, but she was presumably sitting in his room and eating his bread. She drank her tea and decided to keep quiet.

The woman actually laughed. 'It's quite

simple. We have enclosed several acres because we wanted a garden, an orchard and room for poultry and it was easier. The wallabies and wombats ruined our first garden and the birds ate all our fruit, while the dingoes killed the hens. So Angus decided to build the fence and net the orchard.' She paused. 'And then we discovered that the fence helped to keep out the – larrikins, I suppose they are. Lawless young men running round the goldfield. The present gang, they take gold from poor prospectors, they seem to be worse than most.'

'I suppose,' said Jane slowly, 'that it's like the picket fence round our cottage, only on a bigger scale.' She finished her breakfast and tried to dust down her dress. Mrs Duncan looked at her dispassionately.

'Across the yard you'll find a wash house and a privy. I will lend you some clothes and a brush for your hair.'

Washed and changed into a light grey cotton dress, Jane felt a little more normal. There was a saucer of milk outside the door and Lavender soon found it. The compound gate was still locked, but it was sensible to wait for Garth to appear.

Jane wandered about in the sunshine, trying to calm herself and to think rationally. Yesterday had been too much for her to deal with.

There were several wooden buildings next

to her bedroom; one had roses round the door and a lean-to kitchen attached. The wash house was large, with stone slabs like a dairy, shelves of stores and a big copper for boiling clothes.

*Think about gardens, about work, shut out the memory of your own neat little house and garden. It's gone.*

Jane had not been very attached to the cottage, but she felt lost without a home.

A young Aboriginal woman crossed the yard with a pail of milk and smiled shyly. Jane greeted her and she put down the pail.

'That fire very bad, Miss,' she said simply.

'It was indeed ... how do you know, er...?' She was not sure how to talk to a Ganai, but Jane responded to politeness. The original inhabitants of Gippsland had a mixed reputation and in some parts, people were afraid of 'the blacks'.

'My man, Absalom – you know him? He used to go see your dad. He saw the fire, but too late, could do nothing. Bad men did it, he says.'

'Yes, I remember seeing Absalom at the cottage. Well, I'd like to talk to him and so will my brother, Mrs Absalom... What's your name?'

'Dolly ... we work here, my man and me – just going to set the milk for cheese now.' She smiled again and as she went off, the big gate opened and Garth appeared at last.

Half laughing, her brother took both her hands. He looked pale and untidy, as though, like Jane, he had slept in his clothes. His curly hair was tangled and he needed a shave.

'Janey, I thought you were dead!' He choked and tried to start again. 'It was late, I felt guilty – I went home and ... it was just a ruin. I couldn't tell whether you'd been in there ... so,' he finished sadly, 'I'm afraid I went back to the All Nations. It was the only thing to do. Good job I did, that's where Angus found me. And you ... what happened?'

'The house was burning when I got there, I don't know what happened. I wanted to wait for you, Garth, I knew you would come. But that man Duncan forced me to come here against my will. The man's a monster. I'm not staying here a minute longer than I have to. Where shall we go, Garth? Cash your gold and we'll leave this dreadful place, go back to civilisation.' Jane tried to put all her strength into her words, all her horror of the wilds.

Garth sank down on a seat with his head in his hands. 'We're lucky, I suppose. We're alive and poor old Pa's safe in Melbourne ... but – well ... there's precious little gold, girl. The box, my tin box has disappeared. I looked last night and it was gone.'

Jane felt the world swing round for a

moment or two and she fought panic. She sat beside her brother.

'No gold! What on earth do we do?' If raw gold was stolen you could never get it back. Everyone on the Tangil field knew that. It was the common currency in the area and nobody asked where it came from. Some person or persons must have torched the cottage, to get at the gold. It was robbery on a bold scale.

From his pocket Garth drew out a small cloth bag.

'Here it is, all I have left. There was more, but I spent it yesterday, at the All Nations. I was going to keep it, but I suppose we need food and clothes ... isn't it beautiful?' He bent over the pieces of gold, cradling them in his hands. 'I love the stuff ... tell you what Jane, I'll go and work, go after gold until we have built up a fortune! I'll do it for Pa, he wants us to be rich.' He laughed, 'I'll live in a tent, grow a beard and be a real prospector!'

No mention of what was to become of his sister.

Jane was appalled. 'No, Garth. We must leave, you can earn a living in a better way than grubbing in the earth, you're a draughtsman. I'll work too, as a governess or a companion, anywhere, but not here!' She glared at him.

Through an archway, Angus Duncan

emerged and Jane shuddered. The last thing she wanted was his brooding presence, standing over them at this critical time. Their future life was being decided.

'I will not live in a tent! You can't expect it!' She spoke quietly, but forcefully and fixed Garth with another glare.

Duncan stood and looked at them for a while quite peacefully and Jane realized that she could not possibly have got away from him the night before. He was large, much taller than Garth, but so well proportioned that his size was not noticeable. The only thing you noticed about him was that dreadful beard.

'I telegraphed to the police, about the fire and the theft. They'll not be here for a few days, though.'

'Thank you, Angus,' Garth said gratefully. 'I'm off now to find somewhere to live...' but the man had gone.

Garth turned to his sister. 'Angus said to me on the way here that you can stay with them, until we have a home. You'll maybe have to work your passage, though. They are Scottish, after all!'

Jane put a shaking hand on his arm. 'How can you leave me here? I can't do farm work, I'm not strong enough and I – I don't know how. Oh, Garth, don't leave me!' Jane's carefully controlled emotions broke out and she wept.

When she was calm again, Jane realized that it was no good blaming her brother, or expecting him to rescue her. He thought for a while and then said, 'Look, I'll ask round Tangil, see if I can rent another cottage and then you can join me. We'll have to borrow from the store until I earn some money ... but lots of people do that. Give me a week, Janey, you can stay here a week, surely? I'll come back next week.'

A week of the Duncans seemed to Jane like a life sentence in her present state of mind.

'Do you care how I feel, Garth? Can you imagine what it's like to be a woman, completely at the mercy of men? You can come and go as you please, while I have to do as I'm told and stay here.'

'Of course, it's hard for a girl...' her brother looked uneasy.

'I was actually brought here by force, do you realize that? Because that man is big and strong. Men who use their strength on women are despicable! And you will leave me here, in a place like this!'

'A week, Jane, give me a week. I think you misjudge Angus, I must say. He's a decent man and his mother is very ... capable. Angus doesn't talk very much, and that's a problem for some people, but I have found him very helpful and generous. Give him a chance, Jane. And give me a week, there's a good girl.'

That was obviously Garth's last word, for the moment.

Jane sighed; she was weary. 'I wonder what Father would have done.'

When he had gone, Jane felt as though she hadn't known her brother until now. He was almost indifferent to her problems and what was worse, he was a poor judge of character. How could Duncan be helpful and generous? She had never met anyone with less kindness.

## SIX

Jane sat on the bench with Lavender and wondered whether she would ever be happy again. Mrs Duncan found her there, but she showed little sympathy. There was no mention of their dreadful loss. In a matter-of-fact way she said, 'We make soap today. It's not the most pleasant of jobs, but would you like to help me? It's entirely up to you of course, but it might help to pass the time. My son hasn't yet worked out what we can do to help you.'

'How you're going to get rid of me, you mean.' Jane shook her head miserably. 'But I've no idea how to make soap. I thought everybody could buy soap from the store, these days.'

The older woman looked at her critically. 'So you can, but we happen to like the old-fashioned ways of doing things. We buy tea of course, and flour and sugar, and a little kerosene for the lamps, things we can't produce here. Angus has worked hard to build up our farms and save money ... making things for ourselves has become a habit, I suppose. When I was a girl, there was no choice. Soap, candles, bread, cheese – we make them all. So – will ye join me?'

Jane was on the point of refusing. Why should she work for these people? She wasn't a servant or a farm girl. She glared at the woman.

But then, what else should she do? Perhaps this was some form of test. Well, she would show Mrs Duncan and her horrible son that she was quite capable of paying for her board with unpleasant work. Her mouth was set as she said, 'I'll do it. If I have to stay here in prison for a few days, I will earn my keep.'

'That's the spirit!' The woman was friendlier now, or was she being ironic?

They crossed the yard to a sort of scullery. The room was full of smoke from a large fire and it was hard at first to see what was happening. The smell was appalling and Jane wrinkled her nose, then caught Mrs Duncan looking at her. It was some kind of animal fat. Was that really how they made soap?

They proceeded to drain water from two large barrels, pouring it into a third.

'There's ashes at the bottom, wood ash,' the woman said. 'It's been soaking since yesterday.' They worked for some time, pouring water through the layer of ashes to make lye.

*Yesterday, when we buried poor Mr Penrose and we had our house burned down ... this woman was soaking ashes in water.* Jane bit back tears at the thought of yesterday.

'Don't touch the water, it's caustic at this stage, lye will burn.' But Jane had already splashed her hand. 'Don't worry, I have marigold ointment.' Also home made, no doubt. The rural efficiency of this family was beginning to be irritating. How could people know how to make so many things? Surely it was easier to let tradespeople make your soap and cheese.

'Do you make your own shoes?' Jane asked, almost mischievously and the woman laughed.

'No, but we certainly know how to repair them. We have a cobbler's last and we sometimes cure our own leather, when we kill an animal for beef.'

Jane then had to heat the water over the fire in a large pan and add a block of grease. It was cut from a large tub of rendered fat, the origin of the smell, 'From when we last

87

killed a few sheep. We save all the fat, use it for many things.'

Jane added some salt as instructed and as the fat melted, white bubbles came to the surface. Then the woman disappeared and Jane was left stirring, stirring, her face hot from the fire and her back beginning to ache. The smell was quite unpleasant, but she was so intent on not burning herself or spilling the mixture that her mind was firmly on the job.

Mrs Duncan came back with a tray of lavender flowers, which she threw into the mixture. Gradually Jane could see that something like soap was floating to the top of the water. The smell was now much more agreeable; this was quite interesting.

By the time the soap was strained and poured into moulds to set into bars, Jane felt quite proud of her achievement. 'We keep it a month at least, before we use it,' she was told. The longer soap is kept, the more economical it is to use.'

*But I won't be here in a month's time, so I'll never get to use it.*

It was time for the midday meal and she realized with surprise that she hadn't thought about her predicament for at least two hours.

The Duncans and Jane had a simple meal of bread, cheese and salad from the garden. This was all their own produce and it was fresh and appetising; Jane enjoyed the meal, to her surprise. She sat without speaking and was shocked when Angus Duncan suddenly asked her a question.

'Those drawings at your father's house. Whose work were they?'

'Were ... they've all gone now. Mine. Why?' She could be as abrupt as he was.

'Thought so ... Garth showed me some of your work at Bendigo. I would like a drawing of our house. Not this one, the one down river.' Duncan was looking at her, his expression hidden by the beard.

Jane felt like refusing, but that would be childish and in any case, drawing would be much preferable to soap making.

'I'll draw anything, as long as it's not a portrait. I – I want to do portraits, but I need much more practice.'

Elspeth Duncan passed Jane a cup of tea. 'Should we not give Jane a few days to recover? She has been through an ordeal, Angus.'

Was there a sarcastic smile behind the black beard? 'Keep her busy, she needs work. That's my diagnosis and I think Robbie would agree with me.'

'Your brother shows his patients rather more compassion, I think.' His mother turned to Jane. 'Have you met my son Robbie?'

'Yes, Dr Duncan visited my father. He was

– most sympathetic.'

'So,' Duncan rose to his feet and pushed back his chair, 'to keep her active, let her make cheese for the rest of the day.'

'But I don't know how...' Jane caught sight of their faces and stopped. This would never do. 'I suppose I can learn.' Life in Bendigo had not prepared her for this.

Cheese was easier than soap, she found, and the smell of curds was quite pleasant. Dreamily she stirred the warm curds as she was instructed, while Mrs Duncan lined large metal containers with cheesecloth. It was an involved process and Jane began to realize how much work went into the cheese she'd always taken for granted.

Once again, she was absorbed in the work and at the end of the day she decided that hateful though he was, the bushranger had been right; it was better for her to be busy than to have time to think of her troubles. Of course, the only reason he'd suggested it was to force her to earn her keep.

Garth did not come back for her, but Absalom said he was still looking for a cottage. The days passed quickly in a variety of farm work; the prisoner realized she had to be patient.

The next week, Jane was taken to the Duncans' other farm. After breakfast and the morning chores they set out, two silent passengers. The cart creaked its way slowly up the track. The horse was steady, to say the least, and the driver also seemed to be half asleep. Angus Duncan, hat pulled down firmly over his eyes, held the reins but the horse seemed to need few instructions.

Jane was wrapped in a cloak and perched on a cushion beside the driver. Behind them was a load of potatoes and onions, produce of the land, on the first leg of their journey to the stores at Walhalla, a gold mining town to the north that was home to over two thousand people.

Duncan had typically said nothing, apart from giving Jane drawing materials to take with her. From his mother she'd gathered that the other farm was about two hours' drive away and that they'd be back by nightfall.

The cart lumbered uphill, on a track bordered by luxuriant tree ferns and shaded by tall trees. They were leaving the valley of Haunted Creek and eventually came out of the trees into a sunny morning. Duncan turned the horse onto a track across the ridge, from where they could see blue mountains in the distance, covered in forest. The wild country of the Victorian Alps framed their world.

'It's beautiful!' Jane exclaimed in surprise and was rewarded with another of Duncan's looks. She was beginning to wonder why he looked at her like that, but behind the beard it was impossible to judge his expression. Turning away from him with a sigh, she watched the scenery slowly slide by.

Soon they could see to their left the deep valley of the Tangil, the place where she had lived in the dust and the heat until only a few days ago, the place where fortunes were still being made, although she had seen little evidence of wealth. To their right was another river valley, the slopes dotted with trees.

Away from the gold mining areas, Jane was beginning to realize that Gippsland was attractive. The rolling green slopes of well-kept farms and neat houses followed one another in succession. There were no big, imposing residences as at Bendigo, only plain weatherboard houses of one storey. Several had high fences around them and most seemed to have gardens and an orchard, with fruit beginning to turn ripe in the late summer sun. It was a tranquil scene, far removed from the dust and dirt of Tangil.

The little township of Willow Grove lay on their route and Duncan pulled up outside the store. A kookaburra set up its raucous call in a tree above them and he looked up with a grin.

'The settler's chook, that's what they call him.'

He disappeared inside and came out with a newspaper, which he handed to Jane.

'Do you read the *Weekly Times?* You should.' The man seemed to be relaxing a little in the sunshine.

Jane took the paper eagerly. An idea had been forming in her mind, a way forward for her to pick up the pieces of her life again.

'Does it carry advertisements? I hope so, I want to apply for a position as a governess – or something.'

Another of Duncan's looks, as he climbed back into the driving seat. 'What can you offer, as a governess or something?'

'I've been well educated, Mr Duncan!' Jane spoke quite sharply, and then realized that this was just what any prospective employer would ask. 'I suppose I should make a list, before I write a letter. Good grounding in literature and grammar, maths and some science ... drawing and piano playing ... and I can speak a little French.' It sounded quite adequate, listed like that.

There was a slight sigh from under the hat that sounded like 'Mais oui,' but Jane could not be sure. Duncan was gazing out across to the mountains, completely indifferent to her accomplishments.

Off they went again and Jane admired the gleam of the horse's coat in the sunshine. Duncan was just as mean as Garth had suggested, but he looked after his animals well.

Eventually, the cart took a track to the left.

Not far off through the trees, Jane could see a road snaking up into the hills but before they reached the road, they arrived at the farm house. A stone-built house, solid and respectable, framed in trees and shrubs, windows sparkling in the sun.

The Duncans were well established here. The bushranger image of Angus that she'd held was fading, replaced by the impression of a man of substance. Jane smiled to herself, wondering why a prosperous landowner should seem so uncouth.

She must concentrate on the house. Jane could see that it would make an attractive drawing; it reminded her of the pleasant prosperity of Bendigo. Why did Duncan not get a photographer to make a record? Cost, perhaps? She was to make a drawing in exchange for board and lodging, in the Duncans' economical way.

'Oh, Mr Duncan! Thank goodness you've come! Such goings on here, you've no idea!' A female rushed out to open the gate for the cart, keeping up a torrent of words and Jane thought she saw Duncan wince under the big hat.

'This is Marcia,' he said as the cart came to a halt. 'Miss Pendlebury, my mother's house-keeper.'

A young man came out of the farm buildings to take charge of the horse and Marcia raised her voice even higher. 'Jed, take a bag of potatoes into the house. You must come right away, Mr Duncan, the best bull's lame and wild pigs are in the barley–'

Duncan took off his hat and led the way into the house. 'We will have a cup of tea first,' he said firmly and Marcia's chatter subsided. 'And I will show Miss Ashby over the house.' He must be proud of it.

A young girl was scolded into making tea and Marcia turned her fierce black eyes on Jane. 'And who may this be? We don't need any more servants at Blackwood Park, least of all young lasses! None of 'em knows how to work.'

Angus Duncan drank his tea composedly. 'Miss Ashby is our guest,' was all he said. Marcia looked the guest up and down and her conclusion was evidently not favourable.

'I could have sworn that gown was an old one of Mrs Duncan's,' she muttered. 'Thought you was a pauper. Can't afford to feed any more mouths here.'

Jane looked down at her dress. She was clean and neat, but that was all; the dress was worn and the shawl had seen better days.

'I lost my belongings in a fire,' she said quietly. 'Mrs Duncan lent me these clothes.' She was not going to rise to insults.

Jane wondered for a moment what would have happened if Angus Duncan had not dragged her home that night. She was a reluctant guest, but they were kind to her. Not particularly friendly, but they'd certainly rescued her from a night in the bush.

Jane surveyed the housekeeper over her teacup. The woman was about thirty, her black hair straggling from under a cap, her apron wrapped round a meagre body. Of course they had arrived unexpectedly, but Miss Pendlebury did not impress. Her way of speaking to her betters would have earned her dismissal in Bendigo.

'We'll need lunch, Marcia, before we leave. No doubt you have to meet the coach soon.' Duncan stood up.

'But what about the pigs and–' Marcia began loudly, but she was silenced with a look.

'Pass me that bunch of keys, Jane.' She looked round and saw the keys hanging from a nail in the passage. Duncan went out into another room and came back with two shotguns and cartridges. 'I'll tell Tom and Henry to shoot the pigs. If they find any worth eating, they can bring them back and you'll salt them down for bacon.' He paused for a moment. 'I will take a look at the bull.'

He motioned to Jane to follow him and he showed her the main rooms of the house, pleasantly furnished and more elegant than the Home Farm. There was a bathroom with a hot water geyser over the bath and

Duncan explained that hot water for the whole house was heated by a boiler outside. The water closet impressed Jane; she had not seen one since they left Bendigo.

'I like your house very much, Mr Duncan,' Jane said.

'That's good. Now you can draw it.'

Jane was placed by a stone wall in the garden and she had to agree that it was a good position, with the building at a slight elevation. Below the house was an ornamental lake with willow trees and waterlilies; a pleasant scene. Getting out her paper and pencils, she set to work.

Angus Duncan stalked off and she hoped not to see him again for a while; his silences made her feel uneasy. In five minutes he came back with a small table and a folding chair.

The sounds of a late summer morning surrounded Jane as she worked on the drawing. Bees danced in the garden flowers, their humming a pleasant drone. There were red and green parrots squawking through the trees and far off, the inevitable magpies warbled. Occasionally, she heard a distant shot as the men pursued wild pigs.

With a tremendous clatter, the Walhalla coach arrived, coming up from the valley with the mail. It stopped at the front gate of Blackwood Park and four horses were trotted out from the stables. The passengers were

97

offered refreshments, boxes of produce were loaded and then in a short time they were off again in a swirl of dust. The sounds came clearly to Jane as she sat in the garden.

Absorbed in her work, Jane was surprised when a shadow fell across the paper. Marcia stood watching her, head on one side. 'Is he paying youse for that? Waste of money, I call it.' Her face was quite innocent of expression.

'Was the coach on time today?' Jane decided to change the subject. She continued to work, but Marcia was not deterred. She sat on the wall and talked without stopping, the words merging into the background like the magpie's chatter. She talked about the problems of keeping house in the country and the huge amount of work imposed on her by the Duncans, including baking cakes and biscuits for the coach passengers. 'And the pigs, I'm scared of 'em, wild pigs roaming the bush, them as let pigs loose should be hung...' one more hazard, evidently, in country living. Thank goodness there were no wild pigs on the goldfield.

Jane concentrated on a problem with drawing the roof of the house, which was made of corrugated iron. An iron roof was an advantage; rain water could be collected in gutters and drained to a tank, but it was not picturesque. She frowned and tried to fade out the roof a little, just emphasising the dormer window. It looked better and she sighed with relief. The drawing was coming on well, but she only had perhaps half an hour left before the light changed, and the shadows with it.

Marcia was still talking. '...and now I'm asking myself, do youse fancy Mr Duncan? Are youse after him? I'll have something to say if it's so.'

'Good heavens – what do you mean?' This woman was mad.

'I believe in straight talking, Miss – er – forget your name. Doesn't matter. Youse have to realize that Mr Duncan will look much higher than a pauper for a wife, and there's plenty of women after him. So if ye do fancy him and I know that ye do, forget it. There's better than youse hoping to be Mrs Duncan of Blackwood Park.'

Jane realized that her mouth was in danger of dropping open. It was time for a little honesty on her part. 'I don't believe you. Surely, no woman could be desperate enough to marry Mr Duncan!' Then she caught sight of Duncan, standing among the trees close behind them. He must have heard Jane and the man was leaning on a tree trunk, his shoulders shaking. Well, he knew what she thought of him, she had made it obvious.

Marcia hadn't noticed her employer yet. She smiled in a superior way. 'I'm used to his funny ways, see. He doesn't talk because he–'

Angus Duncan strode forward and he was not laughing now.

'Marcia, what are you about? We need lunch immediately, I have to make another call on the way home.' He went off, not even pausing to look at Jane's drawing. She hurriedly completed the outlines; a little tidying up could be done later.

After an indifferent lunch of bread and cheese they were ready for the road and Jane was glad they were leaving. Marcia glared and muttered at Jane when they were left alone for a few minutes, 'You'll not forget what I said!'

This was a lovely spot, but Marcia was unpleasant and the other servants seemed to be afraid of her. Why did the Duncans tolerate the woman?

The horse was yoked up again and Jane noticed that there were several cases of apples and plums on the cart, no doubt for the store at Tangil. Jane would rather not have gone down into that barren valley, but she had no choice. They took the downward track at the horse's usual stately pace. She reflected that the farmers must be making a profit from selling food to miners and their families. Mrs Duncan had told her that once the railway was built, they also had a market for produce in Melbourne.

Duncan was silent until they reached the valley bottom, when he turned to look at his passenger. 'Would you mind if we called in at the cottage? I want to see the damage.'

## SEVEN

Jane hated the thought of returning to the ruin of their home, but she realized why he wanted to see it. This man owned the cottage, as well as several others in the valley, and then, anything left to salvage should be rescued.

'I suppose we should. Will you rebuild the house?'

'Probably, in time.'

The little house was pathetic, a ruin laid open to the afternoon sunshine. The brick chimney stood alone; the roof had fallen in and the timber frame had all burned away.

The iron bed frames were still there, and of course the iron kitchen stove. They looked at the wreckage in silence for a while and then Jane said, 'I hope you don't think I was careless with the kitchen fire.'

Duncan was pushing aside debris in the garden and he looked up at Jane.

'This was deliberate.' Jane could see that the burn marks were black. 'Someone has scattered kerosene and then thrown in a match.'

It was a terrible thought. Jane gingerly picked her way through the mess. As Garth had said, the tin box of gold had gone. And there was something else. Surely...

'Duncan,' Jane spoke without thinking, 'I can't see Garth's shotgun.'

'Where was it?'

The shotgun was kept in Garth's wardrobe, the remains of which were on the floor, but there was no heap of twisted metal. The gun had gone.

'Well, Ashby.' Duncan spoke in an ironic tone, obviously having noticed what she'd called him. 'The gun's been stolen. Unless Garth has been back and taken it himself.'

'Have you any idea ... who might have done this?'

'Not exactly. But the thought of raven's gold is tempting, I suppose...'

'Please explain! I've heard those words before, even in Melbourne. What do they mean, Mr Duncan?'

'Don't know how it originated. Raven's gold is thieved gold, taken from the rightful owners. Garth's tin box is now raven's gold. But the banks can't tell the difference. You won't see it again.'

'Maybe because the raven is a bird of ill omen,' Jane suggested. Ma Dooley had said it would be the death of her lads.

Jane wanted to leave the site and never come back. She was beginning to feel light-headed under the burning sun, having left her hat in the cart. As she walked through what was left of the garden, she knelt down to look at something in the grass. Her father's gold cufflinks ... he'd treasured them because they were given to him by her mother. What would he say when he heard that all their possessions were gone?

The world swung round alarmingly and she slipped sideways in a faint.

'Steady there, Ashby,' said a voice from far away and a strong arm supported her.

Duncan led her over to the shade of the cart. He held out a bottle of water and then went off for another look at the cottage, which gave her time to recover. Jane felt ashamed of her weakness and for once, Duncan's silence was welcome. He didn't ask how she felt, but after about ten minutes silently handed her into the vehicle.

They continued in the cart as before, along the track to the Tangil store and when they got there, Duncan took her in with him and ordered two cups of strong coffee.

Mr Ellis was behind his counter, slicing bacon and he beamed when he saw Jane.

'Well, Miss Ashby, right glad I am to see you, isn't it! After the fire, wicked, that was...' he continued in this way after calling to his wife, 'Myfanwy! Two cups of coffee, right away now!'

Duncan handed over the cases of fruit and when Jane had drunk her coffee, she began to recover. Mr Ellis told her that Garth was looking for a new house for them both. It was good to hear that he'd told the Ellises. Then he drew their attention to a poster on the wall.

'Look you, a dance in the Willow Grove hall. With music and singing, isn't it. My Myfanwy will sing Welsh songs! Everybody will be there and Mrs Duncan will play the piano, she always plays for the dances ... here now, Mr Duncan, you will be coming to the ball, with a lady, it might be?'

The storekeeper looked at them both with his head on one side, evidently weighing up whether there might be romance in the air. Jane felt like telling him there was nothing of the kind.

Duncan glared at the storekeeper. 'Only because I have to escort the pianist.' He looked across at Jane. 'You'd better come too, and help. You are supposed to be musical?' It was a charming invitation, but quite in character.

Jane found it hard to believe that people living in such a remote area would, or could hold a dance. She loved music and had missed her piano, but had not expected to hear any music here. 'I suppose it's another way to get work out of me?' She couldn't resist the sarcasm.

'Of course. We have to keep you working, the harder the better.'

Jane couldn't see the expression behind the beard, but he looked grim. How long was it going to take to get away from him? She turned to the shopkeeper.

'Mr Ellis, if you hear of a house to rent, will you please let me know? I'm desperate! I can't impose on Mr Duncan's – er – kindness much longer!'

There was a silence and Jane realized how rude she had been. After all, the Duncans were giving her board and lodging and had been kind enough in their frugal way. Duncan shot her a look, but said nothing. Mr Ellis agreed that he would ask all his customers about houses to rent.

Megan Ellis came through from the bakery with a tray of scones and exclaimed with delight when she saw Jane. 'And we were wondering if you had left the district!' As her father carried a bag of flour out to the trap, she drew Jane aside. 'You – do you happen to know of any family that needs help in the house, or on a farm? I am looking for a job, see. My sister is coming here to work in the store, so that will give me a chance to try another job, learn something else. But not too far, mind!' She laughed and Jane thought how pretty she was. 'I don't want to be too far from my family.'

As they clopped homewards, a rider came towards them on a big grey. He reined in beside the trap and Garth looked happy as he said, 'My little sister, out for a ride! Good day, Angus. I've just been to Moe, made another bank deposit.'

'Good news, Garth. Now tell me, where exactly are you living? I'd like to visit you,' Jane asked him.

Garth pulled a face. 'It's not very salubrious, Janey, not fit for a lady. That's why I haven't come to fetch you yet. But if you want to see my humble dwelling, it's just down the track a little, you pass it on your way. It's quite close to Home Farm.'

They followed Garth down towards the creek and when she saw the house, Jane was thankful that she didn't have to live there. Duncan said nothing, just sat in the trap and looked around. Jane jumped down and inspected the shanty.

'I suppose you could call it basic,' Jane said. She had to say something, to cover her shock. Garth had bought an expensive horse, but was living in squalor. What would Father have thought? A sagging bark roof supported by rough poles, walls of rough-sawn planks and the window covered in sacking – this was the place her brother called home. The lean-to stable was slightly better than the rest.

They stood in the stuffy kitchen, which was none too clean. Garth was obviously not managing very well by himself.

'How long is this going to go on?'

Garth looked rather sheepish. 'Trouble is, I could be here for quite a while. There's a place up on the ridge, cleared land, plenty of water. I've offered to buy it ... but, no house.' He looked at her as if judging her reaction. 'We might find someone to build a house, but it will take time.' Looking through the open door at the still figure in the trap, he added quietly, 'You could always go to Father in Melbourne, if you don't like it here. The farm work must be hard for you.'

Jane was speechless for a moment, which was unusual, as Garth pointed out.

'Well, what do you want, Jane? If I build a house it will be much better than anything we can rent round here.'

'I want,' Jane said deliberately, 'to get away from Home Farm. Now, not in two years' time! You can't imagine what it's like living with the Duncans, he seems to talk to you. Maybe he doesn't like women? Some bachelors end up like that. His mother works far too hard, especially for her age, but he doesn't seem to worry about it. It's primitive, Garth, that's what it is!'

The bone was thin and sharpened at one end, while the other was wrapped in hide. It was held level with the man's chest, the point aimed straight at his heart.

A gust of wind swirled through the door, the lamp flickered and shadows leapt on the walls. Ma Dooley stared with her mouth open, silent for once, out of her depth. They had not seen this coming. The Law always arrived with shouts and thumped on the door. This was different. The dark man had come silently, stepping out of the mist of a rainy night. It was a night when there were no customers at Mrs Dooley's grog shanty, no living soul for miles except the Dooleys. No help anywhere.

'You know what this is,' the man said softly. 'And you know why.'

'Take that thing away! You've nothing against me ... you can't prove anything!' Roy Dooley pushed back his damp brown hair and looked across at his brother, but he was no help. Michael was slumped with his head on the table, asleep. 'Ask my Ma, I was here that day...' he stopped suddenly, aware that he'd said too much.

Ma snorted. 'Roy Dooley, what have you done now? What day?'

Absalom the Ganai man was intent, his face stern. 'That day, you torched the Ashby house and stole their gold. The gold they had worked for days under the hot sun for.'

'I never! Raven done it!' Roy's voice was high and thin.

'Ashby is a good man, they did you no harm.' He paused, and Roy shivered. 'For this, I point the bone and you will die. I am singing you...' The dark man obviously believed it was true. The bone never wavered.

'You're a savage, you know nothing, take it away!' Roy was squirming, as though he could already feel the influence of the bone. 'Hey, Mike, you know I never done it! It were Raven!'

Michael Dooley raised his head a little, gave a snore and flopped back on the table. Ma found her voice at last.

'Grab him, Roy! We'll throw him out...' she tried to move, but her limbs felt heavy.

Roy Dooley was also motionless, staring at the killing bone.

The voice was soft and low, the words had rhythm like a song. 'I am singing you ... you can do nothing. I wear the shoes, killer for the Ganai nation. Your time has come, Roy Dooley.' There was a flash of white, predatory teeth.

The Dooleys saw a man wearing a cloak of kangaroo skin, wearing it with authority. The man's eyes glittered in his dark face. 'Will not touch you with this thing. I point the bone – you die. There is no escape. This is justice. The old man Ashby, he is sick, he work so hard. You took what was his.'

Ma Dooley looked down and saw the soft shoes of cockatoo feathers, used for ritual killing. It was all true, she'd heard of this but never seen it. She thought the missionaries had banned it.

Time stood still. She looked up and the man had gone, melted away into the shadows. There was silence in the hut except for the trickle of autumn rain. Ma roused herself with an effort and pulled the fire together.

'Get to your bed, Michael. And you, Roy, don't worry yourself about that savage.'

When Michael had dragged himself off to bed, the woman turned to Roy, who was shivering. 'You told him Raven done it. How could he? Mal Raven's been away for months, Marcia says. Police can't touch him. Where's that gold, Roy? I want my share, I'm sick of making grog for drunken miners.'

'I got no gold, Ma.' Roy hesitated, shame-faced. 'Raven ... well, he's back, from God knows where ... and now, that's like Raven, he takes charge.' He scratched his head. 'I might get some of it or not.'

'What will ye do, then?' Ma stood with hands on hips.

'Just have to do another raid somewhere. I feel cold, give us some hot rum.'

Mrs Dooley pulled the kettle over the fire. 'You don't take no notice of a black pointing a stick at you, unless it's a loaded gun and they ain't got none, as a rule.' She lit her pipe. 'Roy Dooley, you stand up to them Ganai, their day is done. There ain't no such thing as black magic, and you know it.'

Roy shook his head. 'How did that black-feller know who done it?' he whispered. 'Nobody saw us. Why do I feel so cold?'

'Cold night, that's all and roof's leaking. Now, you're best to give up raiding with that Raven, he's a criminal although folks think he's a gentleman, and don't take our Michael neither. The lad's got no heart for it. Keep out o' trouble, that's what I say. Dig some gold for yourself.'

Mr Basil Charlesworth sat in his Bendigo office, considering his next move. Clients, mine owners, had asked him to travel to another part of Victoria, to organise the legal aspects of their business in Gippsland; new shares were to be issued and Bendigo experience was valued. He sighed. Bouncing about over mountain roads was not an attractive prospect ... when did the snow season start, up there in Walhalla?

'You'd best go soon, Mr Charlesworth,' one of his clerks had suggested. 'They say you can get stuck up there for weeks in winter. The Victorian Alps are just like Switzerland, in the snow season.'

The mine owner could probably find a local man to work for him, if Charlesworth refused to go. But then, he had papers for Angus Duncan to sign concerning property in Bendigo. Duncan had been to see him about an inheritance, months ago and

Charlesworth's office had sold some property for him. He would write a letter to ask Duncan to meet him in Walhalla. Surely that would not be too much to ask?

There was another client in Toongabbie, which was on the coach route for Walhalla and lastly, there was Miss Ashby. Charlesworth decided he would visit the young woman, on his way through Gippsland. It was time she came to her senses and realized that it was foolish to keep him waiting.

Jane Ashby would never get such a good offer again; by now she would have had time to regret leaving Bendigo. Once her independent spirit was tamed, she would make a good wife. He'd noticed that married life agreed with most women, and it also calmed them down. A lively woman like Miss Ashby would need firm control. He rather enjoyed the thought of bringing her to see the error of her ways.

Charlesworth rang the bell on his desk and the clerk reappeared.

'Buy me a return ticket to Gippsland, Jones, to Toongabbie and make an appointment with Smithers. I believe the train stops there to connect with the coach to Walhalla,' he ordered. 'And write – no, send a telegram – to the Star Hotel, book me a room for – let me see, for three days. I will stay in Melbourne overnight to break the journey, the usual place. And a night in Moe on the way back to Melbourne. That should be sufficient.'

'Do you think the telegraph has reached those parts, Mr Charlesworth?' Jones looked doubtful. 'If you agree, I will write a letter.'

Two weeks later, Charlesworth set out. He had not heard from Miss Ashby, in spite of writing her a letter. Once the business in Walhalla was done, he would make an effort to find her. It would be a long, boring journey and it was inconvenient to leave town. However, if it meant that he returned to Bendigo with deals completed and the prospect of marriage, it would be worth the effort.

After a tedious train journey and a stop at Toongabbie, Charlesworth settled into the Walhalla coach with a weary sigh. This would be the worst leg of the trip. The forest was picturesque, but one soon tired of mile after mile of pale trunks and monotonous green. The day had passed, the sun was in the west. They were supposed to arrive before nightfall.

The road got steadily worse after the second change of horses. It became narrow and dangerous, the track winding round the edge of precipices. As they went higher into the hills, there were fewer trees; they had been cut down for fuel, revealing just how steep the bare hillsides were. It would have been prudent to stay in Bendigo.

Charlesworth shuddered and turned to his newspaper, wondering why anyone would build a town in such an outlandish spot, even if they had found gold there. How they ever managed to cart the heavy machinery up to the mines was a mystery. There were, no doubt, other routes to the town, but none of them could be easy in this wild terrain.

'Lot of accidents on this stretch!' the man next to Charlesworth said cheerfully. 'This is Flour Bag Cutting, the narrowest part, only room for one cart...' he stopped as the coach swayed to a halt and there were shouts. 'Looks as if there's something else on the road. Well, they'll have to back up, coach has right of way.'

'You live up here?'

'Nay! I'm a salesman, come up here twice a year... I wonder what's going on?'

The solicitor let down the window, peered out and found himself staring into disaster.

There were three horsemen barring their way, masked and armed with shotguns.

'We're bailed up!' the salesman said, dropping to the floor.

The coachman was made to get down and one of the masked men opened the door and waved a gun at the four passengers. 'Get out. We'll have your money and jewellery, bags and parcels. Look sharp!' His face was hidden and he had a hat pulled low down on his head and long black hair, tied back. The voice was English, deep and cultured, at odds with the appearance. 'Do as I say and you will not be harmed.'

The solicitor protested. 'My bag contains only papers! It will be no use whatsoever to anyone else!'

Charlesworth was prodded in the stomach by the end of a gun. 'You're a fat gold buyer, we know about you. Let's see your bank rolls, or we'll make it hard for you.'

This was another of the men, a rough voice this time and cold blue eyes looking at him through the mask.

The man with the English voice was the tallest and seemed to be the leader.

'Please restrain yourselves, gentlemen,' he said to the others. 'We are here to do business, not to upset the passengers.' He seemed to be enjoying himself.

'But I am not a gold buyer...' Charlesworth watched helplessly as his document case was turned out onto the road. His money was found and pocketed, and then the man flung the bag over the side, far into the gully below. It was followed by the other bags and the salesman lost his temper.

'That's my samples, my living, you swine!' He fronted up to the man, but was pushed back and hit with the butt of a shotgun. He retreated with a bleeding nose.

The smallest of the three bushrangers said,

'Don't! You've done enough, don't hit them!' Charlesworth tried to get out of range on the narrow road, without falling over the edge. Suddenly, the weapon was swung the other way. A young male passenger tried to fend off the blow, but was hit over the head himself.

'I deplore the use of force, but sometimes it is necessary when the passengers get excited,' the Englishman said, sitting on his horse and taking no part in the proceedings. 'I trust you will respect the lady.' The only woman passenger was a spirited old lady, wielding a large umbrella. She lay about with it and commanded her own respect. None of the men went near her. 'For your own good,' he added with a laugh.

The passengers eventually huddled together in a group. Looking at his victims, the Englishman told them in a conversational tone, 'If I were really professional, I would shoot you all. Then there would be no evidence.'

There was something sinister about all the bushrangers, shadowy, faceless figures in dark clothes, but Charlesworth was most afraid of the leader. It seemed quite possible that they would all be murdered and thrown down into the river far below. Why had he ever come to this uncivilised place?

# EIGHT

A cart came into view, lumbering along the track and the bushrangers swiftly galloped off, causing the cart-horse to rear. The smallest man looked back over his shoulder for a moment and Charlesworth recovered himself enough to shake his fist.

'You shall hang for this!' he shouted and then feared he had been too theatrical.

The whole incident had lasted only a few minutes, but it had left two passengers injured and the others badly shaken. The carter sized up the situation, shook his head and slowly backed the cart away to where there was room for the coach to pass.

The coachman opened the door for the passengers to board. 'Thank goodness they didn't take horses. Them cattle's worth a bob or two and I'm responsible,' he said. 'If you gentlemen and lady will come with me, we'll report this at the town, and let's hope they catch the villains, else we'll not be able to sleep in our beds.'

'Does this happen often?' Charlesworth wanted to know. The old lady was busy trying to help the salesman, who was obviously in pain.

The young man spoke up, 'Never before on this run, to my knowledge. Gold's always sent out with an escort of troopers and there's not many pickings on the inward run, it's mostly food wagons.' The horses shifted and stamped restlessly and the driver went to them. 'We thought there'd be no more of this business, after Ned Kelly was caught. There's no profit in bushranging, if they could only see it.'

'They got quite a lot of money from me.' Charlesworth was bitter. His trip was ruined and the papers for Duncan would take months to replace. It had been a grave mistake to leave Bendigo for this Godforsaken place. In the future, Charlesworth decided, he would only accept new clients in a city.

The town of Walhalla lay at the bottom of a steep-sided valley from which the sun had long since disappeared, although evening light still touched the tops of the hills.

Smoke rose into the cool upland air. Many buildings were crowded together, banks, schools and hotels, with cottages perched on the hillsides above the single street. There were people everywhere and a pervading clank and thud of heavy machinery.

Charlesworth was thankful to see the lights of the Star Hotel at journey's end, but before supper, the passengers had to be interviewed by the police, who seemed as surprised by the raid as they had been.

Trying to give a description of the men, Charlesworth told the constable that the biggest one was dark and he thought the smallest was fair-haired. It was hard to see anything else because of the masks. Their horses were ... he could remember the big man rode a chestnut, that was all. Charlesworth had never been interested in horses. The guns were of the type owned by any farmer, he supposed, knowing even less about firearms. The other passengers could add nothing to his description.

'No, sir,' the policeman said in response to the solicitor's question, 'you won't be able to get papers back from the bottom of that gully. There's no track down and there's the river at the bottom, they'll be washed away by now.' Charlesworth felt murderous; that man with the cold blue eyes had acted out of hatred.

The solicitor spent a restless night, troubled by his thoughts. He had no money to pay the hotel bill, let alone getting out of this place; he would have to go to the Bank of Victoria and see what they could do. Even worse, Duncan's deeds, signatures were all lost. But what could he have done? Resistance to the robbers would have been futile.

Walhalla was the name of the home of the Nordic gods, entirely inappropriate for this frontier town. There was no peace at all in Walhalla. The bedroom windows rattled, the very ground was shaken by the relentless thud of a quartz-crushing machine close to the hotel, a machine that ran all day and all night. Presumably it stopped on Sundays. Charlesworth did not intend to stay there long enough to find out.

When sleep eventually came, Charlesworth had nightmares of being pushed off the edge of a precipice by a brigand with a big black beard. He was not at all his usual confident self at breakfast the next morning and in no mood to see black-bearded Angus Duncan coming into the dining room with his long stride at eight o'clock, far too early for a business meeting. He shook off the memory of the dream with an effort and greeted his old colleague in a subdued manner, which Duncan ignored.

'Got here yesterday to sell some timber. They're short of wood for the mines now at Walhalla, they've used most of the big trees.' Angus accepted coffee and watched while Charlesworth consumed his ham and eggs. 'Bad luck that you met the bushrangers on the way, everyone here is talking about it. Did you suffer any damage?'

'It's your bad luck, as it happens,' grunted the solicitor. 'Your papers were thrown out, they're at the bottom of the river. And of course they took my cash.' He thought that the news would shock Duncan, but the man seemed unconcerned. Did he not realize the gravity of the offence? It would take weeks to get over such a setback, including settling the nerves.

'I expect you can get copies ... the main thing is no loss of life.' The farmer took the bad news lightly. 'The gang thought there was a gold buyer on the coach, they may have decided you were the man they were after.' He paused, 'We've ... had a few crimes lately, but nothing like this.'

Charlesworth took another cup of coffee and wondered how soon he could get rid of the tiresome young man. When they were students, he'd always found Angus too energetic, too restless.

'This means that we can't complete your business. I will send the documents to you in due course, by the mail. I do not intend to visit this part of the world again.' The quartz-crusher maintained its regular thudding, making normal conversation a strain.

It would be good to go back to Bendigo, right away from Gippsland and never come back. Then he remembered Miss Ashby. Perhaps he would call on her, on his way home and persuade her father to bring her to Bendigo.

'It's nigh impossible to attack the gold transports, but the buyers will carry cash on the way in, I suppose.' Angus put down his cup and leaned back in the chair. 'I'm afraid that the robbers are likely to be local men.

There has been trouble here for some time. Some person or persons unknown set fire to one of my houses and stole gold from my tenants.'

'Can your police do nothing to stop them?' Charlesworth asked irritably. 'Robbing a mail coach is a hanging offence and so it should be!' He glared at the empty coffee pot. 'I'm not a criminal lawyer, but I would have liked to bring those wretches to justice. It's extremely inconvenient, a complete disruption of my plans and yours.'

'It's very bad luck, but don't worry on my account. I can wait for the Bendigo sale to be finalised, there's no particular urgency about it.'

That was a relief; Duncan was usually in a hurry. Charlesworth nodded and went on to the next problem. 'Now, Angus, are you known in this town? I will have to ask you to accompany me to the Bank of Victoria, to identify me so that I can endeavour to obtain some money in order to pay my way. I don't suppose anyone's word will be trusted in this uncivilised place.'

Duncan seemed to be amused by this. 'The bank won't be open at this hour, Basil. We'd better order more coffee.'

When they eventually left the hotel, a light rain was falling and the hilltops were hidden in mist, adding to the dreariness of the scene. Accompanied by the sound of the crusher, the two men went to the bank and then Duncan showed the solicitor how to find the office of the Deep Tunnel Extended mine, where he was expected. He suggested they meet for lunch afterwards and strode off before Charlesworth could think of an excuse.

As soon as he opened the door, the visitor felt that the day was going to get worse. His wet spectacles steamed up in the warm room and he took them off and wiped them irritably. Able to see very little, he heard a cool voice.

'Good morning.'

Charlesworth replaced his spectacles and looked round. The mines office was well lit by large windows and was unexpectedly clean and neat. There were flowers on the office desk – in a mines office! A woman sat behind the desk: a woman in a man's world. She was dressed severely, with no flounces or bows and her hair was drawn back smoothly. She was beautiful in a sculptured way, and quite young.

Charlesworth stared. A woman's place was in the home, not in an office. Surely there were enough clerks in the world without employing women?

'I have an appointment to see the manager, Mr D. Pearson, if you would be so good as to tell him I am here,' he said, in the condescending tone reserved for servants. 'Tell him Mr Charlesworth is here.'

The woman pushed some papers aside, stood up and held out her hand.

'I am the manager. Good day, Mr Charlesworth. I have made some notes on our requirements for the legal agreement and I think you will find them quite – satisfactory.'

She called herself a manager! Charlesworth ignored the outstretched hand.

'There must be a mistake,' he said coldly. 'I want to see Mr Pearson, not a clerk! I have travelled all the way from Bendigo and my time is valuable!' He was almost shouting, he realized. That damned machinery must make everybody shout. 'Get me your manager.'

'I am Miss Pearson, Daphne Pearson, and I was not quite happy with your first draft of the papers, Mr Charlesworth.' She smiled, a beautiful smile that lit up the room. 'My company entrusts these matters to me and I am afraid that the other directors are out of the office until next week. I am sure we can come to an agreement.'

'Did they not know I was coming? I made a specific appointment!'

'They did, and replied to you that you would meet me. We discussed the whole matter before they left. I act with their fullest confidence, Mr Charlesworth. And now, will you sit down?'

The visitor sat down heavily. He felt humiliated. To think that he should travel all this way, through discomfort and danger, to be told his business by a chit of a girl!

For some minutes he could not gather his thoughts and shuffled his feet awkwardly, lost without the familiar briefcase.

'My papers were stolen yesterday, you will have to excuse me, Miss ... Pearson.'

'Here are our copies, Mr Charlesworth, with changes in red,' the woman said smoothly and sat back to watch his reaction.

Charlesworth left the mines office exhausted, feeling the sweat trickling down his spine. Miss D. Pearson, with exquisite politeness, had almost reduced him to tears; he had never dealt with such a client before. That woman was obviously well used to dealing with any problem that the business could throw up and any type of man who presented himself. 'I have worked in this business for some years,' she'd told him sweetly.

Of course, he'd started at a disadvantage, with no papers and after a terrible ordeal and a bad night. Charlesworth had thought that he would soon be able to dominate the interview, using his male superiority together with his lawyer's training, but it had not happened. Her version of the new share certificates was better than his. It was diabolical.

This was one of the richest mines in the world and they were entrusting vital legal business to a woman! That was his first incredulous thought, but after an hour of her company, the solicitor had to acknowledge that the work was in capable hands. She had a good knowledge of the law and a quick brain, and she kept calm in the face of his hostility. The changes she suggested were good ones and the outcome was satisfactory, except for the damage to Charlesworth's feelings.

It was irritating to do business with a competent woman; they were so smug. Occasionally a widow would like to air her knowledge, when he was administering a deceased estate, but as a rule, women were pleased to take his advice humbly, as befitted their station.

Before he joined Angus for lunch at the Star Hotel, Charlesworth booked a seat on the next coach out of town. He would get out of this hole, retreat to Moe in the valley, drink a good bottle of wine with his dinner and try to get a proper night's sleep. He might possibly interview Miss Ashby on the next day. But there was another surprise in store.

'Do you happen to know where Mr John Ashby resides?' Charlesworth asked Duncan casually, as they ate mutton pies. 'I believe he and his family removed to Tangil, some months ago.'

A smile twitched behind Duncan's beard. 'John's gone to stay in Melbourne, his health is not good. His children have been some-

126

what unlucky, but Garth has made some good gold finds and will soon set up on land.' He looked across at the lawyer. 'Miss Ashby is currently staying with my mother, on our home farm. She seems to have taken to country life.'

The talk turned to other things, but when Angus invited him to stay the night as his guest, Charlesworth decided that his planned dinner in Moe was not so urgent after all. It was hard to believe that Miss Ashby enjoyed country life, especially in this part of the world. Perhaps she would be in just the right frame of mind to accept his offer.

The men would both travel on the Moe coach and be met by Mrs Duncan at the town. 'We can take you to the Melbourne train the next day,' Angus promised.

The smart trap with gleaming brass work bowled along through the town of Moe, fairly smoothly in spite of ruts in the road. It was the first time that Jane had driven a horse and trap and she loved the feeling of speed and freedom. The horse was well trained, responsive to the slightest touch of the reins. She had to admit that the Duncans ran their business very well.

Jane had driven all the way from Blackwood Park to Moe, Mrs Duncan beside her, ready to take the reins if anything went wrong. Bluey was a stylish horse, but he was old, calm in the face of sudden noises and experienced enough to teach a novice driver. 'May I drive him home?' she asked, but Mrs Duncan laughed.

'Angus will want to drive, once we pick him up. The coach from Walhalla is due in an hour, so we have time to look for some dress patterns before Angus takes over.'

So his mother had noticed that Angus liked to be in charge.

The last few days had been peaceful, since Angus had been away at the Park and then on a trip to Walhalla. Jane had been able to relax and concentrate on her work, instead of watching what she said. She had tried not to dislike the man, but without much success and it was good to be rid of him for a while. His intelligence was too sharp; she felt that she was under observation when he was there. It was like being under a microscope. But worse of all was his silence; when people were silent, you wondered what they were thinking. When he did say something, his speech was hesitating, minimal, even though the voice was deep and pleasant. He must have spent too much time on his own, Jane thought.

Elspeth Duncan had talked about her sons, and Jane listened as they churned butter or made cheese.

'Robert worked hard to be a doctor, he was so determined,' she said. 'But Angus is the clever one, make no mistake, he's like his father.' She sighed. 'Angus qualified in the law, he trained at the same time as Mr Charlesworth and do you know, he was a very good lawyer in Melbourne. But he decided to come home to the farm when his father died. He is making a success of farming, thank goodness.'

'Rather quiet for a lawyer, is he not?' Jane ventured. 'Farmers don't need to talk quite so much, he might prefer that.'

'Angus would always rather listen, I think. But of course when he was a small child, he had a speech problem – the words wouldn't come. He formed the habit of thinking before he spoke. He still hesitates slightly, have you noticed? Robert helped him, when they were young, made him read aloud.'

Apart from meeting Angus to take him home, the women were in town for a shopping trip. For the first time since coming to Gippsland, Jane had money to buy material for making clothes and it was high time she replaced what had been lost. There was limited choice in such a small town, but she'd found some fabrics she liked and a warm shawl for the colder weather. Stockings, shoes, ribbons – there was so much to think of, when you had to buy all your wardrobe at once.

Mrs Duncan had spotted a pretty peacock-blue silk, but Jane had thought it too fine for country wear.

'If we work quickly, it can be ready for the Tangil dance,' the older woman suggested. 'Every woman needs at least one pretty dress.' She seemed to be enjoying the occasion, having dressed in a new bonnet for the trip to town. This was a different person to the rather grim matron Jane had first met.

Thank goodness Garth had been generous with his gold finds, keeping his promise to give Jane and their father a share of what he'd acquired since the robbery. Father was delighted that the Ashbys were now provided for, and his son on the way to buying some land. His letters were full of hope, but hinted that his health was still a concern.

Now that she was not totally dependent on the Duncans, Jane was beginning to enjoy life again. The skills she was learning from Mrs Duncan would be very useful on Garth's farm. Perhaps she should learn to milk a cow? The milking at Home Farm was done by Dolly. Garth probably would marry in the future, but until then, Jane planned to keep house for him.

Clutching dress patterns, the women came out of a shop to find two men walking towards them; Angus Duncan and Basil Charlesworth, who raised his hat.

'Good day, Mrs Duncan, Miss Ashby.' Jane gasped with shock; she had not expected to see him here. She felt herself blushing and was vexed by Angus Duncan's sardonic smile.

'The coach was early, so we came to look for you,' he said.

The solicitor looked less smooth, less complacent than Jane remembered him. His suit was creased from travel and he had a worried frown. Angus's bushranger looks, on the other hand, were fresh and bright. He swung his bag up into the vehicle with ease. To his mother he explained that since they had met at Walhalla to do business, he was bringing the man home with him to stay for the night.

'I hope it is not inconvenient...' the visitor began pompously, but was brushed aside.

'We're always ready for guests, in the bush,' he was told. 'You must realize that for isolated families, visitors are very welcome.

'Jane drove us here, it was good experience for her,' Mrs Duncan told her son.

To her surprise, Angus handed the reins to Jane for the homeward trip and sat beside her.

'You might have to drive a wagon next week.'

Was he joking? Blushing, Jane replied meekly, 'Thank you, kind sir.'

'Do you think it safe?' Charlesworth asked nervously. 'I am not accustomed to seeing a lady drive a passenger vehicle. It is a grave responsibility. And my nerves were badly affected by the coach hold-up, yesterday.'

'Dear me! Would you like to tell us about it?' Mrs Duncan asked.

The solicitor looked round at the trees on either side of the road. 'Perhaps I should not have mentioned it, until we were all safely under your roof. I have no wish to alarm the ladies.'

'Come on Basil, tell the tale. The ladies are quite equal to hearing it,' Angus told him briskly.

'Three ferocious bandits held up my coach, assaulted some of the passengers and – they threw my legal papers into the river ... my nerves are affected.' His voice shook a little with emotion. 'So as I said, I am apprehensive, I think that is the word, about being driven by a lady.'

## NINE

Jane had to stifle a giggle and she thought she detected a gleam of amusement behind Duncan's beard. She was not asked to stop, so she continued to hold the reins. Bluey plodded up the hills sedately and the solicitor subsided, hunched his shoulders and appeared to go to sleep.

The autumn twilight had descended, the last rays of the sun touching the hills with gold by the time they reached Blackwood Park. Jane thought how beautiful it was, a house and gardens with fences and paddocks about it, carved out of the primitive bush. It was an achievement to create a home that was both practical and attractive to look at. Some settlers' homes were ugly, built with no thought for aesthetics, but some of the simplest wooden houses had a rustic look.

At Blackwood they stopped, but Mrs Duncan decided they should push on to the Home Farm.

'We have carriage lights,' she said, 'and it's not a dark night.' A half-moon was rising as she spoke. Mr Charlesworth looked dismayed, but said nothing.

The farm men put a fresh horse in the shafts and Angus took over the driving. Jane saw Marcia look the visitor over, but the housekeeper said nothing to her. Perhaps she was the reason that the Duncans didn't want to stay at the Park.

'I'm surprised you will travel at night, considering all the perils of the bush,' Jane said lightly, as they took to the road again. 'Dingoes, snakes, criminals, drunken miners...' she heard a quiet laugh from Angus.

Charlesworth, who had been on edge from the start, looked even more alarmed.

'What if we meet the bushrangers? I understood you to say that they come from these parts. I have no desire to go through that ordeal again.' He must have been wishing he'd stayed in Walhalla.

Angus urged the horse on faster. 'I still have the pistol in my belt. Don't worry, Basil, we can put up a good fight if we must.' His mother shook her head at him and the solicitor sank down in his seat once more.

Fortunately the pistol was not needed and all they saw that night were possums, wallabies and owls. Dolly had prepared an evening meal and Angus lit a fire in the big open hearth. The dining room was cosy in the lamplight, but the visitor was ill at ease and ate little, although the home-killed beef was excellent.

The solicitor treated them to a detailed account of the incident on the Walhalla road, with descriptions of the miscreants, so far as they could be described.

'There were three. One was quite small and had fair hair, while another was large and broad-shouldered. He spoke with an educated English accent. One would not expect it. There is something disgusting in the thought that one of the educated classes should stoop so low. The third was I think the most dangerous; he struck passengers and he threw my papers...' And so on, and on, while his listeners went from apprehension to boredom.

Jane took part in the conversation at table as she usually did, while Angus listened. She noticed Charlesworth looking at her severely whenever she expressed an opinion.

After the meal, Angus excused himself for a while and Mrs Duncan went to supervise in the kitchen. Jane and Charlesworth stayed at the table. There was a silence and then Jane said, 'I was sorry to hear you had a difficult time at Walhalla, Mr Charlesworth.' Somehow he seemed diminished, less of a threat to her now.

The solicitor sighed. 'None of my plans have succeeded, I'm afraid. One of them was to visit you and your family, Miss Ashby.' He looked weary. 'I expected, indeed, to see you with your father and to find you ready to discuss my offer of marriage. But I see it is otherwise.'

'Do you?' What could she say to the man? He had never asked her what she thought, but perhaps it was time that he was told. 'I believe that I am too independent-minded for your taste, from what you said in your letter.'

The lawyer looked almost relieved. 'Exactly. Instead of making you more appreciative of the guidance of a husband and of the better things in life, I see that this ... experience in a rougher part of Victoria has made you more confident of your own abilities, however mistakenly.' He smiled; the insult must have made him feel better.

'It has,' Jane admitted, hiding her own

smile. He was still trying to show his superiority.

'In my opinion, and that of the world I may say, Miss Ashby, ladies of refinement do not drive, or perform farm duties best left to servants.' He looked at her hands, clean but slightly roughened from work.

Jane wished Mrs Duncan could hear him. How boring to be a lady of refinement!

'My mistaken pride in my new skills does not impress you, Mr Charlesworth? I'm surprised. I am hoping to learn to work with sheep, before long. A shepherdess, now that used to be quite fashionable, did it not?'

'You are facetious about a serious matter, but I gather that your present way of life seems to suit you. It is so far from what I could have offered you, or wished for you, that it is clear you are not the woman I believed you to be.' Charlesworth looked down his nose. 'I wonder how your poor father will view the changes in his daughter.'

'Father always wanted me to do useful work,' Jane said demurely. 'There is nothing demeaning in learning to work.'

The solicitor did not agree. He sat back and folded his arms, distancing himself from Jane and the table.

'This leads me to a statement of my future intentions. I formally withdraw my proposal of marriage, Miss Ashby.' He drew out his handkerchief and mopped his brow. 'This is my final word on the subject.'

Having said more than enough to upset him, Jane needed to say nothing more.

She sat with a straight back, looking at a bowl of fruit on the table.

The doorknob rattled and Mrs Duncan came in with a tray. Charlesworth accepted a glass of port gratefully, while Jane breathed a sigh of relief. It was over, she would never be pestered by him again. She must write to her friend Susan, telling her that the eligible bachelor was looking for a wife of refinement, someone like herself. Susan had the patience to deal with Basil, she thought.

Later that night, Angus escorted his guest to a room across the yard and lit the lamp. He leaned on the bed post and looked round.

'Got everything you need? I hope the bushrangers didn't steal your razor!'

Charlesworth yawned rather pointedly. 'Everything, I thank you, Angus. This is very kind of you.'

'And you managed a talk with Miss Ashby, too. I do hope you don't still plan to marry her, Basil. It would be disastrous.' Angus kept his face impassive.

The visitor flushed and said irritably, 'How did you know?'

'Don't worry, she didn't tell me, I heard you speaking to her at the concert in Bendigo. I didn't mean to eavesdrop, but you spoke quite loudly. Then when you asked me where she was, I realized you intended to visit her.'

'And what has it got to do with you, may I ask?'

Angus stood up and went to the door. 'Miss Ashby has spent several weeks here with my mother and I have come to know her character. I don't think it would be a suitable match Basil, speaking to you as an old friend. The lady has a mind of her own and too much confidence in her own opinions. She is too forward, she would make any man miserable. Her husband, if she marries, is doomed to constant anxiety lest she should embarrass him in public.'

'That is now my opinion, as a matter of fact,' the other man said gloomily. 'Just imagine, if my wife were to embarrass me in Bendigo! A man in my position must be very cautious in approaching matrimony.'

'Quite so,' said the farmer heartily.

Jane, preparing for bed in the next room, could not help overhearing this character analysis. The wooden walls were quite thin and neither man had lowered his voice; it was as though they wanted her to hear them.

Now Jane knew for certain what Angus Duncan thought of her. Of course, she didn't care a straw, but it was surprising to hear the silent man talk so much.

'Most of the dances are in waltz time, I'm sure you'll play very well.' Mrs Duncan was leafing through her music while Jane played scales on the piano. For the first time since she left Bendigo, she was playing music again, in the large, comfortable sitting room at the Duncans' Home Farm. 'It's a mixture of waltzes and quadrilles – the Lancers, that kind of thing.'

They were preparing for the Willow Grove dance, which Mrs Duncan said was held twice a year, in spring and autumn. 'Musicians are scarce out here, ye ken, although some of the miners play the harmonica, mainly the Germans. If you will play the piano for some of the time, that will be a relief. It's hard work for an old woman, playing the whole evening.'

'It's so long since I played ... and surely, the tempo will be very fast? I am more used to playing to accompany singers. My father used to sing, before he was ill.'

'Most of the waltzes are fifty-two beats to the bar, you can manage that!' Mrs Duncan was bracing and it reminded Jane of her first few days at the farm. 'The polka is faster, but you will only be playing to give me a rest, so we can choose the easy ones for you. I wish we had a violin.'

A thought struck Jane. 'My brother has a concertina, he might be willing to play.'

'Will you ask him?' Mrs Duncan passed

over some music. 'These are the tunes for "Pride of Erin," that's in waltz time, it's popular. And we might get someone to sing a song or two, for variety.'

The other pressing need was to finish the silk dress in time for the evening, with the little time they had after the day's work was done. Jane discovered that autumn was a very busy time on the farm, preparing for winter. Bee hives were robbed of some of their honey, endless pots of jam were produced. Two pigs were killed and she had to learn how to salt down the hams, in a stone trough in the dairy. Every day she turned the hams and rubbed in the salt.

'How can we be sure that the hams won't go bad?' The day was warm and they had been hoping for colder weather. Jane had kept the doors and windows closed, trying to keep the meat cool.

'A German settler has a smoke house near Willow Grove and we sometimes take our hams there for smoking. They will keep quite well then, even in warmer weather. I'll remind Angus about it. He's planning to come back here, the day before the dance.' Duncan was at Blackwood Park. No doubt Angus would drive them to the dance, but would he take to the floor? Jane doubted it.

Malcolm Raven threw the reins over his horse's neck, tied it to a tree and strode down the track that led to the tunnel. Roy Dooley saw him coming in the distance and muttered to his brother, 'He goes about as if he owns the place. 'What makes him think he's so much better than us?'

Michael grinned. 'He is better, at most things. Marcia told me his da's an English lord or something, owns a place called Raven Castle. That's why he walks like that, head in the air. Our ma hates him, you know that.'

Roy looked doubtful. 'English castle? Sounds too good for Mal.'

'Marcia took up with Raven cos she fancied to live in a castle, but I doubt she'll not be invited.' Michael liked to know more than Roy, but it didn't happen often.

Roy's blue eyes glared at his brother. ''Twas English lords pushed the likes of us out of Ireland, and we don't forget ... what else did Marcia tell you?'

Michael watched the tall figure looming nearer. 'This lord, he's called Black Jack Raven and no woman is safe within five mile of him, she'd heard. An' if he sees something he wants, be it land or loot, he takes it.'

'Sounds just like our boy, then.'

'What are you two muttering about?' Raven reached them.

'Not much, we was waiting for you. Where've you been?' Ma Dooley said get in first, she said it often. Roy tried to look truculent.

Raven laughed and threw down his whip on the tree stump that served for a table.

'I've been putting my ear to the ground, a thing you might do more often. Sit down. We have much to talk about.'

'It's cold in here,' Roy complained. 'Can't we go outside?' The tunnel led to a disused reef, known to be haunted. Some folks had heard the sound of ghostly picks, working the quartz in the darkness as dead miners went on digging for gold...

Michael looked at him with a frown. 'You're always cold lately. Sickening for something?'

'Shut up and sit down. Nobody can creep up on us, in here.' Raven seemed to be in a hurry. 'Do you want to do business, or not?'

Obediently, the brothers sat at the table on rough stools.

'What d'ye want, then? Why we here?'

The man thumped his fist on the table, dislodging a couple of spiders.

'First of all, that fiasco the other day on the Walhalla road. Whose stupid idea was it to stop the inbound coach to a gold town? An Irish idea, that's what.' Raven threw back his long hair and glared at them both. 'You would have it that the gold buyer was loaded with cash and on that very stage, positive certain. All we got was a poxy lawyer with a few measly pounds, and a ratty little sales-man. Oh yes, a lad and a little old lady who hit you with her umbrella! It made me sick, I can tell you. Fronted up for nothing, reports to Walhalla police, warrants out for arrest.' He sighed, 'I really don't know why I associate with you two. Only went along that day because I had nothing better to do.' The upper class drawl was more pronounced when Raven was angry.

That wasn't fair.

'But Raven, we planned it for when you could come with us.' Roy looked at the dark, implacable face, and was afraid. Being Irish and playing stupid paid off at times. 'Right, you plan the next one. What do you want to do?' The dank air of the tunnel weighed on him and he wanted this to be over, to get out into the sun.

Raven folded his arms and looked down his nose at his associates. 'One: we will work at night, next time. In the dark, in and out, fast. A snatch.'

'What? Where?' Michael looked uneasy.

'Hold on, old chap, and I will tell you. It has come to my notice that young Ashby has struck it rich – again. He's won a lot of gold. But...' he held up his hand. 'This time, it's in the bank.'

'Sure and you're not planning to rob a bank?' Roy Dooley's eyes were wide.

'Ha. You haven't heard? A couple of cow-men from down the line held up the bank at Moe last month. The local doctor, that fellow

Duncan, bravely chased them off. He'll get a medal for it. Then they were followed on a train, would you believe, by the constables from Sale. It wasn't long before the hapless youths were locked up, but now the bank's ready for anything. New bars, new locks. I have personally inspected their arrangements. So we won't think about the bank.' Raven smiled and it was not a pleasant smile.

The Dooleys sat dejected, shoulders sagging. 'What you telling us this for?'

'To give you a taste of reality. We have to think of the unexpected snatch, not the predictable one. People's health and safety are sometimes worth money, gentlemen. If we take the man's sister to parts unknown, Ashby will pay us money to get her back. Understand?'

'No!' Michael sat up straight. 'Jane Ashby's a nice girl, you can't do that. She might get hurt! Since the fire, she's been at the Duncans'. We'll never get her from there.'

Roy sniggered. 'Always thought you fancied her.'

Raven ignored this. 'Now, I will tell you exactly what to do.' He sounded just like the owner of an English castle. 'And make sure nothing goes wrong. You, Michael Dooley, will have to find out the woman's movements and we will snatch her when the Duncans are elsewhere. Roy, find a safe hiding place...' He had it all worked out.

144

'You'd think he'd have enough gold by now,' Roy grumbled when Raven had gone. 'He's got most of what we took from Ashby, won't share it out, just keeps it. I want my share.'

'I reckon he likes gold, Roy. It's like Ma with grog, he can't live without it. He wants more, some to keep and some to spend. He might go back to England.'

Michael looked at his brother. 'I don't like this latest idea at all... Jane never hurt nobody.'

'You do as you're told, our Michael.'

Angus had not arrived at the Home Farm before they were due to leave for the dance, but his mother was quite calm.

'He must have been held up at Blackwood. I'll drive, and we'll hope that he'll meet us there and escort us home.'

Jane was pleased with the blue-green dress; it fitted well. Getting dressed to go out for the evening felt strange and reminded her of the very different life in Bendigo. If only Susan could be there, or one of her other friends! She gave her hair an extra brush, put all the sheet music into a case, picked up her shawl and was ready to go when Mrs Duncan called. The steady horse, Bluey was in the shafts, having been brought back from Blackwood. The full moon was rising as they trotted down the track.

The Willow Grove hall was in the main street, brightly lit and decorated with streamers. Jane helped to unyoke the horse and she led it over the road to a stable where they could leave it for the evening.

The hall had been festooned with green branches and the fresh eucalyptus scent filled the large room. Chairs were arranged round the walls, and in the kitchen, women were preparing supper.

'All the women bring some food – some of them make wonderful sponge cakes,' Mrs Duncan said.

A grand piano had pride of place on a small stage. The master of ceremonies, an elderly man, seemed relieved to see them, even though they were early.

'This is Mr Brand. Good evening, George.' They discussed the plan for the evening and Jane was introduced as the second pianist.

Garth came in, looking very smart in a new suit and Jane thought that prosperity suited him, while the hard work had made him slimmer and fit-looking. He carried his concertina and Mrs Duncan asked him to play straight away. The room was quiet and people were talking in whispers, rather shyly; something was need to break the ice.

Garth started with some popular song tunes and the atmosphere lightened immediately. Small children started to twirl to the music. Jane was surprised to see children at such an affair, but this was a family dance, whole families in their best clothes, ready to enjoy themselves. More people came in and a queue formed at the cloak-room door.

'Leave all firearms here in the cloakroom, if you please,' a man called. Most of the men and one or two women surrendered guns, which were stacked on a table and guarded by the cloakroom attendant. No doubt Angus would have to leave his pistol there, if he carried it tonight. But where was he? Angus Duncan had not arrived by the time the first dance was called and Jane sat by the piano to turn the pages.

Jane played the piano for several dances without too many mistakes, but she was glad to take a rest when Mrs Duncan took over again, accompanied by Garth. She went to sit down at the side of the hall and noticed two women eying her and whispering. Marcia, the Duncans' housekeeper, sat with Ma Dooley, both dressed in shiny black. They appeared to be on good terms with each other, but judging by their expressions they were busy criticising the appearance, dancing proficiency and probable fortune of everyone else in the room – including Miss Jane Ashby.

# TEN

The dancing was energetic and a certain amount of dust was raised in the hall as the couples whirled around in the 'Pride of Erin' to several lively folk tunes. When it finished, a rather solemn young man took the stage and sang 'Home, Sweet Home', a tenor performance that brought a tear to several eyes round the room. Many of the diggers and settlers had come from homes across the sea.

Jane found herself thinking of Bendigo, the more formal balls there and the home they had left. Life there had been pleasant, but oddly enough she no longer felt a sense of loss. That morning she had picked apples in the sunshine, sorting them into boxes for sale in Melbourne. The dappled sunlight in the orchard and the delicate scent of new apples came back to her now. Life in the country suited her very well.

The next song was for the Scots in the hall: 'Ye Banks and Braes of Bonny Doon.' It was sung well and Jane knew Mrs Duncan had asked for it. For the first time, although she knew the song well, Jane realized that the tune imitated birdsong with its rise and fall.

It was so good to be hearing music again! The hall was hushed and even the children sat still.

'You won't be allowed to sit down long at a country dance,' Mrs Duncan had warned, and now it was to be proved true. A tall man came towards her with a purposeful stride and held out his hand.

'May I have the pleasure of the next dance?' he asked quite formally. Jane thought he must be a settler, rather than a prospector. He was quite handsome, with a lightly tanned face and crisp, short black hair. He had a determined chin with a cleft in it.

Jane didn't know the man, but she would have to dance, or risk being rude to a neighbour. They hadn't been introduced, but this affair was very informal.

There was something familiar about this man's voice and the way he looked down at her with serious eyes. 'Are you enjoying the evening, Miss Ashby? I hope they won't work you too hard.' They moved down the set in a quadrille, parting and converging.

Who was he? Jane gave a gasp. 'Angus! I didn't recognise you!' She stumbled and her partner caught her with an arm round her waist. 'Sorry, I mean Mr Duncan.'

'Angus sounds better, Jane.' He paused for a long time. 'You look very ... well in that dress. It suits you.'

'Your mother chose the colour, and she

helped me to make it. She's very good to me.' Jane smiled at him, while across the room, Marcia glared ferociously, then said something to Mrs Dooley. Both women leaned forward to watch and Jane turned her back on them.

'What happened?' The bushranger beard had gone and the man was transformed. Without it, Angus Duncan had a keen, intelligent face and was very like his brother Robert. He also looked about ten years younger; not so very much older than Jane, in fact.

Angus said nothing, but he smiled and now Jane could see that it was a generous smile, with even a hint of mischief in it. The grumpy bushranger had gone. Was this the same man who had dragged her off the night the cottage was burned? It was hard to believe; Jane wondered whether the loss of his beard would affect his personality. To change one's appearance so drastically must have some effect and it would be bound to change other peoples' view of him.

'So you won't grow it back? I do hope not!' That was rather forward of her, but Jane liked him much better without the beard.

She went back for duty at the piano, where Mrs Duncan was looking astonished.

'I didn't know my own son!'

Jane smiled as she sat down and prepared to play, wondering whether Angus would be more normal in future.

The Lancers, The Alberts and all the other country dances were requested, with the Master of Ceremonies calling out the moves as they went. The atmosphere was light-hearted; Jane looked round the room to see smiles on nearly every face. The Ellises from the Tangil shop were there, as well as some of her former neighbours at Tangil who came up in a friendly way to ask how she was doing.

The supper was obviously the highlight of the evening to some people and several women brought the food proudly out of the kitchen, to display it on trestle tables.

Jane could soon see that it was a fierce competition, an exhibition of the baking skills of expert cooks. Deep yellow sponges were compared for lightness and depth of cream, before the cakes were cut and passed round. Cold meat was laid out on plates with salad and the ham was analysed and debated. The dancers were hungry after their exercise and fell on the food with enthusiasm. Mrs Dooley and Marcia had not danced, but they were in the front of the queue and helped themselves to piled plates of supper. This was what they had come for.

'Who cured this ham? It's delicious!' one of the women asked, and a blond young man stepped forward to take the praise.

'That's Mr Meyer, he has the smoke-house,' Mrs Duncan whispered to Jane. 'I wonder what his secret is.'

'Thank you,' Mr Meyer said happily, 'I knew you would like this ham, it is my best this year. But no,' he waved away the questions, 'tonight I am not here to talk about my work.'

'What are you here for, Johann?' asked a jovial elderly prospector. 'Looking for a wife, maybe?'

'Of course. I am always looking for a beautiful woman who would like to make sausages.' He turned to Jane, who was standing near him. 'I think you would like to make sausages with me?'

'There's an offer for you now, Miss Ashby,' the prospector grinned as a general laugh went round, not laughing at the German, but with him. There were various nationalities gathered in that hall, all learning tolerance of each other's ways as time went by.

Jane smiled and murmured that he could easily find someone more skilled than she was, but that was not the last she saw of Mr Meyer. He asked her to dance, the moment she was free.

'I would really like you to see my smokehouse,' he said seriously as they waltzed. 'This is not a joke. I built it myself, out of the wood I chopped down. And I experiment with different types of wood sawdust, to see which smoke has the best – flavour, is the word?'

'You're a farmer, I believe.'

'Yes. Johann Meyer. I came from Germany for gold, and when I found some, it was soon used to buy land. I grow pigs and cattle, so I need a smoke-house.' He whirled Jane round quite expertly. 'But of course we have the different trees here, not the oak and ash as in Europe, so my sawdust is different. When they see my smoke, people bring their meat to the smoke-house, to make it safe – to make it keep. Smoke preserves, as they say.' He smiled at Jane. 'But I am not here to talk about my work. Where do you live, Miss? I think I know your brother. The man called you Miss Ashby. I know Garth Ashby, he played the music tonight as well as you.'

Jane nodded. 'I work for Mrs Duncan, at the moment,' she told him. 'I have to go back to play the piano after this dance and you haven't told me the secret of your wonderful ham.'

'Come to see my smoke-house and I will show you.'

Well before midnight, the last dance was announced, Sir Roger de Coverley, to end the evening according to tradition. Everybody in the hall took to the floor in long lines, Mrs Duncan with Angus and Jane with Johann Meyer. Garth, fresh as ever, played the tune energetically and in strict time on the concertina. Marcia and Ma Dooley danced together.

The German bowed over Jane's hand at the end and told her he hoped to see her again. If only she would visit his smoke-house, he would be very happy.

Afterwards, Angus brought round the trap and tied his horse to the back so that he could drive them home. At the same time, Marcia Pendlebury and Ma Dooley were getting into another vehicle and Angus stared hard at them. 'I wonder,' he said, half to himself. 'Marcia might be keeping bad company.'

Jane looked around as they drove away, pulling her shawl closer against the chill night air. The moon was bright, filtering through the trees along the track and lighting the trunks of grey gums to a silvery whiteness. 'I thought the evening went well,' Mrs Duncan remarked. 'You played well, Jane and so did Garth.'

Jane smiled. 'Thank you. I enjoyed it, I think we all did.'

Angus, as usual, said nothing. Jane wondered what on earth would please him, what would he ever be enthusiastic about ... but he had liked her dress. That was astonishing, when you came to think of it.

The dance had been enjoyable, but Jane's talk with Garth had been rather unsatisfactory.

'Have you found a house for us, Garth? The Duncans have been good to me, but they won't want to put up with me for much

154

longer. Just a little house will do, something of our own.' She had spoken quietly in case they were overheard.

'Of course I want you to join me, Janey,' he'd said while Mrs Duncan was playing. 'But not yet. I'm into a good seam and we might really strike it rich. No time for playing at houses, you see.'

'When we're rich, you won't forget to tell me, will you?' Jane looked at her brother, casual as ever about the future – her future in particular. 'And – put the gold in the bank when you can, Garth. I don't think it will be safe at Tangil.'

'Of course, of course. That's what I'm doing, girl, I promised Father I would. You know we've started an account in all our names, Bank of Australasia. Nobody will be able to make off with it this time!'

Quite near to where they stood, Marcia and Ma Dooley had looked at one another meaningfully. Jane caught the look and decided that they didn't like the cut of her dress.

Jane was disappointed that Garth had as yet no home, but not bitterly so. For one thing, she expected little of her brother these days and for another, life at the Duncans' was full of interest. She would sleep a little better knowing that their gold was safe in the bank.

They were nearly back to the Home Farm.

Mrs Duncan was dozing in her seat, tired after an evening of playing the piano. The horse was plodding along quietly when a kangaroo bounded across the track in front of them. A small joey peeped out of her pouch, quite visible in the moonlight, its little paws over the side.

Jane thought for a moment how sweet the baby looked, but then the world seemed to erupt. The horse, frightened by the kangaroo, whinnied and tried to throw his head up. Bluey jumped sideways and dragged the trap and Angus's horse with him with a rending sound. The whole vehicle moved across and off the track and ended up sliding down a bank, which stopped its movement. One wheel was in the air, still spinning. The whole thing appeared to Jane to happen very slowly; she clutched at the trap and missed. The passengers were all tipped out into the undergrowth at the side of the road.

Jane was stunned by the fall and when she could see clearly again, Angus was out on the track with the pistol in his hand, looking all round and into the dense bush. Mrs Duncan was soothing Bluey, who seemed to be none the worse. The horse Angus had ridden stood waiting patiently, resting one leg.

Scrambling out onto the road, Jane joined Mrs Duncan and the older woman looked her over.

'You're not badly hurt? That's good. We

think we can get home, the harness is broken in places but Angus can tie it up.' Angus was still looking into the scrub, pistol at the ready. 'He suspected a hold-up, but I think it was only the kangaroo. They seem to move about at night and they can do a lot of damage to a vehicle.'

After a few minutes Angus gave the pistol to his mother and went to look at the broken leather on the shafts. 'Just keep a lookout behind us,' he told her. 'Jane, you look the other way. Shout if you see any movement.'

Jane stood shivering without her shawl, looking up the track and into the bushes. Nothing stirred; the autumn night was silent except for the distant hoot of a boobook owl. If this was the type of experience the Duncans expected, she was beginning to see why Angus had dragged her off on the night of the fire. Looking back, she realized that it had been the only thing he could do. She had been foolish; the fire had shaken her, and she'd refused to take his advice.

It was far from clear what the danger might have been. Surely, the kangaroo was the whole cause of the accident tonight? Perhaps settlers were used to expecting the worst and saw a bushranger behind every tree.

When he had secured the harness, Angus told the women to get back into the trap.

Mrs Duncan still held the pistol ready as they went slowly up the stony track. Bluey had had a fright and the harness was only temporarily holding.

Jane felt rather dazed and her head ached; she hung onto the side of the vehicle to stay upright on the seat. In the moonlight she could see Mrs Duncan's set face. It was a pity that a pleasant evening had to end like this. The music of the dances was still running through her mind.

Angus said nothing more until they were safely at home with the gates locked behind them. Once it had felt like a prison, but now Home Farm was a haven and to Jane, it was beginning to feel like a home.

As though he were a doctor like his brother, Angus looked Jane over briefly and ran light fingers through her hair. 'Back of the head, it will ache for a few days.' So this was how country people dealt with a mishap, Jane thought. No fuss, just get on with the job.

The next morning Angus seemed to be more concerned about Jane's bruise, but she assured him she felt quite well. They were finishing breakfast and Mrs Duncan had gone to the dairy when he said quietly, 'Did you see anything last night, Jane? I suppose you saw stars, once you hit the bank.'

'I've been wondering whether to mention it ... I thought I saw a man in the shadows, where the kangaroo came from.' Jane started to clear the table of breakfast dishes.

'I think there were two,' Angus said grimly. 'Didn't want to alarm Mother, so I didn't mention it. I wasn't ... entirely sure. I suppose the pistol put them off.'

Jane was puzzled. 'Why would anyone want to attack us? We had no valuables to steal and as far as I know, we have no enemies.'

'Who knows? P'rhaps they fancied the horses.'

That was quite possible. Garth had told Jane that the Duncans always bought the best when it came to horses. Last night, there had been Angus's riding horse as well as the one in the shafts and they would fetch a good price if sold. She was beginning to realize that the pistol was not for show; there were hazards among the trees during the hours of darkness.

Angus jumped up and went to the door. 'I wish I could find out who they are and who held up the Walhalla coach, whether they are local men or a gang from outside. I've been uneasy for a long time now about those Dooleys in that unsavoury shanty, but there's no evidence against them. They ... just hate everybody, because they had a bad deal in Ireland. Michael told me once.'

Jane took the dishes into the scullery for washing, thinking that this was the longest conversation she'd ever had with Angus. Maybe she could talk to him more normally, now that she could see his face.

At lunch that day, Mrs Duncan told them her own scrap of gossip. 'Did you know, Angus, that Marcia is a widow?'

'I knew she'd had a hard life ... does it matter?' Angus looked as though he didn't want to think about Marcia. 'It's time she found another job.'

'She was married to a Dooley, Mrs Dooley's eldest boy. He was shot as a bush-ranger, some time ago. Mr Ellis from the Tangil shop told me, I don't remember hearing about it. She's used her maiden name with us.'

'So that's the connection... I noticed them together at the dance,' Jane said.

'Perhaps it does matter.' Angus sat up straighter. 'We ... need to keep an eye on Marcia.'


Raven was furious, coldly furious with the Dooleys.

'You failed. I might have known it. You Irish...' he swore, loud and long, the words sounding even worse in that impeccable English accent.

'I tell you, they had a bodyguard with 'em,' Roy Dooley said plaintively. 'They went down to the dance, just two women on their own. It looked easy, grab her on the way back, so we told you to be ready ... but then there was this great big savage bloke with a pistol ... he'd ha killed us both, surely. He was driving, his horse was tied on the back.'

Michael took up the tale, although he couldn't meet Raven's black glare. They were at their rendezvous, explaining why they had no prisoner with them.

'We chased a kangaroo up and across the track, then the horse shied and the trap went over. That all went well. But this bloke, his horse was tied to the back of the cart. He had the pistol ready and he let the old woman look after the horses. The young lass was out cold, I think. There wasn't a squeak from her, he was covering her and watching for us. So ... we moved away, in case they saw us. We hadn't a chance to snatch her.'

Raven moved impatiently.

'Idiots! That man was just Farmer Duncan, he took his beard off last week when he was at Blackwood. He's too soft to shoot anybody.' He looked at them with distaste.

Roy looked shocked. 'That was Angus Duncan? Well, he says nothing but I reckon he'd be handy with a pistol, all the same. He was ready for us, surely.'

'Do you know him? He's a big bloke,' Michael said nervously. 'I never guessed it was Duncan, but...'

'You are a chicken when it comes to a fight.' Raven was contemptuous. 'Marcia told me all about Duncan. He's weak. Scots are never as tough as they think they are! Swaggering about in kilts while the English walk all over them. Remember that. Marcia can say anything she likes to him and he still doesn't turn her off. She uses his stores, she does as she likes. He hardly talks at all. Too soft for a settler, she says.'

'You soft on Marcia, then, Raven? You spend a lot of time with her.' Roy laughed.

'She is useful,' Raven said with menace in his tone. 'Marcia knows where people are, she gets the news from the coach drivers, she knows what goes on. If you have to ... to make up to a woman to get information, that's all in the day's work. Besides, we owe her – she lost Liam. And so ... you failed again.'

'Well, we didn't know Duncan was going to turn up to take them home,' Michael reminded them. 'How could we? Did our best, Raven, you know that.'

'You failed again, you stupid Dooleys.' Raven slapped Michael lightly across the head with his leather glove. 'It will soon be too late, people will know us – the Walhalla coach job has seen to that. One last good haul and we can leave – that's what you want to do, isn't it? Get out of this hole and live a quiet life. I shall go back to England.'

'You don't like Australia?' Michael was surprised.

'I have property in England waiting for me. One last try, and make sure you get it right this time.' Raven glared at them both and they dropped their gaze.

'Remember, we need to get the cash and get away. Or you might swing. Your mother can't afford to lose you.'

Roy shivered in the night air.

## ELEVEN

Angus Duncan stayed on the Home Farm for the next few days and seemed pre-occupied, more silent than ever, which was disappointing. Jane had hoped that his improved appearance would make him more talkative, but it hadn't happened. If he would only say what worried him, perhaps something could be done about it. Surely he wasn't brooding about bushrangers?

Mrs Duncan took Jane out in the trap several times, driving different horses. One day they went to collect the mail at the post office, on another they travelled on tracks across the paddocks to pick up sacks of potatoes. Jane wondered why she was being taught horsemanship so carefully and one day she was told that everyone on the farm had to be able to drive.

'It looks as though you'll be here over the winter,' Mrs Duncan told her as they un-yoked the horse in the stable. 'We'll be glad of that, Jane, we are short of people to do the work.' The two maids were very young and only worked part-time, which left Dolly, Elspeth and now Jane to manage the work of a busy household.

Well, it was true that Garth would hardly have a house ready before next summer.

'I could join my father in Melbourne,' Jane suggested and then realized that she would hate to go to Mrs King's for a long visit.

Elspeth Duncan looked glum. 'If that's what you would like, of course you could. But I'd like you to stay, Jane, if it suits you. I enjoy your company.'

'As long as Angus can put up with me, it must be hard for him! He thinks I have too much confidence, you know. I'm too forward.'

Jane spoke lightly, but Mrs Duncan looked serious. There was a silence, in which Jane could hear her own words echoing. 'I like your confidence, Jane and I would never describe you as "forward". I'm not sure that you've understood Angus correctly.'

Jane could hardly say that she'd heard his conversation with Charlesworth, but she couldn't resist saying, 'Mr Charlesworth told me he thought so too. He believes that men are far superior to women.'

Mrs Duncan gave her a rather cynical smile. 'We know the truth, dear, don't we? Mr Charlesworth has no experience of country life and I know he thinks the work I do is not suitable for a lady. But Jane, I think you really frightened him when you drove the trap from Moe. He looked terrified, did you notice?' They both laughed at the memory.

They walked out into the stable yard; dusk was falling quickly. 'We'd better go in and light the lamps, Angus should be here soon for supper.'

Mrs Duncan was obviously still thinking about their conversation when they were preparing the meal.

'It is hard for you, Jane, when we see so few people. Farming does isolate us, I'm afraid. To be honest, I think Angus is worried about criminals at the moment. He's on the watch for thieves and he's trying to find out who they are. He's put more locks on the doors.' Mrs Duncan, Jane noticed, had shut the stable door and locked it. 'I hope the police catch them soon.'

'Well, that's a relief,' Jane said. 'I had thought perhaps he must be worried about his health. He looks so serious sometimes.' Miserable, she'd nearly said.

Mrs Duncan put down the loaf she was holding and turned to face her helper. 'I think myself that the threat is quite serious, Jane. We have no police nearer than Moe and there is a large population of single men at Tangil, that's almost on our doorstep. If gold prospectors have no success, sometimes they turn to crime. It's easier to steal from some-one else than to go scratching the soil for gold, day after day. You can imagine that goldfields can be quite lawless.' She sighed. 'I don't want to alarm you and neither does Angus, which is why he doesn't talk about it.'

'When we came here, people told me that Tangil was very quiet and law-abiding,' Jane remembered. 'When we lived at the cottage, when Father was here, the men who came to see him were quite respectable. Things must have changed, over the past few months.'

'I'm sure most of the diggers are harmless, hard-working men. It's just the few that cause the goldfields to have a bad reputation.' Mrs Duncan stirred the stew in the pan. 'People used to be afraid of the Chinese, I don't know why. They were hard-working, in-offensive people ... but of course they weren't Christian. There are very few Chinamen left at Tangil now.'

Angus must have continued to worry about their safety; the next day, he offered to teach Jane to shoot with a pistol.

'My mother can use firearms, it's quite important,' he told her.

Mrs Duncan thought it was a good idea. 'Twice I've had to shoot a sheep that was badly damaged by wild dogs,' she said. 'I was glad of the gun then, in case the dogs came back.'

'Is this anything to do with the outlaws?'

Jane suggested.

'Of course we wouldn't shoot anyone! But it is good in these wild days that people know we carry a gun when we go out. The word soon gets around, you know. The man at the post office told me that several horses have been stolen this month.'

Angus showed Jane the pistol that his mother carried and encouraged her to try some target practice. She found she had a natural aptitude and could sometimes hit the bullseye more often than Angus. It was a game, but would she be able to use a gun if a real situation arose? Living on a farm was so very new to her, even now.

'You'd feel safer, out in the paddocks on your own,' Angus told her. They practiced often and Jane learned the safety drill, and how to load and unload quickly.

As yet, she had not been sent out on her own, but Angus said the day might come when she was the only person available. The routine at Home Farm had to include regular inspections of the farm animals, sometimes in paddocks that were at a considerable distance from the homestead. The Duncans owned nearly a thousand acres round the Home Farm; some of it was uncleared forest, some was ploughed to grow crops and the rest was pasture.

As the days grew colder, Jane was very glad she did not share her brother's primitive hut.

Gippsland seemed to be colder than Bendigo and it was certainly damper, now the summer drought had broken. A big wood stove stood in the centre of the room where they sat in the evenings, and thick curtains kept out draughts. The Duncans had a good library of books, so there was always something to read, as well as plenty of sewing. There were socks to knit and Mrs Duncan was making clothes for her son Robert's third child, expected in a few months.

Jane admired the tiny vests and jackets, but Mrs Duncan sighed. 'I don't know when Angus will get married ... he never seems to consider it. I would like to see him settled down before I die.'

Angus had no hope of finding a wife, Jane thought, but she kept it to herself. She was trying not to be too forward and embarrassing. It was a pity; he was quite an attractive man since the beard had gone. But he'd been so gloomy lately and the silences were too much for a wife to bear. She couldn't imagine how anyone could live alone with him; they would go mad and start talking to themselves. For him, marriage would no doubt be a trial if he was expected to talk.

'I'm sure Angus is a very busy man,' she said consolingly to Mrs Duncan. 'He may be happy to stay single, you know.'

A few days later the Duncans went to Blackwood Park, leaving Jane at the Home

Farm. 'We both have work to do there, but we'll be back by Friday,' Mrs Duncan said as they left on Monday morning. 'Angus has to draft some sheep for sale and I – well, I want to see to the housekeeping and check the stores for winter.' That meant she was going to check up on Marcia and the maids, especially now she'd discovered the connection with the Dooleys. 'You and Dolly can make cheese while we still have some milk to make it with.' She looked at her helper with a hint of a smile. 'I noticed quinces are dropping off the tree.'

Jane had found Dolly to be a pleasant companion. It was interesting to talk as they stirred the cheese curds in the vats, to hear about Dolly's life, so different from anything she had encountered before. Dolly and Absalom were the only regular staff living there, but the Duncans employed several other people who came in as needed.

Dolly said that they liked working for the Duncans and respected their Scottish traditions. Hogmanay was a spiritual time for them according to Dolly, and Burns Night celebrated one of their famous elders, a man who gave them songs.

'Mrs Duncan, she's asked me about our own Ganai customs,' Dolly said. 'She gives us time off go up to Baw Baw in the spring. Did you see big moths, Bo Gong, in the spring?'

'I saw one or two when we first came here,

the biggest moths I've ever seen. Are they special to you?' Jane asked.

Dolly's dark eyes sparkled. 'Absalom and me and our cousins, we go up the mountains, up Baw Baw way, when the moths come over. We roast them on the fire, good tucker!' Her smile was bright.

Jane repressed a shudder at the thought of eating insects. 'Where do they come from, Dolly?'

'Dunno. Way, way over the country up there.' She pointed to the north. 'They stay in the caves and such and then, when the sun's not so hot in the autumn, they go back again where they come from, way, way up country.'

'The ones you didn't eat,' Jane reminded her.

'There's plenty Bo Gong, we only have a few good feeds. Moths are good for the Ganai.'

'I saw Absalom in a kangaroo cloak, once,' Jane remembered. 'Is that – part of your Ganai traditions?'

Dolly looked grave. 'Best not talk about that, forget you seen it. Now Jane, time to strain the curds.'

The days went quickly, two of them sticky with quince jelly. This was new to Jane, but she got down the well-used copy of Mrs Beeton's Book of Household Management, as the Duncans had encouraged her to do.

Jelly-making was quite simple; the fruit was sliced and boiled in water with a little lemon juice. Then the liquid had to be boiled again after sieving, and sugar added. The thrifty Mrs Beeton suggested that the residue after sieving should be used to make 'common marmalade.' By then, Jane felt she'd done enough boiling and stirring, so she gave the residue to the pigs.

A row of rose-coloured jars of clear jelly on the pantry shelf was evidence that she had not wasted her time while the Duncans were away. The fruits of the quince tree had been put to good use. She was learning that every season had its own tasks, as well as its own flavours. The new knowledge she would carry with her for the rest of her life; Jane was now a practical woman and proud of it.

On the Thursday night, Jane was walking across the yard to go to bed when her mind was abruptly wrenched from satisfying thoughts of the week's achievements.

A voice called her urgently. She looked round; it was coming from the other side of the high fence that surrounded the compound.

'Miss Ashby! Jane! You're wanted!'

Startled, Jane went across to the fence and found that a small hole had been made where one of the knots had fallen out of the wood. 'What is it?'

'It's Michael Dooley, Jane.' Jane put her eye to the hole and saw Michael, a shadowy figure on the other side. 'Can you come? It's your brother, Garth's taken real bad and he … he says you'll know what to do, he's got the stomach pains, he's in trouble, with no physic.'

Poor Garth! He was usually so healthy, but he'd had several bouts of stomach problems since they came to Tangil. They had decided that the trouble might have come from their drinking water, which was none too fresh on the diggings. Their water supply at the cottage had come from the tank which held rain water, drained off the roof. No doubt Garth had the same arrangement for his hut. Jane had boiled their water, but perhaps Garth had grown careless.

She'd always kept remedies in the cupboard and since she came to the Duncans, Jane had learned more recipes. She could make up some mint tea, add a little ginger and give it to young Michael, whom she'd always liked, to take to her brother. But then, if Garth were really ill, she should send for Dr Duncan.

'Oh, Michael… How bad is he? Perhaps I should go to him.' And check on his water supply, too, as well as his food. It would be hard to keep food clean in that hut.

Michael said anxiously, 'He is bad, miss, I think you should come. I'll show you the way, if you like.'

'I'll bring a lantern. Wait for me.'

In a few minutes Jane had dressed in a warm shawl and her strong boots and had made up a bottle of stomach physic, mint and ginger, to which she added willow bark for the pain. She also took a fresh loaf and a few stems of mint leaves for him to chew. She would tell him to grow mint in a pot near his hut ... if the doctor was needed, she must send a telegram in the morning, as soon as the post office opened.

Mrs Duncan's pistol lay in a drawer; should she take it? After a moment's hesitation she strapped the belt round her waist and slipped the gun into the holster.

She was confident that if a dingo came too near her, she could shoot it ... best not think about criminals that might lurk in the bushes.

It was difficult to unlock the big door, but at last it was done and Jane put the key on a ledge above the door. She hoped to be back before Dolly found she had gone, but if not, she would be locked out. It was not fair to disturb them at night, after they'd worked hard all day. The Ganai were early risers and would be already asleep.

Michael looked worried by the light of the lantern when she joined him on the outside and Jane remembered again all the perils and dangers of the night that Angus had warned her against. Perhaps dingoes would be frightened by the light, but then, 'miscreants' might be attracted to it ... the men who'd attacked Mr Charlesworth's coach. 'Do you think we're safe, Michael?' she asked and the lad laughed nervously.

'Aye, miss. Just let's hurry there as fast as we can, it's not far off... Can you walk a bit faster? I'll carry your things.' Jane gave him the lantern, but did not give up her basket in case he dropped it.

She knew that it was not far from the Home Farm to Garth's hut, but it seemed a long way in the dark of a winter night. There was a crescent moon, and the stars were brilliant.

Then the attack came, as Jane had feared; it had been at the back of her mind ever since they set out. Out of the forest a dark form materialised, huge against the stars, and another behind him. Michael came to a halt. 'Run for it!' he shouted to Jane, but it was useless. He took off with the lantern and Jane followed the light, but the large figure overtook her and grabbed her in his arms.

There was a soft laugh in the darkness.

'If it isn't little Red Riding Hood, going through the woods on an errand of mercy!' The voice was mocking, deep and musical. It was the voice of an educated Englishman.

'Let me go! What do you think you're

doing?' Jane struggled, furious, making not the slightest impression. She tried kicking, but he only laughed. The other man took her basket and tied her hands together, while the big one held her.

'Too late, Red Riding Hood. You have just met the Big Bad Wolf.' He tightened his grip, holding her close. 'And he eats young ladies from Bendigo for breakfast.'

His hands encountered the gun underneath her shawl. 'What's this? Little Red Riding Hood with a deadly weapon strapped round her waist? My, my... The girls are dangerous these days!' He was shaking with laughter, but his grip tightened. 'Wolves beware! Take it off her, you.'

The gun was savagely pulled out of the holster. It had been of no use at all in this situation.

Rigid with fear, Jane tried to think. Had Michael brought her here for this – or had they been unlucky to meet men who were looking for trouble? Michael had gone; he'd not stayed to help her, or them, either. But these men knew who she was. What on earth could they want with her?

'Give up, let her be. She's tied now for sure,' the second man muttered.

'I like holding them down, and the more they struggle, the better,' the big man told him. Jane was utterly powerless to move. 'But I'm a gentleman.' He kissed her on the lips and threw her over to the other man. 'You take her. I'll walk behind. Where's that useless brother of yours?'

Brother...? This man now holding her must be Roy Dooley, Michael's older brother.

Michael must have delivered her up to them and had been expected to stay to help them. Michael was not her friend. He was what Angus had suggested, a shady character, as he'd warned her when they lived at Tangil.

Understanding dawned. Garth was not sick at all, it had been a lie to get her out into the forest. That was something to be thankful for, in spite of her present predicament. Jane realized how stupid she'd been to believe the tale. If only she'd sent Absalom, this would never have happened. But why on earth did they want to take her away from the Home Farm? Where were they going?

'What is all this about?' Jane asked angrily, but there was no answer.

She was pushed along narrow bush paths, brushed by overhanging branches, until the Wolf called a halt. He took out a scarf and bandaged Jane's eyes and they led her forward, stumbling on rocks, for about five minutes. They stopped and she could hear running water. When they took off the bandage she could see the outline of a roof. The smaller man quickly untied her hands before pushing her into a building with her basket. The door slammed and she was alone.

Jane could see nothing. The place had a musty, disused smell; it was probably a miner's cottage, abandoned when the owner left the area, as so many of them did.

Where was she? Beside a creek somewhere, by the sound of it. Shivering with fear, she peered into the shadows. By the faint light, Jane could gradually make out the outlines of a table, a chair and a bed in the room. She tried desperately to think. Were these the bushrangers and if so, why would they want to lock her up and when, and how, could she escape?

There was a small window with stout bars in one wall. The Southern Cross constellation hung low in the sky and below it, the darkness of wild bushland. There were the stars, familiar since she was a child; they made her feel calmer. This meant that the window faced south, and that she was on a slope above some kind of creek. Where it was, she couldn't visualise.

Time passed and Jane's beating heart grew calmer. Angus would be furious when he found out about this – and with her, as well as with the criminals. He would have expected she had more sense and he would tell her so. She'd learned nothing from her months with the Duncans; when it came to a crisis she had still made the wrong decision, let her heart and concern for her brother rule her head. How could she be so simple?

Thinking about Angus, she wished desperately that he were at hand to rescue her.

She would endure the criticism, the cold words, the silence if only she could see his strong face again. But Angus was far away at Blackwood; he would only know she was missing when he returned, on Friday or maybe even Saturday. There would be no clue to tell him where she had gone.

## TWELVE

She was almost defenceless against these men, but not quite. Jane's dress had deep pockets and one of them held another weapon, a small pair of scissors she used for cutting threads when sewing. If they assaulted her, she would fight back and the thought held a shred of comfort.

Waiting for daylight, Jane fell asleep in the chair. She woke in fright when a sudden light shone in her face. The Wolf was standing over her with a lantern and at first, Jane thought she was going to be moved on, but the man turned and locked the door behind him. He came back and stood gazing at her with a slight smile.

Jane's heart beat violently as she stood up to face him. Deliberately she concentrated on slowing her breathing; she would not give in to fear. With a great effort she said, 'What do you want, Wolf? Shouldn't you be out there, howling at the moon?'

The man took off his hat. 'I would rather talk to a beautiful woman.' That voice was seductive, deep and resonant and the accent was that of the ruling classes, clear and commanding. 'When we started this prank I had no idea of your quality, Miss Ashby. I thought you would be a typical mousy spinster... I regret to say I am impressed, after close acquaintance of only a few minutes.'

Jane thought of those terrifying minutes when he had held her close and she had not known what would happen next. She studied his face in the lantern light, a hard, handsome face with prominent nose and chin and dark eyes. His long black hair was tied back. Was this the face of a murderer? She might soon know.

'Let me go, Wolf. You have no reason to hurt me!' Jane stood up straight and looked him in the eye, trying to look braver than she felt.

'And now I see you in the light, I admire your beautiful eyes.' He traced the outline of her cheek with a gentle finger. 'However ... much as I enjoy looking at you, I must get to the point. What would your brother pay, to have you back again? He's been rather careless, hasn't looked after you properly at all, Jane. Left you with the mean Scottish Duncans.'

Jane said nothing and concentrated on trying to look defiant.

The Wolf sat on the table, swinging one of his long legs. 'Garth could feel guilty. That would make things easier, he would pay up straight away and we would let the little bird out of the cage.'

'So that's the point. I see now.' They were after Garth's hard-won gold, now safely in the bank. It was safe until tonight ... and now they had thought of another way to get their hands on it. Jane said no more; she had failed to imagine that they could get at Garth's gold through her.

What would happen if Garth refused to be blackmailed? It was the correct thing to do, to refuse to give in to criminals, Jane knew that. The consequences didn't bear thinking about.

After a long silence, the man spoke again. 'My name is Raven, Malcolm Raven. I am at the moment, only temporarily I hope, by profession a bushranger. It's a calling that has very few advantages. For example, I have never been lucky enough to abduct a pretty girl before. It's quite exciting, isn't it?'

She had to keep up the defiant front.

'Mr Raven, I am not enjoying this experience. Perhaps you need to find some more conventional ways of meeting people?' Jane glared at him. 'For heaven's sake, this is not a game. You lock me up in a rat-infested hole and then pretend to flirt with me. I will not put up with it!'

Raven shook his head sadly. 'You question my methods, Jane. Remember, this is business. Perhaps I should also point out that correctly titled, I am now Lord Raven, my dissolute parent having expired last year.'

Well, it could be true. He stood and spoke like a lord and by all accounts some lords were just as horrible as he was. All this theatrical posturing to make the blackmail seem less criminal!

'A member of the nobility should be able to choose a more suitable career,' Jane said forcefully. A thought struck her. 'Of course, in the past some of your class have kept busy grinding the faces of the poor, as they say. I'm sure you would be good at that.' Her voice trembled a little, but Jane kept her head up.

He laughed, a genuine laugh. At least, so far he wasn't assaulting her, although he was looking her up and down intently. 'You are absolutely right, we made a habit of it. My own forebears enclosed the common, so then the peasants couldn't keep their geese. It made us most unpopular, but it is a mean trick, when you think of it. I would rather steal from people who can afford to pay.'

'So bushranging is almost moral, by comparison. Do you intend to go back to claim your inheritance, Lord Raven?' This was developing just like a bad dream ... soon, she would wake up.

'Ah ... Raven Castle, on a rock above the sea ... a medieval fortress, with battlements, so romantic.' Raven sighed and then snapped upright with a quick change of mood. 'That's why I need your stupid brother's money. I plan to go back to England, repair the castle and set about the undeserving poor again.' He looked at her. 'Would you like to come with me, Jane? You might enjoy helping to spend Garth's money.'

'Would you invite me?'

He stood there, tall and almost elegant, handsome in a hawkish sort of way, looking steadily into her eyes as if he would read her soul.

'I couldn't abduct you, all that way, though it's tempting. You would have to fall madly in love with me. Such things have happened.' Raven paused, still gazing at Jane. 'If your brother is stubborn, I might be obliged to remove some small portion of your ... anatomy, say, an ear or ... a finger, and send it to Garth to concentrate his mind.' He lifted her hand and inspected it, then let it fall. 'Of course, I wouldn't care to take a mutilated woman to

England with me, I must bear that in mind.'

Was he joking? Jane felt she was running out of courage; she was shaking. She fingered the scissors in her pocket and wondered where to stab him, then felt ashamed of her violent thought.

'Go away, or I might be tempted to mutilate you, Lord Raven.'

'You terrify me.' Raven moved quickly from the table, gathered Jane in his arms and kissed her, a long kiss. 'We could be made for each other, Jane. You are very like me. Think about it.' He strode out and the door was bolted on the outside.

Jane gave a sigh of relief, left in the dark on her own. Against her will, she too had felt the attraction. It was a pity that Raven was a criminal. Another sigh, this time for a lost soul. Sooner or later, he would hang. Perhaps there was no such thing as a wholly evil person; perhaps everyone had a light and a dark side.

Some time later, a rat ran over her foot. Jane suppressed a scream. Bush rats in the dark were after all not so dangerous as the men who had locked her up in here. She tried to think of the rat as an ordinary animal, going about its business. Her basket was on the table; she hoped the rat wouldn't find it.

After that, the hours of darkness seemed never-ending, while Jane's mind went round in circles. As the first light crept into the sky, she realized that to help Garth as well as herself, she would have to get out of this prison. He would lose everything if she didn't move quickly.

Daylight brought disappointment, a blank despair. A thick blanket of fog shrouded everything outside the window. Tangil often had winter fogs, while the hills above might still be in sunshine. The fog hid every landmark, isolated the hut in a white world.

Shivering with cold, Jane ate a little of the loaf in her basket and drank some of the ginger tea. Thank goodness they had unbound her hands. She would have to do something to help herself before the Wolf came back.

Jane looked at the walls carefully. In one corner was a pile of fine sawdust; white ants had been at work, as they often were in this part of the world. They demolished woodwork with ease and were a constant threat to wooden houses. She kicked at a plank and hurt her foot, but it gave slightly and clouds of sawdust fell out.

Picking up the chair, Jane attacked the wall with vigour. The chair broke, but she was relieved when nails gave way and the plank of wood hung free at one end. She rested for a minute or two and then pushed at the next plank and hit it with a chair leg.

'Thank you, white ants!' Jane said shakily as she crawled out into the fog. She was free for the moment, covered in dust and totally lost. At any moment the gang could come back.

Listening, Jane heard running water again and wondered whether she should find the creek and walk along it, which would at least save her from walking in circles. She'd heard stories of people who died in the bush and she knew that even in a comparatively settled area like Tangil, it was easy to get lost among the dark trees.

The birds were silent in the morning cold, but there was another sound, faint and far away. It was a rooster, the call of civilisation. Jane smiled to hear the homely sound of a poultry run. There must be a little farm somewhere not far away, where she could get help or at the very least, directions. It would be possible to walk back to the Duncans' farm, if only she knew the way.

The cock bird's hoarse cry came intermittently and Jane went towards the sound. The fog was so thick she could see very little in front of her and had to move slowly through the dark trees, her feet sinking into the deep litter of the forest floor. Bark had peeled from the trees and piled into mounds that in places were almost as tall as Jane was. Dead branches, limbs sticking out at grotesque angles, caught at her clothes as she passed. The bush had quickly grown up again round the abandoned cottage.

The evergreen Australian forests were gloomy in winter, the leaves shutting out what little light there was. Jane shivered at the thought of the mile upon mile of dark woods that surrounded the little human settlements. Europeans would never be safe in this part of the world. The Ganai themselves walked the winter woods in fear of their ancient spirits; they preferred to keep to the coast.

The Ganai would, however, have been able to survive here. Shut off from home and its comforts, from food and shelter, Jane began to realize how fragile their 'white civilisation' was, how easily it could be destroyed. People should help each other, she thought angrily, not harm each other through greed. Nature here was hostile enough for the settlers and prospectors, without their having to go in fear of their fellow men.

Eventually, the dark shape of a building emerged from the gloom and there was a smell of bacon frying. Jane hurried forward, hoping to meet a pleasant-faced settler's wife and to be invited in for breakfast, with a steaming cup of coffee. It would be so good to be among normal people again. Her troubles would soon be ended; they might even drive her home. And then she froze in horror.

Far from being the cosy farm of her imagination, this was Ma Dooley's grog shanty.

She had walked into the enemy and any moment now, one of them would see her. Jane almost wept with disappointment. There was no help here, only danger.

And – she knew too much! Jane could now name the bushrangers. If she were allowed to go free, they would eventually be hunted down.

There was the squalid veranda with its upturned barrels, where a flock of hens was busily foraging for scattered grain. A pig ran out of the kitchen door. Michael Dooley, the traitor, was outside the shanty. He was shaving and his bowl of water stood on a tree stump, steam rising into the foggy air, while a towel hung from a nearby branch. He looked up and straight into Jane's face.

Angus Duncan was angry, deeply angry. He found it hard to believe that Jane had gone. After all his mother had done to help Jane Ashby, the ungrateful woman had taken off while they were at Blackwood, without a word. She hadn't even told Dolly where she was going. She was probably in Melbourne, perhaps she had gone with her brother. There was no note in her room and the only thing missing was the outer door key, which nobody could find.

He had only himself to blame for the desolate feeling when he saw the empty room: Jane's dresses hanging up, some of the sketches she had done. It was foolish of him. He knew that she disliked him, he should have been able to stay detached.

Instead of that, he was feeling devastated and also furious with himself, as well as with Jane.

Ever since their first meeting at the concert in Bendigo, Jane had fascinated Angus. She'd been so good at the Home Farm, had learned quickly and she was prepared to tackle anything. Jane Ashby would make a wonderful settler's wife. In fact, he had discouraged Charlesworth deliberately, hoping that he and Jane could ... but there was a huge barrier, her obvious dislike. She was such an independent person; he admired that about her.

Angus now had to accept that Jane Ashby must have hated the Home Farm. She'd put up with it only until she got the chance to get away. The stupid girl must have thought that he would have tried to stop her. She must have felt that she was still a prisoner, and jumped at her chance of freedom.

'Where's the pauper?' Marcia had jeered, when they'd arrived at Blackwood. 'I thought you took her everywhere with you. I suppose you know, that there German's after her? He was very friendly with the pauper at the dance. She'll be off to work for him, one of these days.'

After several days at Blackwood, Marcia's

chatter and her spiteful remarks had got on Angus's nerves. She often referred to Jane and seemed to hate her for some reason. 'Pauper's in for trouble, she'll get what she deserves, mark my words,' she said darkly. 'Her and that brother of hers.' The Duncans had no idea what she was talking about and said so, but Marcia would tell them no more.

The housekeeper was annoyed that Mrs Duncan had taken too close an interest in the running of the house and asked many questions about missing meat and cheeses. Marcia's ill-temper affected the whole household, even the farm men.

'She's hard to work with,' one of the men had whispered to Angus in the stable, looking over his shoulder in case she could hear him. 'We all hope she'll get wed soon to that bloke she's friendly with. I reckon he's a shady character, that one. Though why he should bother with her is a mystery, she's not the type he would fancy, being gentry.'

Angus, unyoking the cart, was only half listening to the gossip. He wanted to dismiss the woman; she spoke rudely to his mother and she was a slovenly worker.

Later, the Duncans discussed the housekeeper problem. 'Try to be patient, dear,' his mother had told him. 'You know how hard it is to get servants here, especially women. Marcia will probably look after the stores rather better, now that she knows we keep an eye on them.'

'It seems she's got a follower, a shady character too, Tom says,' Angus said gloomily. 'That's probably where the missing stores went.'

His mother brightened. 'That's all to the good! I dare say she will get married soon and then we can look for another housekeeper. It might suit an older woman, perhaps a widow who might be looking for a home.'

'The sooner the better,' Angus had growled. 'But who would marry a woman like that?'

It was a relief to arrive back at the Home Farm on a cold, foggy day, but then came the news that Jane had vanished. At least they knew that she wasn't at the German's smokehouse, whatever spiteful Marcia had said. Angus had called there on the way home, with two hams from Blackwood to be smoked for Christmas. Johann was his usual industrious self and he asked after Jane in a completely innocent way. Angus was sure he was an honest man.

Elspeth Duncan was quiet when she heard that Jane had gone and Angus saw a tear in her eye. 'I'm disappointed,' was all she said. 'I thought better of the lassie than that.'

After an hour or two at home checking on the livestock, Angus could bear it no longer;

he would have to do something. He sent Absalom off to see whether any tracks might still be visible in the damp ground and the Ganai man went off eagerly, glad to be of help.

He and Dolly were most upset, but Absalom had not known what to do until Angus came home. The Ganai people believed Jane had been carried off against her will. How else could you explain it?

'She was happy, we were all happy,' Dolly sobbed. 'Something bad came in the night.'

What next? Angus couldn't just wash his hands of her and get on with the work.

His mother deserved an explanation and an apology, therefore he would find Jane for that purpose. He would also tell her what he thought of her lack of courtesy.

'She has no grace,' he said to his mother. If he could only see her again, he would get over this hollow feeling of loss.

Angus decided to saddle up and go to see Garth Ashby. He surely should know where Jane had gone – unless they had gone off together. Surely someone on the goldfield would know if Garth had gone to Melbourne. Shrugging on a big riding coat, he was going into the stable when a horseman came into the compound through the open gate.

Garth Ashby, haggard and white-faced, dismounted quickly and hurried up. 'Angus, dreadful news! Jane has been taken away – she's being held somewhere, for a ransom. What on earth shall I do?'

Angus went rigid with shock for a moment. He'd been so busy blaming Jane that he had not seriously thought of this possibility. 'We've been away, just got back,' he explained. 'What happened?'

Garth tied up his horse and slumped down on a bench. 'This morning I found a note at the door. They've got Jane, whoever they are, and they want me to draw out our money from the bank and pay them cash for her release. If I don't, or if I tell the police, they threaten to kill her.'

'Jane – poor Jane!' Angus hit the bench with his riding crop. 'I'll kill them if they harm her!'

Garth swallowed. 'I put all the gold in the bank, so they couldn't steal it. So they thought of another way to get at me.'

Angus swore comprehensively, under his breath. Poor Jane, taken away forcibly. He thought of the shining row of quince jelly she had left on the shelf and the way she had driven the trap. The girl had courage, as well as grace and he had misjudged her.

'How could they get her out of here? The whole place is locked up at night. We're very particular about it. If only I hadn't gone away...'

'Don't blame yourself, Angus. I can't think

how it was done, I knew she was safe, here with you. But what to do next? Should I go to the police? Father – it would be the end of him, if we lost Jane. It's worth anything to get her back... What shall I do, Angus?' He was sweating in spite of the chill air. 'I don't know who they are...'

He passed a hand wearily over his face. 'It could be those bushrangers, I've been finding out more about them. They probably torched the cottage and took our gold. Raven, he's the leader. He's dangerous. He has no morals at all.'

Raven ... the name of Marcia's follower, Tom had said. And Marcia had been making veiled threats about Jane. 'She'll be waiting for us to turn up. She won't be far away,' Angus said, trying to sound calm. 'We'll go to look for her. I've already sent Absalom, he's a tracker. If he finds out where she is, he'll come back and get us.'

Garth looked relieved. 'If we go out in different directions... I'll try the old tunnel, the disused mine over the ridge. Jane could be in there...'

'I hope not, in the dark and the damp. But wherever she is, we've got to find her quickly, poor wee lass.'

# THIRTEEN

Jane stared at Michael Dooley, paralysed by fear. The fog swirled around and from the house Ma Dooley called hoarsely, 'Michael, you're too slow, come for your breakfast, now.'

Deliberately Michael put down his razor and wiped his face with the towel.

'Coming, Ma.' He waved to Jane, a shooing motion. 'Get out of here, for all love,' he said quietly, turned and went indoors without looking back. He hadn't told the others. Michael had given her another chance and she must take it.

Jane was very cold. Drops of moisture beaded her shawl and her hair was wet with the fog, but walking should warm her up a little. She found the track that led down towards where their cottage had stood, but then she realized that to stay on any kind of road might lead to trouble. The others, Roy Dooley and Raven, would be out looking for her as soon as they found she had gone. Michael might even tell them, to protect himself.

When Raven found out he'd lost his source of income, he would be determined to get her back. There was much at stake; he wanted the money. She feared violence if he found her, feared his anger and what he would do. Losing a finger might be only the start. She was not deceived by his pleasant manner; Jane felt instinctively that Raven could be very unpleasant indeed. The Dooleys must be afraid of him, so what chance did a weak female stand?

The Home Farm represented security and Jane longed to be back in the compound again, ironically enough. Once a prison, it now seemed like a haven to her and Angus Duncan and his mother had become friends. If she could escape, Angus might be less annoyed with her.

She remembered that the Duncans were due to come home that day. What would they think of her? She felt even colder when she realized that they might decide she was an ungrateful hussy. They'd assume that she had run off to Melbourne in search of an easier life ... and not try to find her. But Garth, surely, would tell them what had happened, once the bushrangers had contacted him.

The best option was to try to go across country to the Home Farm along the tracks, but step aside if she heard a vehicle coming. Walking across this type of country would not be easy. Much of the land had been cleared of trees for gold mining, but there were shafts, pits and heaps of stones everywhere. It was a dismal, degraded landscape, even worse in the fog and without a distant view.

The fog closed in, wrapping Jane in her own world and soaking her to the skin. Sounds came through the blanket more clearly than usual, because of the moisture in the air. The rooster still crowed at intervals and someone at Ma Dooley's dropped a tin plate with a crash.

Listening, Jane thought she heard something else. There it was, hoof beats; a horse was coming briskly down the track, iron shoes striking the stones.

Blindly, Jane scrambled down a bank to get out of sight. She found an area of level green, soft going for her boots after the stones. She would stay parallel with the road, a few yards away, until the horseman had gone by. Thank goodness the fog was so thick she would not need to move far.

Jane found the going easy at first, but the surface changed to a more vivid green and soon her feet started to sink into the soft ground. Mud bubbled up in her footprints and oozed into her boots. She was in swampy ground, a treacherous place at the best of times and worse after the winter rains.

Trying to keep calm, Jane looked round as far as the fog would allow. Here and there were rushes and tussocks that might give her a foothold across the deep green of the stagnant water. She stopped on a tussock in case she could be heard squelching through the mud.

This was a natural basin where springs rose, a place where the water had once been used by miners to wash dirt and extract gold. An old gold cradle lay drunkenly at an angle, almost submerged. There must be hard ground here somewhere.

Not far away, the horseman went by unseen. She had avoided that danger, but now she had to get out of the swampy area and back on to high ground. With such a restricted view it was hard to see which way to go, but Jane tried hard to keep her sense of direction. Now her skirt was wet too and felt heavy, she was being dragged down. Because she had stood still, she was sinking.

Jane had to fight panic. She needed to step carefully but quickly from one tussock to another. She thought of snakes, but then remembered that they hibernate in winter; no snakes today... The tussock she was on gave way and in leaping to another, she lost her footing and fell. She could feel the swamp sucking her in; now she could not lift her legs out of the mud, she was trapped. She was going to die, out there in the fog.

A strange calm seemed to fill the small world of mud and water. Jane decided to try her best to go on living as long as she could. She shouted loudly in case the sound would travel through the fog ... where was Garth? He must be looking for her by now but where would he begin? Tangil was a wide area and he might think she was being held in the town. None of them had known about the existence of the cottage in the trees where she had been locked up last night.

Hanging on to a clump of rushes, Jane felt herself sinking lower into the slime.

Not long now ... another horse was going by, this one more slowly.

'Help! Help!' she yelled, as loud as she could.

The horse stopped and a man's voice replied. 'Where?'

'Here! Here!' Jane kept on calling until a shape loomed out of the fog, a tall man.

'Angus!' she called and closed her eyes, concentrating all her strength on dragging her legs out against the suction of the swamp. Angus would get her out, she was going to live, after all. They both struggled together until gradually, the swamp gave her up and she was dragged clear.

Jane found herself lying at the side of the track. She looked up at her rescuer and said, 'Thank goodness ... oh, no!'

The dark face of Raven was looking into hers. 'Thank goodness indeed, a few more minutes and you'd have gone. Jane, my darling, I have just saved your life. It is I, your faithful jailer. Is that not romantic?' He wrinkled his nose. 'Except, my dear, that you smell terrible.' He looked down at his sodden clothes. 'And so, no doubt, do I.'

Jane tried to wipe the slime from her face. She had failed miserably, she was back as a captive.

'Saved your chance of getting money out of Garth, you mean. I'm just a commodity to you.' Anger swept over her, in spite of exhaustion. 'I have no illusions. If I hadn't been useful, you would have let me die.'

'May I say how much I admire your spirit?' Raven was smiling. 'What a woman! Still fighting, still resisting me. I must try to exert more charm, to keep you with me by force of character.'

'You have none,' Jane said wearily.

Raven's horse had wandered and he went to retrieve it. When he came back he was still smiling; rage was not going to be a problem, not just yet.

'You are a lovely girl with nerves of steel, an unusual combination. You were not afraid of me last night, and you got away from the place by your own efforts. You managed – just – to stay alive after falling into the swamp. Many people who get into swamps die, because they panic and start flailing about.'

'I was lucky you came by just now.'

'I'm so glad I did, happier than you would believe. You are the kind of woman I can admire, Jane. There are so few women who would fight with no advantages on their side.' Raven was reminding her how hopeless her position was.

*How I wish Basil Charlesworth could hear him!*

'You didn't know about the scissors in my pocket, Raven. I was going to stab you, if you assaulted me.'

Relief was making Jane light-headed. She struggled to stand up, pushing her wet hair out of her eyes with a muddy hand.

'What are you going to do now?' Wet, cold and miserable, she must keep up the brave front. He may be praising her, but she had lost the fight. Raven was back in charge and she was at his mercy. 'Please don't take me back to that hut!'

'Not safe, my dear. I hadn't realized that you would be able to fight your way out.'

He thought for a minute or two, trying to clean his hands on the sparse grass at the side of the track. 'What would you really like, just now?'

That was a simple question. 'A hot bath and a change of clothes.'

'Come with me, then. I will put you on the horse and you will not struggle, or try to escape.' Raven spoke quietly, but there was a dangerous edge to his voice.

Stiffly in her wet clothes, Jane climbed onto the big chestnut's back and Raven sat closely behind her, holding the reins. They set off at a brisk walk. What would happen if they met another traveller? But there must have been few people out in the bitter weather and no one loomed out of the mist except a surprised cow.

Raven took them on tracks Jane didn't know, down into the valley and out the other side. They rode for an hour or more and warmed by Raven's arms around her, she was drowsing when the horse stopped and he said, 'Here we are. Let me lift you down, my angel.' He dropped his voice to an intimate whisper. 'And remember, mud is very beneficial for the female complexion. You will be lovelier than ever, after this.'

They were in a farm yard next to an open stable door. The place was familiar! With a shock Jane realized they were at Blackwood Park. At Blackwood, a few hours too late; the Duncans would have gone home.

Marcia screamed when she saw the bedraggled pair, but on orders from Raven she hurried Jane off to the Duncans' bathroom immediately and brought her some clothes, including a warm black dress and shawl.

'Mrs Duncan's, these, you've worn her clothes before.' She looked as though she was going to ask questions, but the Walhalla coach arrived with a rattle and she hurried off.

With a sigh of relief, Jane slipped out of her

slimy garments. Hot water came steaming out of the tap, there was lavender-scented soap and lavender-fragrant towels. This was sheer luxury and for some time, she forgot she was the prisoner of a dangerous criminal. The hot water soothed her aches and bruises and her nerves settled down

Soon, however, the problems came back. What would happen next she had no idea, except that once she had some food and a rest, she would have to escape again. The thought of Garth losing his gold for a second time was unbearable. Marcia had shown her a bedroom and she was evidently to stay at Blackwood for the night. She was bound to be locked in. But what if she had a key herself?

Marcia's keys were like a badge of office, a great bunch always worn at her waist, jingling as she walked. They were unattainable. Angus had his own set of keys ... now where was it they had been standing, when he'd asked her to pass them over, on her first visit? Jane remembered clearly; it was when he'd given guns to the men, to shoot the wild pigs and she had been in the doorway to the main passage through the house.

As she dressed, Jane wondered how Raven had the effrontery to come here and to give orders to Marcia. He must know the Duncans' movements exactly; he must have known that when Michael came for her last night – was it only last night? – they were away from home, but that they would be back there by now. Of course – Marcia would tell him, it was obvious. The widow of his dead associate, working with the bushrangers and against the Duncans.

Jane crept quietly out of the bathroom and along the passage. Sounds came from the kitchen; the farm men were eating their midday meal, with Marcia and the maids.

Heart beating, she took the keys and wrapped them in her towel, praying that no one would notice they had disappeared.

She was not to be locked up just yet. Raven came to join her in the large room which was both dining room and parlour and soon they were sitting beside a log fire with bowls of hot soup and fresh bread. He too was bathed and changed; he looked quite civilised, less of the ruffian, sitting there as if the place belonged to him.

'Do you come here often?' Jane couldn't resist the question.

Raven looked up and smiled. 'Not as often as I would like. I think I should install a bathroom or two in Raven Castle, do you not agree? So necessary, when you have demolished a building and then fallen into a swamp.'

When they had eaten, the bushranger stood up. 'I must go now, Jane, but I will return for supper. Marcia will bring you anything you need.' He bent over her swiftly, kissed her cheek and was gone. He was a strange kind of jailer, but he did not forget to lock the door.

Jane slept for a while, then roused herself, inspected the Duncans' books and read a little, but it was hard to concentrate. She tried the door, but it was still locked. Marcia was taking no chances.

In the late afternoon, the fog lifted and through the window Jane saw the shreds of a red sunset in a stormy sky. If she managed to get away from Blackwood Park she would have a long walk, down through Willow Grove and along the ridge to the Home Farm. She sighed and then tried to pull herself together. However long it took, she would do it. At least she had her boots with her, drying by the fire.

Raven came back as darkness was falling, looking pleased with himself.

'I have just concluded a business deal – a legal one, my dear, don't look at me like that. We shall celebrate with a bottle of Australian claret, a much underestimated beverage, given to me by a grateful client.' He found two glasses in a cupboard and poured the wine, then sat back and beamed at her. A criminal, enjoying Blackwood Park.

Jane felt the wine warm her to her toes. She looked at the man over the rim of her glass. 'If you have ... legitimate business, why do you style yourself a bushranger and gallop about doing harm to innocent people? Lord Raven, you are too intelligent, surely, to be a criminal ... and possibly not evil enough.'

*I hope you're not evil enough, I can't be sure about that just because you're in a good mood at present.*

Jane looked at him intently. 'You might not like that suggestion.'

Raven reached over and took her hand. 'Jane, I ask myself this question. I can only think that it's bred in me. The Ravens answered to no one, up there on the border between Scotland and England. The castle can withstand a siege. They stole cattle from either side, Scots and English, whichever were the fattest, I should think. They were Border Reivers, brigands, for about three hundred years. Cursed in the sixteenth century by a Bishop – Gavin Dunbar was his name – for all time. Then one of them happened to please the king of the day and was ennobled for it. Now how can you expect me to stick to the straight and narrow, when I've been cursed? By a Scot, which is why I don't like the Scottish race.'

'You can't blame your ancestors, or the Scots,' Jane said firmly. 'I believe that everyone is responsible for their own actions.'

Raven put down his glass. 'So you think I should reform.'

'Can you not see the advantage? If you go on as you are, you will hang. There is a certain amount of law and order in Victoria. And I don't think you can blame your ancestors, or a bishop's curse, if you end up in court. It won't convince a judge.' Jane wanted to say a lot more, but she felt she sounded like a Sunday school teacher.

'They sent me to an expensive school, to teach me how to behave properly. Kindness to widows and orphans, that sort of thing. We were taught to be young gentlemen and to protect the poor. It was a complete contrast to the Raven way of life, I can tell you.' Raven smiled, looking into the fire. 'Sitting here with you, I can see the advantage of being an upright citizen. I could enjoy domesticity. I'm sure you would not ... consort with me, if you were free to go, and yet – you might.' He took a sip of wine.

Jane herself preferred not to think about it. She pushed the glass aside; wits were needed and wine would make her sleepy.

Of course, Raven noticed her movement. '*In vino veritas* ... I rarely drink, it does not help either horsemanship or ... harrying the population. I admit it, I am tired of the constant fear of being caught, not to mention the odd bout of conscience. I sometimes think of Ned Kelly, shut up in Melbourne jail, then taken out and hanged. A dreadful end.'

'Give it up, before it's the death of you. I mean it, Lord Raven.' Jane was surprised how much she wanted him to see sense, and not just for her own sake. She put a lot of feeling into her words and she thought they had an effect on him.

'Please call me Malcolm... Nobody does, these days. The lads call me Mal, the French for evil, as you will know. The evil raven, they like that.'

'Give it all up, before it kills you, body and soul.'

'Perhaps I should try to be good. I promise, once Garth's cash is safely in my hands, I will consider it. Ah, here is Marcia with supper.'

The housekeeper put the meal on the table and went out, muttering. Raven looked at the dishes and smiled.

'Roast beef, perfect! The Duncan beef is Scottish, you see, Angus beef, the breed of the cattle as well as the name of the owner. The wine we are drinking will be exactly right.'

'Poor Angus Duncan! We're eating his beef.' Jane shook her head; remorse didn't stop her enjoying the meal.

Lord Raven shook out his napkin. 'One day, perhaps I will entertain Mr Duncan at Raven Castle, to repay him for his fine hospitality.'

The evening with the bushranger was unlike any Jane had experienced. They talked about England, and he told her more about Raven Castle. He took her through a broad sweep of history from the Norman Conquest onwards, his ancestors playing various roles, both saints and sinners.

Marcia cleared the meal, a little unsteady on her feet.

'The lady is partial to gin,' Raven remarked as he closed the door. 'I must warn her not to drink too much tonight.' Jane had seen her eyeing the wine bottle, which was still half full, and hoped she would finish it off.

As they went back to sit by the fire, Jane asked him, 'Malcolm, what is the connection between you and Marcia?'

A shadow passed over Raven's face. 'A bad one. Her husband was Liam Dooley, the oldest Dooley boy, and the cleverest. A born bushranger, that one, without a shred of conscience. He saw the English evict his family from their land, you see. The younger brothers only heard about it.'

Jane said slowly, 'So the Dooleys hate the English, that explains a lot. But they surely should hate you, as well?'

'I'm sure they do. It happened that Liam married Marcia, she was more reasonable then ... and he was killed in one of our raids. She became slightly deranged after that. So I've tried to help her, since then, and she helps me. I've never stayed long here before, this is in your honour, my lady. I have a house of my own in the bush.'

So that explained why Ma Dooley and

Marcia were allies.

Suddenly, the mood seemed to change. 'I suppose you realize that you are in very grave danger, Jane Ashby.'

Jane sat up a little straighter. 'I've been in danger ever since you tricked me to come away, out of the Duncans' farm,' she snapped. 'You are a villain.'

'You're angry, and with good reason. An innocent victim of the plan.' Raven laughed. 'You are in danger of falling in love with me. You actually care what happens to me.' His eyes were hypnotic. 'I could take advantage of the situation ... but I have honourable intentions towards you. I want you to come to England, I swear I would lead an honest life with you beside me. Do it, Jane. Marry me.' He stroked her hair. 'I will show you the world. I care about you.'

'This is rubbish. Don't be so dramatic.' He was playing with her, knowing she was his prisoner.

Jane was surprised at herself; a tiny part of her was almost tempted. What was it about this man? Then she thought about Angus Duncan, that honest, decent man who had taken her to his home when she was left with nothing after the fire. Angus was her type of man, not Raven. That last thought was something of a surprise. Not long ago, she'd disliked Angus intensely and now, she longed to see that clever, sensitive face again.

'The last man who proposed marriage to me was a solicitor, but he found that I was too bold, too forward. He thought I would embarrass him,' Jane said thoughtfully.

Raven laughed. 'I begin to have sympathy with him, whoever he is. He had a lucky escape.'

## FOURTEEN

Garth and Angus went out on their horses, but could find no trace of Jane, no sign of where she might have gone.

'They must have told her some tale to get her out of the farm,' Garth said. 'She was safe here.' He paused. 'I'll have to give them the money.'

Angus, who had not slept since he came home from Blackwood, wondered wearily whether it was worth going out again. By now Jane could be miles away; they might have taken her to Moe, even to Melbourne. He had never felt so wretched in his life before. Now, when it might be too late, he realized what Jane meant to him.

Jane meant light and life, and the faint hope of a future with a family. She was dear to him in a way he had never experienced or

210

imagined. She was independent and spirited ... would she ever agree to share his life? It was hardly an enticing prospect for a young lady. Angus knew he was too quiet. He found it impossible to express feelings. But for now they must concentrate on getting her back, unharmed.

There was despair at the Home Farm when Absalom the Ganai tracker came back to report. Angus and Garth were sitting in the stable in silence when he came in; they were defeated. But his news was not good.

'Man came to the side fence, I saw marks of his boots in the earth,' Absalom told them. 'He went away with Jane ... then met other men. They went to a place, under trees.' He looked at Angus. 'That old place of Mac's, he went away years ago. The hut, it's still there, windows with iron bars. That was to keep his gold safe.'

Angus and Garth both shouted, 'Is she there?'

'No, she gone. There was hole in the wall and nobody there. She ... Miss Jane's boots came out of the hole, she must have got herself out.'

'That's like Jane,' Angus said very quietly. 'Do you know where she went?'

Absalom nodded. 'She walked up to Dooley's shanty, not quite all the way, and then away ... down to the swamp. I lost her then, no more tracks.' He wiped his eyes. 'I hope ... I hope I am wrong. No sign in the swamp. Nothing after that.'

The others were silent, imagining what might have happened. Jane, sinking into the swamp...

'It was so foggy, she wouldn't have known where she was.' Garth got up and paced about. 'What else can we do?'

Angus shook his head and said nothing. He could see her vividly, Jane walking and walking through the fog, trying to get home, and her end when she sank into the mud of the swamp. Nothing would ever be the same again. How could they tell John Ashby what had happened?

How could he get through the rest of his dreary life?

Marcia marched along the passage and locked Jane into her room with a flourish.

'You can have yer own clothes back in the morning. You won't get out of here until I say so! Serves you right, pauper, for getting ideas above your station. And you needn't bother telling Mr Duncan about me helping Raven. If you see him again...' her look was full of hatred, 'if Raven lets you go, you can tell Mr High and Mighty Duncan that I'm leaving. Got better prospects in Melbourne, so I'm off next week.'

Jane smiled into the sour face.

'When I tell Mr Duncan what you've said,

it will give him the greatest pleasure. Thank you. Goodnight.'

Jane sank into the big feather bed with a sigh of relief. It seemed that there was to be no guard on the door, no savage dog patrolling the passages. The only dog in the house, an ancient sheepdog that looked more like a hearthrug, had made friends with her on her first visit. All was quiet and Jane was asleep very quickly; she had decided that a few hours of sleep were essential. Raven had left, saying he would come back in the morning to take her to a safer place, but by then she intended to be gone.

The night was fine, but the moon was partly obscured by dark clouds when Jane woke. The clock in the hall struck three; it was time to make a move. She carefully arranged the bolster in the bed to look like a body under the blankets. When Marcia came to let her out, it might fool her for a little precious time.

Jane dressed quickly, picked up her boots and quietly tried a key in the door. At the third attempt, the lock clicked and the door opened. Thank goodness – one hurdle over. Trying to remember the layout of the house, she pictured a room with an outside door where stores were kept. She padded along the dark passage carefully; the hearthrug dog came up and licked her hand, but that was all. Regular snores came from the housekeeper's room, so the wine or possibly the gin had done its work.

She found the turn into the store room, but fell over a bag of potatoes. Jane listened for a while, but there was no movement in the house, no sound except the snores and the slow tick of the grandfather clock. Thank heavens, the key for that door was soon found. She pulled on her boots and in a minute was free again, in the cold air.

So far so good, but she was a long way from being safe, a long way from the Home Farm. Her main concern was to get a message to Garth, in case he handed over the money. Once that was done, it was unlikely he could get it back. The robbers would all disappear, Raven had said as much. This was their last throw of the dice and they were determined to win.

In the yard, the farm dogs started to bark and she slipped out onto the road like a shadow. No one must catch her now; she would not be able to escape for a third time.

Walking briskly down the track, Jane tried to calculate how long it would take her to reach the Home Farm. The cart had travelled about twice walking pace and had taken nearly two hours on her previous visit with Angus, so she would need four hours to cover the distance. By then, the dawn would be breaking and the household at Home Farm would be stirring. She had never walked for four hours at a stretch, but she knew that hikers could walk for much longer. She would be a hiker.

One stage at a time; the first stage was to reach Tangil South, the cluster of houses at the side of the track that led from Blackwood Park to the township of Willow Grove. Small settlements on the track were surrounded by paddocks and beyond them, the immense, silent bush.

It seemed an age before she achieved her first goal. At Tangil South, there were no lights in the houses and the fires had died down. It was a lonely feeling, passing those houses where people slept; Jane felt like a ghost, an outcast, walking in the night. In her black clothes, she would be hard to see, unless a light was turned on her.

What would happen if she knocked on a door and asked for help? A dog barked and Jane jumped in alarm, but it was chained up and couldn't harm her. She hurried along in case it roused the household. People were always wary of anyone who wandered in the night, when all decent people were in their beds; it put you outside the law. The folk of Tangil South might have been friendly, but maybe not in the middle of the night. And then, where was Raven? It would be her luck to fall into his arms again, to knock on his door. It was safer to avoid everyone.

The moon disappeared entirely and there

was a flurry of rain. Jane pulled her shawl tighter and tied it round her waist, keeping up the brisk pace. It was important to get right away before Marcia found out she had gone. Her boots had dried out, but the leather was now hard; her feet would be sore before the end of the walk.

The events of the last two days kept revolving in Jane's head. She was appalled and furious that the bushrangers would try to blackmail Garth, but then another thought crept in. She had not been harmed; they could easily have tied her up or assaulted her. Or cut off bits of her to send to Garth, as Raven had kindly suggested.

As Jane left Tangil South, the rain began in earnest, a steady downpour and soon she was soaked; her clothes weighed her down. This would make the journey much more difficult. She struggled along, but couldn't keep up the brisk pace and she soon began to tire.

'I'll walk as far as Willow Grove,' she said to herself. 'The rain might have stopped by then.' On this part of the road the forest was quite close, and Jane dared not think about what was rustling in the undergrowth, just a few yards from her. The rain beat in her face, whipped by a sudden wind. Fatigue overwhelmed her and she sank down at the side of the road.

Where was the bold, forward woman Jane

Ashby now? She felt the loneliness of the bush and the wild places, the darkness of Gippsland. There was no sign of civilisation, only the track, almost invisible in the dark night.

In her tiredness, Jane felt an aching sadness for Raven, a man who had lost his way. She gave herself a mental shake; she should hate Raven and the other bushrangers, but it was tragic that they had ruined their own lives. Michael Dooley had seemed to be a pleasant, gentle young man. Raven had such energy, he could have been a force for good in the world. The addiction to gold and to adventure had ruined him; he'd admitted it. Was it true that sometimes prisoners grew to love their jailers? But not Jane Ashby.

The rain grew heavier and Jane forced herself to move, to stand up and start walking again. It took all her willpower to put one foot in front of the other. She was almost upon it before the first garden fence in the village appeared through the driving rain.

Perhaps she could find a shed or a stable for shelter? There would be no one about at four in the morning. Jane realized that she was not going to reach the Home Farm without rest, it was impossible. She stumbled on, wondering what to do and then she saw a light. This must be Willow Grove.

Surely the bushrangers wouldn't have friends here? The risk must be taken, or she could die of exposure. Her hands and feet were numb and she began to feel drowsy.

It took Jane a few minutes to realize where she was. There was the scent of wood smoke in the air; this was the German's smoke-house. He must keep a fire going all night when the smoking was in progress. Perhaps she could creep in there if it wasn't too smoky, and give in to sleep? All she wanted to do was to sleep.

The wind was driving rain into her face as Jane struggled towards the light. As she got there, the door of the shed opened. Jane backed away into the shadows, but then saw it was Johann Meyer who came out. At first he looked terrified as she walked forward, a black, dripping figure like a drowned woman.

'What... What is this?'

'Mr Meyer, it's Jane Ashby,' she quavered. 'It's a long story, but I'm walking back to the Duncans' farm.'

He must have thought she was a ghost. For a long moment he stood quite still, staring at her.

'Please.' It was an effort to stay upright; Jane felt herself swaying with fatigue.

Johann seemed to pull himself together. 'But you poor girl! Come inside, I have a fire in the house also!' He led the way along a flagged path to his kitchen door. 'Mutter! Come, there is need of your help!' he called and in a few minutes, a white-haired woman appeared with a candle, looking alarmed. Johann explained quickly in German that the Mädchen needed towels and warm clothes, and she hurried off to find them. Jane stopped herself from falling with one hand on the kitchen table.

She was making a pool of water on the floor.

'I'm sorry to be a nuisance,' she whispered.

Johann pulled the fire in the grate together and threw on more wood, talking all the time.

'Mr Duncan was here yesterday, his hams are smoking at this moment. I usually tend the fire once in the night. Mr Duncan was chatting and I asked him about you, Miss Jane. He said you were very well. He had noticed that we danced together at the social evening.' He looked puzzled. 'He said you were at the Home Farm, and well.'

'I was very well, until … this happened,' Jane whispered. 'The bushrangers locked me up, but I managed to escape. Mr Duncan didn't know about it.'

Johann shook his head in disbelief. 'I have heard of the bushrangers … robbers and criminals. Why would they do such a thing to you?' His mother came back and motioned Jane into another room, to change. 'My mother speaks little English. It is hard for old people to learn a new language, you understand.'

Jane tried to summon her small stock of German words, but could only manage, 'Danke.' Sipping milky coffee gratefully and wrapped in blankets, she told Johann how the bushrangers were after her brother's money and were holding her until he paid them. He was horrified and translated the tale into German for his mother, who also gasped in horror.

'You will stay here for the rest of tonight, of course,' the young man said. 'And in the morning I will drive you to the Home Farm. Can you sleep on the couch yonder, do you think?'

'Easily,' Jane said thankfully. 'Thank you so much, Johann.'

Surely the bushrangers wouldn't find her here? The danger might be in the morning. They would probably patrol this road, knowing she would try to reach Home Farm. Thinking of this, Jane put her clothes in front of the fire to dry as soon as Johann and his mother had gone to bed.

After a few hours the German household awoke: roosters were crowing, pigs squealing for their food and a cow was swinging into the milking shed of its own accord. Jane quickly dressed in her fairly dry clothes. Johann milked the cow, while Mrs Meyer cooked breakfast, the famous Blutwurst sausages and eggs, with dark rye bread. Jane felt light-headed and less than hungry, but

220

she realized that they would be offended if she didn't eat.

'Mother says you look too thin,' Johann told her. 'Please to take another slice of the bread, it is our own.'

'Lovely sausages,' Jane said politely and Johann seemed to glow. 'I will show you one day how to make them, but not today. Today you must go back to your place.'

The Meyers had a fast pony and a stylish trap; the farm and the smoke-house must be prospering. Johann wrapped Jane up in a large rug before they left. The rain had stopped and a watery winter sun was trying to prevail.

'If we meet anyone, I will hide,' Jane said nervously.

Johann gently tucked the rug over her head, so that very little of her could be seen. 'How would any person see you now? They think it is my mother, she goes in the trap with me.'

The young German continued to talk as they trotted along. 'If ever you should think of leaving the Duncans, Jane, I would like for you to work for us and we would pay you good. You would learn to make sausages, my mother wishes for a helper. I can build with wood, so I could build you a little room of your own to live in. You would like that, yes?'

He obviously thought she was a housemaid, which of course she was, in a way. 'The

Home Farm must be lonely, in Willow Grove you would see more life. Angus Duncan does not talk.' He beamed. 'I, I talk all the time!'

Jane said tactfully, 'I would love to learn to make sausages one day, Johann. I have learned to make cheese, butter and soap at the Duncans.'

'And,' said the farmer hopefully, 'with you, I would learn English better.'

A thought struck Jane. She knew a young woman who was looking for work.

'Why don't you ask at the Tangil store? Mr Ellis has a daughter who's looking for a place and a change of scene.'

'Ja? I will ask today, thank you, that is a good idea.' He paused. 'I would have liked it to be you, Jane. But the other young woman, she will be a good worker?'

'I think so. She's been very busy in the shop.'

They met one or two people on the road, but no one who might be looking for Jane and they arrived at the Home Farm as the gates were being opened for the day.

Angus was in the yard, looking curiously hunched and unlike himself. In a sudden insight, Jane realized that he thought she was never going to come back. He stopped dead as Johann drove in, pulled up and then helped Jane out of the vehicle. Jane watched; his face was so much more expressive without the beard. It registered amazement, delight at seeing her and this was followed by dismay as he looked from one to the other with a frown.

'Meyer ... I can't imagine what is going on.'

Johann beamed and proceeded to make things worse. 'Jane is in great danger, so I rescue her, is this the word? I admire the young lady, I am pleased to do it. She slept at my house.'

'Did she indeed!' He looked thunderous. Angus Duncan was jealous! That was the only word for it. Jane blushed, which probably made her look guilty, but a sort of joy was rising and she couldn't help smiling. She was free, the sun was coming out and Angus was jealous. She wanted to hug him.

'But do not worry, Mr Duncan, she came to no harm. My mother looked after her.'

Mrs Duncan emerged from the kitchen and her eyes widened as she looked at Jane. 'Those clothes are mine! How on earth did you – what has happened?'

'It's a long story,' Jane said wearily. 'But first I need to tell Garth that I'm safe.'

'I'll send Absalom,' Angus said briefly, and went off. Mrs Duncan gave Johann a basket of apples and he declined a drink of coffee. He went off smiling, saying to Jane, 'You have made me pleased.'

'That young man seems very pleased with himself,' Mrs Duncan observed when he had gone. 'Jane, we thought you ... we might have lost you. Absalom tracked you as far as a swamp, and then – nothing. Imagine how we felt.'

'Absalom is amazing. He was right, I left that place on a horse. Raven pulled me out of the swamp. I'll tell you when Garth comes.' Jane wanted desperately to sit down; her legs were trembling.

Sooner than it seemed possible, Garth rode in and threw his arms round his sister.

'Janey! How did you get away? I was on the point of giving them some money ... I felt so guilty, letting this happen to you. Now tell us all about it.'

Safe in the kitchen at Home Farm, it all seemed like a bad dream. Angus came in to hear the tale and Absalom, having run back from Garth's house, squatted in a corner.

By the time all the questions had been answered it was time for lunch and Dolly made bread and cheese for them all. As Jane had expected, there was general jubilation at the news that Marcia was leaving.

'After this, she would certainly have been dismissed in any case,' Mrs Duncan said severely. 'She should be arrested as an accomplice in crime. I wonder how much from our stores she gave to the criminals?'

The police would have to be informed, the bushrangers should be rounded up. 'They are a menace to society,' Angus growled.

Jane shrank from the thought of giving long statements to the Moe police. 'I think they will disappear for a while,' she said. 'They'll expect to be arrested.' The Dooley boys had been suspected for a long time, but Raven had been elusive. He would know that the whole neighbourhood would be after him, once Jane's story got out.

In the end they agreed that Garth should tell the police and he went off to the town. Jane went over to her room to wash and change into her own clothes, but she fell onto the bed and slept until evening.

Sitting opposite Angus at the supper table that evening, Jane caught his eye and they smiled at each other. 'I'm so glad to have you back,' he managed, looking as though he would have liked to say more.

## FIFTEEN

The next morning, the sun shone and Angus was whistling as he went over the yard. Jane was tired, but said she was ready for work again. Sleep had taken away some of her aches and relief still flooded her. Relief, and the secret joy that Angus had cared so much what had happened to her.

Mrs Duncan had other ideas and had

planned no work for her that day.

'You need to rest,' she said firmly.

Angus also had a plan for the day: 'If you've recovered ... would you like to come with me to move the sheep? We can ride there through the paddocks – you can ride a horse?'

'I've only tried side-saddle, but I'd like to come.' Jane had driven, but never ridden the horses. Angus saddled an old steady mare called Bonnie for Jane and brought out his own horse. They set off at a walk down the track that led to the lower grass paddocks near the creek, followed by two working dogs trotting behind.

'I could get to like horse riding,' she said happily, looking round at the green rolling fields in the winter sunshine.

This was where she belonged, with Angus Duncan. Still shocked and bruised from her ordeal, Jane was relieved and thankful to be back from the dark world outside the farm. She never wanted to go into the forest again. The warmth of her welcome back had touched her and made her feel valued.

'Jane ... I want to talk to you,' Angus began.

'That will be a nice change,' Jane said and then regretted it when she saw the pain in his eyes. 'I'm sorry. But you say so little, Angus.'

'I gather I don't measure up to the social graces of Lord Raven,' Angus said bitterly. 'Or even of Herr Meyer. I must bore you, Jane.'

She should have been more critical of Raven when she'd told her story, put him in a worse light. Angus evidently thought she had been attracted to the ruffian. Jane made an effort to lighten the atmosphere.

'Never! You are so mysterious, you keep me guessing. Now tell me Angus, what were you going to say? What are you really thinking?'

Angus Duncan got off his horse and tied it to a tree, then helped Jane down. He took her in his arms beside the horse and held her close. To be with Angus felt entirely natural; Jane relaxed.

'A man of deeds, not words,' she murmured and Angus laughed.

'I know how you saw me at first, I heard you tell Marcia. Now, Jane...' again, the hesitation. 'That was some time ago. In the light of fresh evidence, could you revise your judgement?'

'That sounds like Mr Duncan the lawyer. I suppose they never tell what's in their minds!' So he cared what she thought about him...

The dogs sat down in the shade to watch them, paws crossed on the grass. Angus took a deep breath. 'I'll tell you what I'm thinking. When we came back from Blackwood and you'd ... disappeared, I thought you must have hated us, to go off like that. But I realized that I'd find it difficult to live without you, I wanted you here, for ever. So I was going to find you, Jane, and – try to sort things out. However long it took.'

That was a very long speech for Angus. Was it a door into Paradise that had just opened – or a life sentence? Jane wondered whether she had what it took to be a settler's wife. Which was stronger: her growing love for this man or her independence? It would hurt him if she backed out now. There was a strong attraction, a physical one when they were close like this. It might lead her astray...

'And then when Absalom said he thought you'd drowned in the swamp, I was in despair. I don't want to let you out of my sight, Jane.' Both the dogs thumped their tails on the ground. 'Thank goodness you're here. I can hardly believe it.' Angus was still holding her.

Jane looked up at him. 'But I heard what you said, too! To Charlesworth when he was here. I didn't mean to ... you said I was ... the assumption is, we don't like each other, Angus.'

'I was warning him off, even then I wanted you myself, or ... at least, to save you from life with him!' He bent his head and kissed her and she felt very secure in his arms. Words were not always needed. 'Can we agree that we perhaps do ... like each other? You like kissing me. I rest my case.' Angus was laughing, now. Then he kissed her again.

'Oh yes,' Jane said, rather breathlessly. 'We can agree ... on some things. I would like to know you better, Angus, to know what concerns you. But now, shall we go and move the sheep?' Jane needed a little space and time; too much had happened, too quickly. Time to get used to the idea of Angus ... as a lover.

Side by side they rode over the grassy slopes, the dogs working the sheep smoothly to a gate in one corner. Along the creek, golden wattles bloomed, heralding the end of winter. Jane felt happiness spreading through her in a warm glow. Her feelings for Angus had been growing for some time and she could hardly believe now that once she had disliked him. But was this a trap, the one that caught so many women? The trap of romance, of the excitement of falling in love.

'Promise me one thing,' Jane said when the sheep were safely in the new paddock, heads down into the fresh grass. She saw his alert look, and smiled.

'Only if I can keep the promise... I ... can't promise that Home Farm will be the best in Victoria, but I'll try.' They turned back to the home track.

'That you won't grow a bushranger beard, ever again.'

Angus laughed. 'I promise.' His horse moved closer to hers and that was the excuse for another kiss. Jane hadn't imagined that it was possible to kiss someone on horseback. 'Do you promise to marry me? We belong to each other.'

'I can't promise you anything yet, Angus. Give me a little more time.' Jane saw his look of disappointment and wondered whether she'd been too forward once again, possibly too flippant, and raised his hopes too high. It was cruel to kiss a man so enthusiastically if you didn't intend to marry him, and the last thing she wanted was to hurt Angus. When he looked vulnerable, she wanted to protect him.

Angus Duncan felt that his life was at a crossroads. He and Jane had progressed so far and no further. Part of the problem was his own nature; he found it difficult to talk about his feelings, difficult to talk at length about anything. He'd been a listener since childhood and a thinker.

The training in law had been enjoyable; strangely enough, Angus loved words and he loved reading. Advising clients was interesting, but appearances in court demanded a fluency and a showmanship that he knew was beyond him. It had been a relief to give it up, to go home to the farm and to take on the management of what had become a fairly big enterprise.

Jane thought he was too quiet, and Angus

was beginning to care very much what Jane thought. She was affectionate, but would she want to spend her life with him? She was so capable of looking after herself. How many other women would have done what she did to get away from the bushrangers?

It would be foreign to his nature to try to control a woman in the way Charlesworth thought was necessary, but Angus felt protective of Jane, now more than ever. The night he'd dragged her away from the burning house and into the safety of their farm, she had resented his interference and she wouldn't thank him for protection now.

There was business in Melbourne, to arrange a sale for his wool bales and Angus decided to take a trip, although he hated the thought of leaving Jane at the farm. Absalom had toured the countryside and reported that the bushrangers seemed to have left the area, so she should be safe. Before he went, he told Absalom to shadow Jane if she went outside the homestead yard and to guard her if necessary.

The wool was sold and Angus had a little time on his hands before catching the train home the next day. Why not visit John Ashby?

Mrs King's house was easy to find; Ashby had asked him to visit, before he left Tangil, and had given him the directions to the coach house at the back of the property.

John Ashby was shocked. 'I didn't know you at first, Angus! Without the beard, you look completely different. May I ask why? How does it feel?' They shook hands warmly.

'Chilly at times, since it's winter,' Angus said briefly.

The older man was pleased to see him and seemed lively, but Angus thought he looked very frail. 'I believe Garth has been doing well. He told me the cottage had burned down when no one was there. I was sorry your property was damaged, Angus.'

Angus gave him an edited version of the news. He said that Garth was well on the way to buying a farm and that Jane was enjoying country life at the Home Farm, but didn't burden him with the latest adventures of Miss Ashby. He showed John the drawing of Blackwood Park that Jane had made.

'This is very good, I'm pleased with her progress. What a pleasant house!' Ashby paused for a while and then said, 'If you agree, we could enter it in a competition. An art gallery here is offering prizes in several categories... Jane's drawing might have a chance. I will have it framed.'

Angus looked round the pleasant room and spotted a drawing board near the window. 'You're doing some work, then?'

'Yes, a little, just to keep my hand in.' He showed Angus the plans of a house and they looked at them, while Angus wondered whether to say what was on his mind.

Eventually he said, 'I should tell you that I very much want to marry your daughter, but I'm not sure ... whether it's the right thing to do, and whether in fact she will want to spend her life with me. Or – whether you will approve.' It sounded far too hesitant, to his own ears.

John Ashby sat back and looked at him. 'This is another surprise! Angus, I've known you for some time now and respected you. But Jane – you will know by now that she has a mind of her own. I really don't think that she wants a husband.'

They watched the fading light outside the window for a while and then Ashby added, 'Jane wants to keep house for Garth, but when he marries, what then? I am concerned for her future, Angus. She's quite determined not to marry, as far as I can see. Of course I wish you the best of luck. I would be very pleased to have you as a son-in-law.'

That was encouraging, at least. Angus felt himself struggling with the words; there was always the struggle.

'Jane ... is a lively girl, is she not? Farming is a quiet life, lonely sometimes ... and I'm not very good company, I'm afraid. She thinks I don't talk enough.' He squared his shoulders. 'But she ... enjoys living at the Home Farm and she would be well provided for.' She was happy with him, was that not enough?

The winter sun was setting and the shadows deepened in the pleasant room. John Ashby lit a lamp, then poured two glasses of whisky and gave one to Angus.

'It's good to see you, you know. I would like to come back to Tangil, but the doctor won't let me – and neither will Mrs King. Here comes the dear lady now; I will pour her a glass of sherry.'

Mrs King loved visitors, it was clear. Angus had to give a brief resumé of his career so far and she smiled at the law training, but frowned at the farming. Then, asked for news of Jane, Angus told her what Jane was doing. The lady was horrified.

'Making cheese! My dear, in no time at all she will be a settler's wife!'

'That's what I'm hoping,' said Angus quietly. 'If she'll have me, it's by no means certain.'

'But I warned her against it, when she was here! I have seen those poor thin women ... Mr Duncan, you can't make Jane into a drudge! Could you not go back to the law?' She sipped her sherry, but kept her eyes fixed on him. 'You would both have a much better life in town than you would shut away in those forests, with all manner of dangers! They tell me there are snakes, wild dogs, bushrangers and Heaven knows what else in Gippsland!'

Angus kept very quiet as John defended Gippsland. 'Now that the railway has gone though, the western part of Gippsland is quite civilised. Garth is thinking of buying some land there and settling... I'm sure there are no bushrangers, those days have gone.'

As the farmer left, Ashby clapped him on the back. 'Carpe diem, my boy, seize the day. You lawyers like your Latin!'

The next day, Angus went home on the train in a lighter frame of mind. The change of scene had somehow helped to put things into perspective. The wool was sold and the sale of property in Bendigo had gone through. With the help of a bank loan, he could buy a good stretch of land adjoining Blackwood Park, which would give him a bigger business and if all went well, more profit. He would explain it all to Jane, if ... if she wanted to marry him.

The plan was now clear; he would employ more workers – they were to be found, if you could afford to pay good wages. Some of the settlers on smaller blocks of land might be happy to work for him and they would probably be the most reliable workers. Settlers were bringing in more wives and daughters, who could help in the house and dairy.

Mrs King had been right; many settlers' wives had a very hard life. Angus wanted to be able to offer Jane a good life. With plenty of help, she could supervise the work at Blackwood, where they would live for most of the time. Jane would have time for her art, designing a new garden and anything else she wanted to do. They would both manage the farms together, as she learned more about the business.

All this depended on Jane, of course. Or did it? John Ashby had said 'Seize the day.' Only he could do that, he himself would have to overcome Jane's reluctance and he knew what he must do. Angus Duncan must learn to talk, to share his thoughts, so that they could really get to know each other.

He felt that he knew Jane quite well; at meals and in the evenings, she and his mother had talked and Angus had listened. Until now, he hadn't realized that he would have to join in. He had held too much of himself back.

He smiled as the train left Warragul; not much further now and he would be home before night.

As Angus travelled home, the youngest bushranger walked fearfully into the Duncan stronghold. It was afternoon and the gates were open, but Michael Dooley knew he wouldn't be welcome.

'What are you doing here? Get out!' Jane was shocked to see him. All the events of the previous week came back vividly to her memory and she recoiled in horror. 'Absalom! Where are you?'

Mrs Duncan emerged from the kitchen with a rolling pin in her hand. 'Who is it, Jane?' She looked ready to do battle.

'This is Michael Dooley and he should be arrested. He should be in jail!' Then Jane caught sight of the woebegone look on the lad's face. 'Why did you come here?'

'Please, Miss Ashby ... I'm sorry for what I did, real sorry. I did want to see you, to say so. And I've come to get Absalom. Me brother's dying, Roy is dying.'

Jane glared at him. 'Get a doctor, Michael. I don't believe you. Go away and never come here again.' He had fooled her, and she had thought he was their friend.

Michael brushed the fair hair out of his eyes with a hopeless gesture.

'He pointed the bone, Absalom did. And Roy knows he'll die, and Ma too. Only I thought if he could take it off, the curse or whatever it is...'

Absalom appeared, a stern look on his dark face. 'Dooleys never welcome here.'

'Roy's dying, he wants you to come...' Michael was almost crying. 'They say it's only marsh fever, but we know what you did. You've got to see him...'

To Jane's surprise, Absalom nodded. 'I will come.' He walked over to Jane and Mrs Duncan and spoke very quietly. 'If you say

237

yes, I will go to this Roy Dooley. It may be that I can do some good. Please lock the gates behind me. Mr Duncan said I was to stay with you.'

When he had gone, the women looked at each other. 'This isn't another trick, is it?' Mrs Duncan said doubtfully.

'Not if we lock the gates,' Jane said as she moved across the yard. 'The Dooleys must have been let out on bail... I thought they would have been in prison.'

The winter afternoon was not cold, but Roy Dooley was shivering in his bed as well as sweating, tossing from side to side and barely conscious. His skin was clammy and a deep yellow. Absalom looked down at him in silence. He had a plan and would let it unfold. Michael watched fearfully and he was waved out of the room.

'Swamp fever, that's what got him,' Ma Dooley said. She sponged Roy's face and hands with a wet rag. 'He won't fight it, because of the curse. You'll have to take it off. Where's the kangaroo skin? You don't look right at all in that woollen shirt.' She looked at Absalom. 'For all love, take it off, man. The shirt and the curse both. One son of mine has gone to God, I can't bear to lose another.'

'I do not know that I can,' Absalom said deliberately in his deep voice. He took off the shirt and immediately looked more like a proud Ganai man. Roy opened his eyes and looked at the dark skin, the glittering eyes.

'The spirits are still angry. They want your death.' Absalom pulled out a pouch from his pocket and gave some leaves to Ma Dooley. 'Boil these and make a tea. Manna gum, for a fever. Do not come back.'

Ma hurried off to the kitchen and Absalom stood at the foot of the bed with his dark eyes fixed on Roy Dooley, who looked back, terrified. He stood there for about fifteen minutes, motionless.

Eventually Roy croaked hoarsely, 'Can yer not take it off? I haven't got much time left. I can't sleep, haven't slept for weeks...'

'A wrong was done. The spirits say it must be put right.' Absalom believed this, in his own blend of Ganai and mission teaching, believed that wrongs must be righted. He knew the swamp fever, the missionaries called it malaria. It affected many men on the diggings, but he believed that pointing the bone had brought it on. The manna gum leaves would only work if the man's own spirit was calm again. The bone was strong, it tormented the victim before he died.

There was another silence until the sick man said, 'What then?'

'It is out of my power. You must put it right and your soul will have rest. Whether in this world or the next, I cannot say.' Absalom wondered where his words came from; it must be the spirits. But he would stick to his plan.

'You want the gold.' Roy Dooley groaned. 'Raven will kill me...'

'Back to its rightful owner. Gold has no use for me.'

'How can I...?' Absalom continued to stare as Dooley tossed and turned.

'Your spirit will have no rest,' Absalom warned him.

'Get Michael,' he said at last.

Michael came in and Roy muttered, 'Take him to the box ... or I'll die. Don't tell Raven.'

The Ganai man passed his hands above the bed and chanted, a strange mournful sound. 'When the gold is given back, you will lose the guilt. You may sleep at last. 'What after that, who knows.' He left the room with Michael and told the victim's mother to give him the manna gum tea.

'Will he live?' Michael asked anxiously.

'I do not know. Now, how do we bring back the gold to Mr Duncan? We must do it now.'

Michael Dooley looked sick. 'It's Raven's gold, he'll kill me.'

Absalom put on his shirt and stood over Michael. 'Raven is not here. I am here, Michael and you do as I say.'

# SIXTEEN

Angus decided to take things slowly, since that was what Jane wanted. In the days that followed his trip to Melbourne, he spent more time with her and they talked about the farm, about books, about art. But at his heart was a real fear; if he asked Jane to marry him again, and she refused – what then? She might not like to stay on at the farm, and indeed, what future would there be in it for either of them? He would leave it for a while.

As plans will, this plan went wrong; it was suddenly interrupted when Garth rode in one sunny afternoon. Jane and Angus were in the farm office; he was adding up accounts and Jane was dusting the shelves and filing documents away.

Garth flung himself into a chair and looked at them, eyes shining. 'Good news!'

'More gold?' Jane asked.

'Didn't Absalom tell you anything?' They both shook their heads. After going off with Michael Dooley, Absalom had been at work as usual the next day. Angus never asked the man about his secret Ganai business, so nothing had been said.

241

'Well, good old Absalom went to see Roy Dooley... Roy was convinced that he would die, so Absalom made him tell where my gold was hidden. He'd guessed they wouldn't try to move it straight away ... it was in the old tunnel, you know those workings on the hill? There's a slate tunnel goes a long way in.'

Angus stared at him. 'Did you get the gold back? That's amazing.'

'Not all of it, that was too much to ask, but some. We took my horse, Absalom helped me and we found it. Michael told us that Raven kept some of it there, couldn't bring himself to part with it. Raven's gold is a sort of obsession with him. So it's in the bank at last, and Dooley was told he might live. Only might, mind you.' Garth laughed, 'I really think he would have died, because he believed in the curse. But then Absalom says he has marsh fever and that could get him, in the end.'

Angus could find no pity in his heart for the wretched man. 'Good riddance. One criminal less.'

'What will you do now, Garth?' Jane wondered.

'So, my plans, I moved quickly. I'd already put a deposit on a nice house, you know that place of the Forsyths' at Wattle Tree? It's close to the land I've bought. They've moved out onto a new selection. So now I've paid up and it's mine, I move in tomorrow. And

I'll pay off the debt for my land. Anything left will be needed for furniture. You'll have a share in the house, of course.'

'Goodness! You haven't wasted any time,' Jane told him. Why hadn't he told her earlier, or asked her opinion? Her share had been disposed of without her knowledge.

Garth grinned from ear to ear. 'I know you'll be thrilled with it, a decent house at last.' He looked round rather disdainfully at the farmyard and its cluster of buildings. 'You can come and keep house for me, Janey, the sooner the better. Isn't that good? Father could come too, it's well away from the goldfields and the dust. I thought he might like to come out here for the summer. We can all benefit from the gold we found. And you can look after us both! How about next week?'

Jane was stunned for a moment, realising that Garth had come for her at his own convenience, not hers. He could have found a small house for them long ago, he'd been earning money for some time. And one day in the future he'd want to drop her just as quickly, when he found a wife. She didn't want to go.

There was a silence and Garth looked bewildered. 'I thought you'd be pleased!' He looked at Angus. 'You can find someone else to help your mother, surely?'

Jane collected her thoughts. 'Of course

I'm pleased for you, Garth. It's wonderful and you'll have enough money to stock your farm ... but...'

Angus stood up and shook Garth by the hand. 'Congratulations, Garth, you have a bright future in front of you. Unfortunately,' he took a deep breath, 'Jane is going to marry me, so she won't be able to keep house for you. You'll ... just have to find a wife for yourself.' He went over to Jane and put an arm round her. 'Yes, Jane?'

The new fiancée felt her heart thumping. She was annoyed with Garth, and furious with Angus – what right had he to assume she was only too pleased to fling herself into his arms? She felt like shouting at them both, but well-bred young ladies didn't make a scene. Then she looked into his dark eyes and saw the love there. They stood gazing at each other until Garth coughed theatrically.

'I wish you happy, very happy, this is so sudden! I really thought you didn't like him, that is,' Garth turned bright red. 'I mean, I thought you – er – didn't want to marry anyone, Janey.'

When a rather subdued Garth had gone, Jane decided it was time to deal with Angus. She closed the office door and turned to face him.

'How dare you? How could you assume you know what I will agree to? Men always think they know what's best for a woman! I would like to tell you, Angus Duncan, that I prefer to think for myself.'

Angus took her hot face in his hands and kissed her gently. He was amused by her anger and that made Jane more angry still.

'So you really want to marry me, it wasn't just to save me from housekeeping for Garth? You could have asked me first!' Jane glared at him. 'How can I promise to obey you for the rest of my life? It's – it's a lot to ask of an independent woman!'

Angus said, 'The truth is... I know you're independent... I was afraid you'd turn me down, I've been putting it off. When I saw you hesitate, I thought I had a chance.' He stood very straight and took her hand. 'Will you be my wife, Miss Ashby? I love you very much.'

Jane was too angry to respond to words of love. 'We'll see. I won't be bullied into anything.'

You might fall in love and then wake up later, to find yourself with no freedom and no opinions of your own. That was the catch. It wasn't as though you would fall out of love; just that you might get used to being told what to do and what to think by a loving husband, until one day, you remembered how you used to be. Marriage was an unknown country and everybody had to work it out for themselves.

Jane took a few hours to think things through, weeding in the vegetable garden with the spring sun on her face. She found that she couldn't imagine life without Angus. That was strange, considering how angry she had been. The world would be a desert without his presence.

There were several obstacles to happiness as she saw it. One was the fact that a husband, any husband, would have the right to order her about and make decisions on her behalf. The attitude of Basil Charlesworth had made Jane realize the dreadful fate of many wives. She hoped that the woman Basil eventually married would take comfort in the beautiful house and the life of luxury, and not miss her independence, if she'd ever had any.

Some people hadn't noticed that things were changing with the last years of the nineteenth century and that women were not content to stay in the kitchen or the drawing room, as workers or as decoration.

Angus did like to be in charge, but that was natural; he ran a successful farm.

As far as she knew him, he wouldn't dream of telling her what to think.

Angus was lovable, kind, humorous and very capable. Everything he did was done well. The problem came back to whether he would tell her what he thought and felt, or whether she would feel shut out forever from the real person. That would mean a lonely life. Married people would need to talk things over, to agree or disagree. She would want a share in the decisions, the management of the farms.

It had been obvious that she should refuse Basil; Jane didn't love him, didn't even like him and he was only too eager to tell her how inferior women were, in his view.

Angus was a different matter. She sighed and bent to another row of carrots.

What about children? How would a child feel about a silent father, or would a little one get through this barrier that Angus seemed to carry about with him? And how would she, Jane, cope with a row of little Duncans in any case? Perhaps twenty-three was too young to take on the responsibilities of marriage. It would need courage ... would she have enough?

'What are you thinking, Jane?' A shadow fell across her path and Angus stood there, waiting. He was very still, a tall, handsome young man with his happiness in her hands. She could sense the tension in him.

All the debate, all the doubts left her at once. Of course she dared to take a risk. Jane stood up and took off her gardening gloves. 'About a row of little Duncans. What do you feel about children?'

'There certainly should be some.' He looked at her with hope.

247

'I've decided to live dangerously. I love you, Angus.'

Angus took her hands. 'My dearest.' He led her into the flower garden, where they sat on a wooden seat. Above them, a thrush poured out a song, the notes like liquid gold. 'I don't … know what to say, I'm too happy. I didn't really hope…' their two shadows merged as the thrush sang on. 'I wish I could tell you how much I love you.'

He sounded almost despairing, as though speech was a struggle to him. Perhaps it was. After a while, Jane moved away a little.

'What will your mother say, and my father?'

'Your father didn't hold out much hope for me.'

'You told him, when you were in town?'

Angus looked at her. 'Yes … asked him. He welcomed the idea, but didn't think you would. My mother will be … nearly as happy as I am. As soon as it can be arranged.'

Jane laughed; of course Father would have told Angus there was no hope of taming his independent daughter.

'I do realize that … you'll need to be consulted, from time to time.' Angus was smiling now, his strong face alight with mischief.

'Frequently, but I'll also need to learn a lot more about the business before I can tell you how to run it.'

There was so much to think about, so many plans to be made. Once she'd got over the delight and surprise, Mrs Duncan was practical.

'I hoped it would happen, but I never thought it would! Now, about the wedding ... the church at Wattle Tree of course, we've got used to being Church of England, Scots though we are.'

They were still learning new things about each other. 'I was brought up in the Church of England,' Jane said quietly. She'd thought that Angus would have made a good Quaker; his integrity and his silences would have qualified him. Like the Quakers, Angus gave respect to everybody equally. But then he carried a pistol and Quakers were men of peace.

Angus might say little, but he made many plans and asked Jane for her approval. He thought they should live at Blackwood Park and Mrs Duncan would stay at the Home Farm, with the help of another maid.

'But,' Jane said when he suggested this, 'this will cause a great deal of change.' She knew that the farm at Blackwood was effi-ciently run by the foreman Tom, while the Home Farm was overseen by Angus. 'I think your mother might like to live at Black-wood.'

'Independent thinking has its uses,' Angus told her. Mrs Duncan agreed that she'd always hoped to live at Blackwood one day and take life a little easier as she got older.

Jane had noticed that she looked very tired sometimes.

Jane did have misgivings about managing the household at the Home Farm, as she admitted to Mrs Duncan one day at breakfast. 'I've learned a great deal from you about cheese and butter and so on, but I'm not sure how I'll manage if you're not here.'

'A bold and forward woman, and you're not sure?' Angus teased her.

'You'll manage very well, Jane, and Dolly will help you. I like to make all our soap and so on, but you needn't do things in the same way.'

Blackwood Park was nearer to civilisation – except for the wild pigs. It was much nearer to the town and Jane would have seen more people there, and had a much better house, but it was clear that the Home Farm was where Angus needed to be. Perhaps one day they would install a bathroom?

'Of course,' said Angus. In a few days, a workman appeared with a cart full of pipes and Jane thought that a man who didn't waste words perhaps had more time for action. A new, spacious bedroom was organised, with pretty curtains and bedcover.

There were plenty of rooms in the sprawling buildings inside the fence, plenty of space for a nursery in due course.

An October wedding was planned, with spring flowers decorating the church. Jane's father came on the train and was delighted with Garth's new house. Susan Burns arrived from Bendigo, very excited and she too stayed in Garth's house, which was supervised by their old servant Mrs Moss, dragged out of retirement by the young man. 'She loves it,' he said.

The wedding was quiet and nothing happened to disrupt it, although Jane half expected Marcia to turn up at the last minute and raise objections in church to Mr Duncan marrying a pauper.

Susan admitted that she didn't know how Jane could live in that remote spot.

'No shops, no art gallery ... Jane, you must come and stay with me sometimes, to get away from the forest.' She looked round nervously; they were walking on a track near the farm and the afternoon sun was hot. 'Is it – dangerous, living here?'

'Not especially,' Jane told her. 'Bendigo can be dangerous, you know, in some parts!'

They had a few days of holiday in the sunshine, Robert's children making the most of country life, helping to collect eggs and playing with Lavender the cat. Angus gave them rides on the oldest horse, a creature that could endure their squeals of delight.

The happy couple had very little time to themselves during the day. Newly married farmers couldn't go off on a holiday together, although Angus thought they might possibly take some time off during the winter. At night they climbed into the big feather bed in their new room with a sigh of relief. There was no need for words as they held each other, loved each other. This was a loving partnership of equals, their first taste of the real happiness of a good marriage. Eventually, the guests left. Mrs Duncan kissed her and went off happily to Blackwood Park and a slightly easier life. Silence fell on the Home Farm and Jane began to realize what she had done.

For the rest of her life she would live with so much silence; friendly silence, but so much less than the free exchange of ideas. There was love, but there were barriers and always would be.

Angus loved her, she was sure of that and they were happy in each other's company, but without Mrs Duncan, the place was too quiet. Until now, she'd hardly realized what a good companion she'd had in Angus's mother. They had worked and talked together and now, she was on her own for long hours while Angus was out on the farm. When he came in at night he had little to say, but his tired smile was a happy one. His new life suited Angus very well.

There was one thing she could do. More than before, Jane went out with Angus on the farm and he was pleased, because he wanted her to understand what went on there. To get him to talk, she asked questions about the animals and the crops and her good memory helped her to learn quickly. Who would have thought there was so much science in farming!

Angus sometimes brought home gifts, perhaps to take the place of words. One day he gave her a spinning wheel, after she'd told him of her interest in spinning wool from their sheep. Sometimes he brought in a few wild flowers, grevilleas and bottlebrush. Jane knew he was always thinking of her happiness and trying to make her life easier. The new bathroom was installed, which made life much more comfortable.

By November, the sun was very hot and Jane had to water the vegetable garden nearly every day. Angus looked at the sky, hoping for rain, but none fell and soon they were moving cattle into paddocks by the creeks, because the rainwater storage dams that normally watered the stock were drying up.

'You're not supposed to have droughts in Gippsland,' Jane said. 'Green and wet, everybody told me.'

'We haven't had one for years, but it does happen.' Angus sighed. 'I don't like the look of this weather. We might have to sell some stock, after Christmas.'

Keeping food cool became a problem and Angus brought out the Coolgardie safe they'd always used in the summer. It was a wooden cabinet with canvas walls, down which water trickled into a bucket. Inside the cabinet in the cooler air, butter stayed reasonably firm and bread didn't dry out so quickly.

Angus was interested in refrigeration. Shipments of frozen meat were now being sent from Australian ports all the way to England and he felt that this would in time help Australian farmers by opening new markets. 'Wouldn't it be wonderful if we could freeze our own meat!' Jane said.

In the larger towns you could now buy ice to keep food cool, but not here.

They had a meat house, in a breezy spot underneath a tree, but in summer they couldn't keep meat more than a few days.

Christmas was something to look forward to; the whole family would be together for the day at Blackwood Park. Jane made sweetmeats and pies and a large Christmas pudding that had to be boiled in a cloth for hours, all in hundred-degree heat.

The wood stove made the kitchen almost unbearably hot at times. Christmas food was designed for a northern winter, but everyone felt it was important to keep up the traditions. There would be geese to be plucked and the hams to be fetched from the smokehouse.

It was a heavy responsibility for Jane to

cook for the whole family, so Mrs Duncan undertook to cook the roast dinner. Jane's pudding would follow for dessert and Jane's Christmas cake was to be the centrepiece of the feast. Mrs Duncan had made the wedding cake and she suggested the same recipe for Christmas.

Following Mrs Beeton, Jane assembled the ingredients and mixed the cake with great care. The heat of the oven needed to be just right, not too fierce, and – this was the tricky part – to stay at the same temperature for five or six hours. Jane would need to stay near the kitchen, to keep up the supply of wood to the fire.

Dolly brought in a supply of firewood and then wiped her face. 'Our way, Ganai way is better,' she decided. 'We cook outside in shade of a tree. But you can't make cakes that way, can you?' Dolly believed fervently in all the Christmas traditions, learned at the mission school.

Jane tried her best, but it was not enough. At the end of five hours of suspense, she peeped into the oven. The cake had collapsed in the centre. It was soggy, useless, she would have to begin again. Sixteen eggs, three pounds of butter ... and the rest, all wasted.

All the heat and worry and the silence suddenly became too much, and tears ran down her face. Jane cried for the cake, for her silent, suffering husband watching his farm dry out, for the garden wilting in the fierce sun. At that moment she felt more alone than ever before.

Doubt had began to creep in; doubt as to whether she could stand the life on the farm. Jane wasn't as strong as she had thought she was. She was a failure.

After some time, Jane became aware that a small black face was peering at her.

'Jane, don't cry. This happened many times before. Mrs Duncan made pudding out of cake like this,' Dolly said helpfully, prodding the sticky mess.

'I was going to give it to the pigs,' Jane sobbed.

Dolly brought a pudding cloth and they scraped the cake into it. They could hang up puddings in the cloths to dry and they would keep in the pantry for months, if needed. 'Shearing time, we need plenty tucker to feed the men,' Dolly reminded her.

Jane cooked the evening meal very carefully, in a sombre frame of mind. Angus was quiet, but he was not indifferent. That night he took her in his arms in the kitchen and asked to know what had happened to make her so sad. She had to admit her failure and her loss of confidence.

That was when Angus found the words to tell her of his own early fears that the farm would lose money and have to be sold, that he couldn't farm as well as his father did, or be as successful as his doctor brother. It had taken him years to accept his own occasional mistakes and to take pride in his successes.

'It's a hard life for you, my love. You are coping much better than anyone could expect,' he told her. 'It's human to get things wrong sometimes.'

Jane realized as she washed the dishes that she had learned quite a lot. Angus's silence had once seemed to her to be a form of arrogance. Now she knew that it had started with a lack of confidence; now she knew exactly how that felt. He said no more, but she felt comforted.

## SEVENTEEN

Christmas was a pleasant interlude, with family parties, visits to neighbours and a carol service in the little wooden church.

Houses were decorated with holly and cotton wool snow and the heavy meals were enjoyed in spite of the heat. This was the time of year when Australians remembered their origins and kept the traditions of the northern hemisphere as a matter of pride.

This was a time when farmers tended their livestock, but otherwise took a little time off, a rare occurrence for most of them.

Before she came to the Duncans', Jane hadn't realized that farming was so strictly governed by its own momentum. The seasons and the weather dictated the timing of work. Chickens hatched in spring, cows calved and sheep lambed. Christmas was in high summer, with the spring rush over for the most part, but then there was hay to be made for the next winter, followed by the corn harvest. Fruit picking stretched across late summer and into autumn.

'How do you cope with the boredom, the monotony of country life, dear?' Mrs King asked. She had ventured into Gippsland with John Ashby to spend Christmas with the Duncans.

Jane laughed. In the past year she'd been sad, happy, terrified and exhausted, but never bored.

'It's a very varied life, Mrs King. You never know what will happen next.' She knew that the lady was watching her closely for signs of being a typical settler's wife and she tried not to look thin and faded.

John Ashby reminded them that he'd farmed in England. 'It still seems odd to make hay in December and to pick fruit in April,' he told Angus. 'But I do miss country life. I'm surprised that Jane has taken to it so well – perhaps it's the generations of farmers in her ancestry, she must have loved it from the start.' Jane smiled when she heard this, remembering how she had hated the farm for the first few weeks.

Jane and her mother-in-law had made themselves new dresses, Jane's in a cool green and Elspeth's in lavender. Without the need to dress up in fashionable clothes, it was easier to keep cool. The draped skirts and huge bustles worn by women in the cities were completely out of place in the country. Even Mrs King had discarded her city clothes in favour of more simple dresses.

Robbie Duncan brought his family to the Home Farm for a few days. His wife Isabel was kept busy with three children, but she found time for a few talks with Jane. Isabel had been a nurse and was very practical, a friendly young woman who seemed to approve of the way Jane was managing the household.

Her father said to her in a quiet moment, 'I'm so glad to see you happy, Jane – and so successful!' The episode of the collapsed cake was forgotten and Jane began to feel that she could cope with the settler's life.

Johann Meyer invited the Duncans to a German feast, held for his smoke-house customers.

'Some of my countrymen talk to only each other,' he told them, 'but I, I wish to be Australian, I talk to everybody!' In addition to the inevitable sausages, there were very rich German cakes and excellent cups of coffee. Jane was pleased to see that Megan from the Tangil shop was working there and seemed to be enjoying the experience. She had learned a few words of German and could converse a little with Johann's mother, which was good for both of them. Her employers were learning more English, with a Welsh accent.

At the party, the conversation turned to robberies. A mob of cattle had been stolen from a farm near Willow Grove and spirited away, nobody knew where. This was worrying, because it was impossible to lock up grazing animals.

'If you put a lock on the paddock gate, a criminal, he can cut it off,' Johann agreed sadly. 'Or he cuts a hole in the fence.'

Mr Lewis from the store seemed to know more than anyone. He said he'd heard that the Tangil gang of bushrangers had been mainly Dooleys and the man Raven, but that they had dispersed. Liam Dooley was dead and Roy Dooley had followed him, dying of marsh fever. Michael had been interviewed by the police, had denied any wrongdoing and had then been let out with a stern warning. He was thought to have left the district.

'The police did a deal, then,' Garth said bitterly. 'I was hoping that Dooley would be in prison by now. I'm sure they burned the cottage and all our things, but I can't prove it.

But Roy knew where my gold was hidden.' He seemed to be more concerned about wrong done to their goods than to his sister. Angus said nothing, but looked furious whenever the bushrangers were mentioned.

Jane had not looked forward to the prospect of giving evidence in court, so she was pleased there was to be no trial. Perhaps Michael, who never seemed vicious, would decide to live an honest life. Nobody knew what had happened to Raven; Mr Lewis thought that he was the origin of the phrase 'raven's gold'. They must all have planned to leave immediately they got their hands on Garth's money and when the scheme failed, he would have left quickly. Presumably Michael stayed on because of Roy, who was dying.

Jane still had nightmares about being locked up in dark rooms. Johann Meyer looked across at her and said quietly, 'You will be pleased they have gone, Mrs Jane.' He knew how desperate she'd been after she escaped from them in the winter. She nodded, but said nothing. She planned to present the Germans with a drawing of their house and garden, to thank them for their help on that terrible night. Perhaps one day she would have the time to do it.

Soon after the New Year, which was an important event in Scottish households, came the hay harvest. The yield was poor, because of the lack of rain. Jane made lemonade from fresh lemons for the thirsty field workers and took out baskets of scones and cold tea.

After the hay was gathered in, the cut paddocks dried out in the heat and still no rain fell. The rolling green hills of Gippsland had faded to yellow, the soil baked by the burning sun. Fat Hereford cows, usually knee-deep in grass, were thinning and beginning to show their hip-bones. Angus Duncan usually fattened the calves that were born every year, but this year he decided to sell most of them when they were weaned, because of the shortage of feed caused by the drought. So did all the other farmers, and consequently prices were low.

Winter came and went without much rain, followed by another dry summer. Jane battled with the dust in the yard, blowing through the house. The heat of the kitchen was just as oppressive, but she had got used to it. Her main concern was the fact that so far, there was no baby, not even a hint of one. She knew that Angus was hoping, as she was, for children. His brother Robert's children were often at Blackwood Park, which made Elspeth Duncan happy.

Jane had made gradual changes at the Home Farm. She cut down on household chores by buying soap, cheese and sometimes bread, feeling guilty until her mother-in-law said it was a good idea. 'You can help Angus more, he'll appreciate it,' she said. 'I've decided to do the same at Blackwood, I'll have more time for embroidery.'

'We'd better make cheese occasionally, just to keep up the tradition,' Jane decided.

With the time saved from kitchen chores, Jane could ride out to check the sheep or the cattle on distant paddocks, which was time-consuming, but not hard to do and quite enjoyable. She had sharp eyes and could soon spot a sick animal or a broken fence, so that Angus could put it right.

Angus gave her a horse of her own, a dark bay with a sweet disposition called William and in defiance of convention, she rode him astride. Learning to ride gave her aching muscles at first. Angus took her out on a long rein and told her how to sit properly and give clear commands to the horse. He also showed her how to 'rise to the trot,' which made riding more comfortable.

'Americans don't teach their horses to trot, they canter and sit tight,' Mrs Duncan told her. 'Ours is the British way of riding, of course. Robbie was in America for a while and he still rides like they do.' Jane remembered Dr Duncan coming to see her father and she'd noticed how he rode away.

'I think,' Jane wrote to her friend Susan, 'that the side-saddle is intended by men to keep women in their place. It looks very elegant I suppose, but it's uncomfortable and it can be dangerous. Your balance is all wrong. I don't know what horses think of it, but I suspect they don't like it. It's just a fashion, after all.'

Jane made herself a riding skirt, long and wide and divided up the middle, so she could sit a horse in comfort, looking quite correct with her skirt in graceful folds. Now she could ride out in freedom and enjoy the work of the farm, such as taking refreshments out to the farm men in the harvest. Because of the size of the farm, this was not possible without a horse. Following the hay harvest, there were crops of oats to gather, grown for horse fodder.

Susan wrote back to tell Jane that she thought things were beginning to change for women; one or two brave spirits were asking why women were not allowed to vote in an election. 'Just imagine, women having a say in the running of the country! I think it will come in time,' she said. Her news was that Mr Charlesworth had married a small, nervous woman with a large fortune. 'Good luck to her, I hope he's kind to her. Rather her than me!'

One day in January, Jane went with Angus in the trap to Blackwood Park, to inspect the new land he had bought adjoining his own. Part of it was cleared, but some was still covered in trees and bushes. Like the rest of the area, the new acres were very dry, but under the trees there was still some grazing, so Angus decided to turn the sheep in there. They walked the boundary together to check once more on the fences, Jane wearing a large sun hat.

'Maybe I shouldn't have bought this,' Angus muttered as they went through the burning afternoon. The air was still and the eucalypt leaves shimmered in the heat, while the scent wafted over them. 'If the drought goes on much longer we'll be in trouble.'

'It's bound to rain, sooner or later,' Jane comforted him. 'We'll just have to wait.'

Rain was not likely until autumn, a month or two away. The income from orchard fruit would be down this year, the potatoes were pathetically small and the onions had gone to seed early.

It was the same for everybody after two years without much rain. Settlers were leaving the land, or trying to find other occupations that would help them to hang on to their hard-won acres. The Duncans had been settled in the district for forty years, and had been able to withstand all the extremes of climate, floods and droughts, until now.

They looked across the wide valley of the Latrobe River, to the blue hills in the south. The hills had a misty look. 'Is that smoke?' Jane wondered. 'I hope not.'

'It's a bush fire,' Angus told her grimly. 'If

the wind gets up it could be with us in a day or two.' That was another hazard of the dry summer.

For the next few weeks, smoke drifted across the valley and over the Home Farm, giving rise to a sense of unease. Angus was anxious about this and about several other things. He had to go to Blackwood frequently to sort out the livestock and organise selling; there was no longer an option. He would have to hold on to the best breeding cattle and sheep. 'Maybe we should be farming goats, or kangaroos,' he told Jane one night. 'They can live in barren country.'

The best way to help Angus was to stay cheerful, to try to produce good meals and to take on as much of the routine work as she could. Increasingly, Jane went out to check the cattle and sheep and sometimes to move them, when their water supply was about to dry up. One day she found a dead sheep. It had become stuck in the mud of a dried-up dam and tears came to her eyes at the cruelty of nature. If only she'd found it earlier, it might have been saved.

During February that hot year, when things were at their hottest, Angus went to Blackwood Park for three days, leaving Jane in charge of the Home Farm. The labour force had been cut because of the drop in income, so there were few men to do the work. Dolly and Absalom stayed about the house and farmyard; they had plenty to do there and it was reassuring to have their company.

Jane set out for the far end of the farm in the late afternoon, hoping for a cool breeze to dispel the heat, but there wasn't a breath of wind. A group of breeding cows, due to calve in March, needed moving to a fresh water-hole. Smoke hung heavy in the air, making her eyes smart. The cows were heavily in calf and walked very slowly in the heat of the day. When they were at last all through the gate, she reined in William on a little ridge and sat for a few minutes, looking over the parched land. It was hard to remember this was the same place that had been green and pleasant in her first spring here.

Her eye was caught by movement on a track that went beside the paddock fence.

A horseman had appeared from nowhere, a man on a tall horse. It wasn't one of their workers; who could it be? Jane's heart started to thump when she saw him turn his horse's head towards her and throw back his long hair.

The horse was a chestnut, gleaming with health and the man was Malcolm Raven. She had hoped never to see him again.

William was a good little horse, but he would be easily outpaced by Raven's chestnut if it came to a contest of speed. She couldn't run away. Jane felt for the pistol in the holster by the saddle, but doubted whether she would use it, against either man or beast. If she had the nerve, she should shoot the horse and gallop off for the safety of the farm ... thoughts raced through her mind. What did he want here, if not to do her harm?

Jane sat very straight on her horse and told an outright lie.

'There are farm men over this ridge,' she called, as soon as he was within speaking distance. Raven took both hands off the reins and made a gesture of peace, palms upwards. The chestnut pulled up beside her.

'Jane, I would like to speak to you for a moment. Don't call the men, I won't harm you. I only want to say goodbye.'

Raven was quite close now, their horses shoulder to shoulder. His dark eyes had a serious look. He was soberly dressed and well groomed. Jane reminded herself that he was a dangerous criminal and that his stories of an estate in England were probably lies. But he looked like a prosperous landowner ... like a lord.

'I was hoping you had gone for good,' she said coldly.

'Jane, remember I never harmed you,' Raven said, his eyes on her face. 'We spent a very short time together and I venture to think that you enjoyed my company. You were clever enough to get away and spoil our plans, but I admired you for it, more than ever.' He laughed, a pleasant, easy laugh. 'Red Riding Hood beat the Big Bad Wolf, twice over. What a woman!'

'Never harmed me!' Jane was angry now. 'I nearly died, do you remember? I was dragged through the bush, locked in a filthy hut, fell into a swamp and then locked up again. I walked for hours through pouring rain in the middle of the night. I could have died of pneumonia, after all that. I still have bad dreams about it. Malcolm Raven, you are a heartless criminal.'

William moved restlessly at her fierce tone and Jane drew him away from the other horse, but Raven came up to her again.

'Talking to you reminds me ... as if I could ever forget. You should belong to me, not to that miserable Scot.' He paused, smiling down at her. 'Criminal I was once, but I have taken your advice and given up crime. You made an impression on me, that night at Blackwood. But heartless, only because you Jane, have my heart.'

Jane smiled wearily; she no longer felt drawn to the man. The young girl he'd kidnapped was now a woman, matured by the hardships of farming life.

'Go away, Lord Raven. I have nothing to say to you.'

Raven sighed; he should have been an actor. 'I came here only to see you one last time. I sail for England in a few days. Jane, I want you not to think too badly of me. I will go now, as you wish.' He moved a little nearer and handed her a small parcel. 'This belongs to you, please take it.'

'I don't want it! I want nothing from you! Stolen goods, no doubt. I can't accept it.' Jane glared at him.

Raven said seriously, 'This is the pistol we took from you, Jane. I wrapped it because you would have been alarmed to see me with a weapon in my hand.'

Reluctantly, Jane took the parcel. 'I thought you enjoyed alarming women. Goodbye, Raven,' she said firmly. He blew her a kiss, turned his horse and galloped off. Jane watched him until he was out of sight.

What should she tell Angus? He would be furious to hear that Raven had ridden across his land and had spoken to his wife. Jane knew that Angus was not a jealous husband, but he had a deep hatred of the men who'd abducted Jane and he considered that she had been treated very badly.

When Angus came home from Blackwood, Raven's visit was put out of her mind. He rode in wearily, after a days' work at the other farm and Absalom took his horse to the stable. At the supper table he almost went to sleep over his plate, but then seemed to pull himself together. He was silent as usual, and Jane waited.

'I suppose I'd better tell you how things are at Blackwood,' he said eventually and Jane could see from his face that something was wrong. 'We've had to mortgage the farm ... to see us through the drought.'

'You mean there's no money in the bank?' Jane put her hand over his. 'We can borrow, then, until the rains come.'

'Aye. Blackwood's worth more than Home Farm. I handed over the titles yesterday.' He paused. 'And ... I've had to sell the new land.'

If they'd talked it over, the news would not have been such a shock to Jane. Why could he not share his problems, even now? Things must indeed be difficult, if Angus had sold the parcel of land next to Blackwood. He'd had such hopes for it, such plans. In the middle of a farming crisis like this, no one would pay very much for land. It was the worst possible time to sell.

A thought occurred to Jane. 'Why not borrow from Garth? He would be happy to lend you money.'

'No, Jane. I'll not borrow from a friend, or a relative, that way lies ruin.' He looked beaten, defeated. 'But I don't know how much longer I can carry on like this.' With an effort he said, 'What news have you for me, little wifey?'

'This might not be the best time for my news, Angus. But ... I think, I'm sure I'm pregnant.' Jane sat and smiled at him. She had kept the news to herself before he went away, but Doctor Robbie had confirmed it when he visited the farm the day before, on his way to the goldfield. 'I hope it doesn't make things any worse.'

The effect on Angus was amazing. He jumped up and came round the table to put his arms round her. 'That's the best news we've had! Jane, of course it's a good time, I feel more like going on already. You ... know, in a few years the drought will be forgotten, and we'll have a family, a future.'

Jane realized that she'd never known how much Angus wanted children.

## EIGHTEEN

'You're not afraid of storms, Jane?' Angus tipped his head back and looked at his wife. They were visiting Blackwood Park for a few days while Angus completed some repairs to fencing, after high winds had blown large trees across the boundary fences.

The work was very difficult; it was almost impossible to hammer posts into the hard ground and he was exhausted. If only the rain would come! This was why Mrs King's 'settlers' wives' looked so harassed. They worried about their menfolk in the bad times.

'Of course not. I hope we do get a huge storm, the rain will do so much good.'

Jane smiled at him, to prove she was not frightened.

They sat on the veranda at Blackwood Park at the end of the day, looking across the valley to where lightning flickered on the far hills to the south, dancing along the ridges. Loud thunder rolled, rattling the windows and Elspeth Duncan shivered.

'I hate storms,' she said. 'I'm going indoors.'

The sun went down in a stormy sky, but there was no rain. Angus pointed to several pinpricks of light, showing up in the dark forest behind them as night fell.

'Fires,' he said. 'Lightning strikes.' Volatile eucalyptus leaves burned fiercely even when green and forest fires were often caused by lightning.

The wind rose, a hot north wind blowing across the parched land from the mountains. Jane once again felt the implacable force of nature; they were helpless in the face of a fire. She'd been told long ago that Gippsland was one of the most fire-prone places on earth, but in normal years this had been a far-off threat and not often mentioned. Perhaps those fires were far enough away from human settlements? The bush soon regenerated after a fire; fires were part of the natural system in Australia, allowing for regrowth with the rains. But property was a different matter and settlers could be ruined when the fires tore through a district.

Tom, the Blackwood foreman had taken his wife and children to Moe the day before, in case of fire and then returned himself. This had left Mrs Duncan with no help in the house, as Tom's wife had replaced Marcia and their young maid went with Tom's family.

Their staff had been much reduced as the drought took away the farm's income, but loyal Tom and his wife had stayed on, hoping for better times and content to live on a lower wage.

In the higher country were isolated farms and a few little townships, surrounded by forest of the most inflammable type: eucalypts with their volatile oil and trees that produced ribbons of dry bark, copious quantities that littered the forest floor to a depth of several feet. Jane knew how well it burned because she used tree bark for lighting the kitchen stove. Those people in the bush were in danger, tonight.

The Duncans went inside and ate supper, but little was said. Angus was deep in one of his silences, but eventually he looked across the table at his mother.

'I've filled the house gutters with water.'

Jane realized that they could be fighting a fire themselves, very soon. There were open paddocks and gardens round the house, but really fast fires could leap across such defences. Tomorrow they intended to go back to Home Farm ... what if the fire reached both of their farms? She deliberately put the thought out of her mind. Blackwood was enough to think about for the present.

'The new settlers worry me,' Elspeth said as the women cleared away the supper dishes. 'Some of them don't seem to realize the danger, its been years since we had a bush fire, so they've no experience. Some of them light fires outside on hot windy days! And they're no' prepared ... we've learned by experience. When I was a young girl, our house was burned down in a bush fire.'

Jane was fervently hoping not to gain experience of this kind. 'But there's not much preparation you can do, surely? Not to fight a bush fire?' Take your valuables and run, she was thinking, but she knew that fire could outrun anyone. Perhaps they should harness a horse in the trap and go down to Moe.

Elspeth said to Angus, 'Tell Jane what we've done. We try to do the best we can, we do plan to stand and fight to defend the house and buildings. The livestock too, of course.'

Angus stood up and stretched. 'It's true that there's nothing can be done in a really big fire. But we do ... prepare, every summer. As you know we sweep up all the leaves, cut the grass short round house and buildings. We've a handcart with a pump on it and long lengths of canvas hose, to pump water out of the house dam. Sometimes, a sprinkle of water is enough to keep the buildings from catching fire.'

Tom, the farm foreman, appeared with a lantern. 'Horses are all in the stable ... fire's up to the Walhalla Road, boss. I think we'd better start pumping, keep the buildings wet. There's no rain in sight.'

Angus went out with him, calling to Jed, the young boy who worked for them.

'Jed, ride down and open the paddock gates ... we'll have to let the stock shift for themselves.' The lad went off, white-faced. Sometimes cattle and sheep were caught in a fire, but often they ran away if the gates were open, and came back after it was all over. Jane hoped they would go down to the river and stand in the water.

Jane could feel tension mounting, tension they could do nothing to relieve. The air was almost crackling with heat as the thunderstorm rolled down the valley and echoed in the mountains. She thought about the livestock at risk and the creatures in the forest. Birds could fly out of danger, unless the hot air currents sucked them in, but could the possums and echidnas escape? What would happen to the wallabies?

Elspeth was calm, concentrating on the practical. 'We'll collect all the buckets and fill them with water. With a wind like this, burning embers can easily blow in and cause spot fires. It's our job to put them out round the house.' She smiled at her daughter-in-law. 'It won't harm baby, never fear, not at two months or so.'

Jane tried to smile back, but her face was stiff with anxiety, not for herself but for Angus. He was tired already and with a long night in front of him. He would fight to the end to save his family and his farm, but after two years of worry about drought, he was tense and had not been sleeping well.

The hot wind increased in strength and the darkness made things worse, except for the fact that they would be able to see spot fires. A heavy pall of smoke now blew over them, making it hard to tell how close the fire was. The time for fighting had come.

Tom worked the hand pump furiously and Jane held the big hose steady, streaming the jet of water onto the wooden buildings. The stables were now full of frightened horses and cackling poultry. All the farm dogs and cats were shut in the house and Elspeth filled buckets from a tap.

Angus came back to the women. He was wearing a leather coat as protection against the heat of flames.

'Be ready to go into the house if we have to,'

he told them. He put his hand over Jane's for a moment. 'You're a brave lassie. We'll get through it, never fear.'

Now, in the moment of danger, Jane loved Angus as never before, his quiet competence and his fortitude. She valued every word he spoke to her, recognising the effort it sometimes cost him. She loved the way he looked after his animals, always making certain that they were well fed and watered and checking them constantly in case of problems. Tonight, the cattle, sheep and horses were on all their minds. It was an additional problem in times of fire.

It was by no means certain that they themselves would survive. The stone house was safe, the Duncans hoped, stone wouldn't burn. But smoke could suffocate them, if enough of it got into the house and Jane knew that the roof was supported by timber. Sparks could blow in under the eaves and set that tinder-dry roof on fire.

'Or,' said Elspeth calmly, 'we could get into the house dam. I've put our documents and valuables in a tin box, they would be safer in the water.' The house dam was the one Jane had first thought of as an ornamental lake below the house. It was fed by a spring and supplied water for the house and farm buildings. The small island in the middle might make a refuge...

In Jane's memory afterwards, the night was

a confused jumble of images, seen through smoke. The hose was effective; she saw many sparks and blown embers and doused them with water, too busy to be afraid. Her arms ached, but her muscles were stronger now with the physical work she'd done.

Angus was working with Jed and helping him to keep calm; they were bucketing water over the hay barn and putting out spot fires near the fire front. From time to time he took over the pump from Tom. When Elspeth relieved her at the hose, she moved away, the wind roaring in her ears ... or was it the roar of the fire itself?

'Tom, how close is the fire?' she asked the sweating foreman at the pump.

'Front's no nearer, Boss says,' Tom yelled above the din. 'Wind's veered a point or two, thank goodness. Main fire's going downhill now, that slows it a bit.'

So the poor people of Moe might be in trouble next.

A few minutes after speaking to Tom, Jane felt a spot of rain on her cheek, then another. She hardly dared to hope ... it could be water blown from the hose. In a few minutes she was sure; the rain, blessed rain had arrived. Drops gradually increased to a downpour and the wind lessened. Smoke began to drift away.

In an hour, the firefighting team gathered in the kitchen, where Mrs Duncan gave them

279

copious cups of hot tea. They could hardly hear for the drumming of rain on the roof. Everyone was wet, their faces were black and Jane found that her hair was singed, much to her surprise. The danger was over for the moment, the relief was enormous.

Tom the foreman was a hero, Elspeth said, and Tom turned bright red.

'Paddocks near the road will be burned out with no fences left. I'll go and look for stock in the morning,' he said quietly. On the way out, he turned back. 'Mrs Jane, you're a real settler. Settlers never give up and neither did you.'

Looking down at her blackened dress and sore hands, Jane felt she was now a perfect specimen of the settler's wife. She was glad she'd been there, in the thick of things. Their lives were hard, but at that moment she felt a sense of achievement.

The rain fell steadily all night and they woke to the welcome sound of streams of water running into the storage tanks. Morning dawned grey, but the rain gradually stopped. Angus and Jane walked round the yards and found little damage. The horses and poultry were let out into a fenced area, but they found that nearer to the road the paddocks were black, the trees gaunt skeletons and a row of black stumps were all that remained of their fences.

'Blackwood will never be the same again,'

Jane said sombrely.

'Trees will sprout and we'll mend fences ... do you realize how lucky we were? A few hundred yards more and the whole farm would have gone.' Angus seemed to be quietly optimistic. The air was fresh and cool after the storm, but the overpowering smell of wet ash hung over everything.

Luck was relative. It would have been even luckier not to have had a fire at all.

In the huge barn, the layer of hay on the outside was blackened, but Tom thought there would be some good fodder left in the middle.

By mid morning, Tom and Jed rode in with a motley collection of sheep and cows, and a few goats.

'It looks very Biblical,' Elspeth remarked, just as cool as ever. As far as Jane could see, the animals had not suffered, though they were streaked with dirt. The men had found at least some of their stock, wandering back up the road towards home. The rest might turn up over the next few days.

The next task was to draft out the Blackwood stock from the rest, after which Jed went off to try to find the owners of the extra animals. Sheep and cattle needed grass in front of them all the time, Jane had learned, it was something to do with their digestion. They had to keep eating, but Blackwood couldn't cope with extra mouths to feed and the animals couldn't be turned loose to starve.

There were small paddocks round the house to hold stock for a short time and the sheep were put into the orchard. With hardly any fences left, how could they keep the stock in, let alone feed them?

'We'll have to take some of the cattle to the Home Farm,' Angus decided eventually. 'Drive them across, we can do it in a day.' At least they had fences there and a little feed. 'Three horses should keep them together. We'll go tomorrow.'

'How can we feed them at home?' Jane wondered, as the two women washed the dishes.

'Once or twice before, we've turned cattle into the bush near the Home Farm, into the natural forest. There are shrubs that they can eat, and some grasses. You can't do it here, because of the roads and the traffic. And then when the grass grew again, we went to fetch them. They were in good condition and most of them came back, so maybe that's what Angus will do again.'

'Can I help to drive them?' Jane asked quietly, when Angus came in. There was so much to do; young Jed would need to stay at Blackwood to sort out the mess and feed what stock they would leave behind. There were cows too heavy in calf to walk to Home Farm and the pedigree sheep flock, that had taken years to establish, should stay. Those sheep represented Angus's hopes for the future.

'If you feel up to it... I'm not sure that you should ride...' he looked anxious.

Back in Bendigo, Jane's friend Ruby had put her feet up on the sofa for most of her pregnancy, as ladies were expected to do. But Doctor Robbie had told her, 'Just be sensible, pregnancy's not an illness, it's a natural process. Exercise is good, within reason, ye ken.'

Elspeth intervened. 'It shouldn't harm the baby, Angus, she can ride for a few weeks yet. Not after three months, though.' She paused. 'It's a risk, of course, but riding is always a risk. Everything we do on the farms is a risk, most of all for a pregnant woman! Don't go above a walk, Jane. The cattle will be slow, so it shouldn't be necessary.' Jane knew that Elspeth's rheumatism made it impossible for her to ride.

'You and Tom, with me to bring up the stragglers, very slowly,' Jane persuaded him and in the end, he agreed. Whatever happened, she would not trot or gallop the horse.

For the 'drove' as they called it, Jane was given the oldest horse, Bluey, the one that had taught her to drive the trap. Her own little William was at the other farm. The cattle were still tired after their ordeal and not inclined to hurry, walking in an orderly procession down the track that Jane had taken in her escape from the bushranger. The fire had not reached Tangil South, although burning embers had caused small fires here and there.

Tom rode back at intervals to help Jane, while Angus stayed ahead, leading the herd steadily on. Cattle naturally liked to move on; this was what they did in the wild.

They were used to following Angus to new pastures, so they went willingly. The trick was to keep them from turning aside into other men's paddocks, but everything was so dry that there was little temptation. Where gardens had been watered, cabbages and lettuces beckoned and the cows gazed longingly over palisade fences as they passed slowly by. Children shrieked at the sight of a huge, horned head with big eyes looming suddenly over the garden fence, but fences here were built to keep out stray beasts, both wild and tame.

At Willow Grove, they stopped to drink water and eat a slice of bread and cheese, giving the cattle a chance to drink at a way-side pond.

'How far did the fire come?' a woman called to them. People wanted to know the worst; they'd had the rain, but no fires and were thankful.

'Tom, you could go back to Blackwood now,' Angus suggested as they sat their horses, watching the Herefords in the water. 'We're through the township.'

Tom looked uneasy. 'I'd better come a bit further, Boss. Don't want Mrs Jane to have to gallop, Bluey's past it now!' He was pretending to worry about the old horse.

They skirted the edge of the deep Tangil valley and struck a green road that ran parallel to the track.

'Right, Boss, you should be home in half an hour,' Tom called, and headed back to Blackwood.

Angus waved him off and turned to Jane. 'We'll let them take their time now, Jane. The old girls are tired and we shouldn't have any trouble... How do you feel?'

'Never better, Angus,' Jane assured him. He hardly ever used endearments, but she was beginning to know him and she could feel his deep concern for her, even when no words were spoken.

It was easier going for the cattle's feet on the grass road and there was shade from the trees. Jane breathed in the scents of the bush; it was good to get away from the ruin that had followed the fire.

With relief, they turned the cattle into their own track and pushed them into a paddock not far from the house.

'Well done!' Angus turned in his saddle to beam at Jane.

At that moment, a wallaby jumped out at the horse, which took off. Angus was a very good horseman and kept his seat, but the frightened horse galloped under a low branch. Jane heard the crack as the branch hit Angus and swept him off the horse. He fell and lay still.

Jane dismounted and hurried towards him. As she did so, she could see that in his fall, his arm had struck a large tiger snake. It reared up angrily, mouth open and sunk its fangs into Angus's arm.

'Half of the people who are bitten, die...' Jane had never forgotten what Angus had told her, on the night long ago when he was dragging her home. Since then, she'd been taught what to do. She threw a stick at the snake and it slithered off. Kneeling beside the still body, she found that Angus was still breathing. He now had concussion and snake bite ... what on earth should she do?

'Snake bite first,' she said aloud, trying to stop her hands from shaking. In Angus's pocket was a small bag of Condy's crystals. He'd always carried them because they were the only treatment they had for snake bite. Potassium permanganate, Angus had told her. Robbie thought the crystals would oxidise the poison ... in some cases, when the snake had fed and was not so venomous as usual. Not in all.

A wave of nausea swept over Jane. The baby ... would it survive, would Angus survive? Her head was whirling; their world was crumbling. The fire was over, but now disaster had come back and their life together was in danger of ending too soon.

Shakily, she placed the crystals over the puncture marks in his arm and tore several strips from her petticoat, which she used to bind the wound firmly. Pressure was the other requirement, to slow down the spread of the poison. The patient didn't move and this was a good thing, but how badly was his head damaged?

Blood was seeping from a wound where the branch had struck him. Jane wiped it gently and then bound it with another strip of cotton petticoat.

'Angus, my darling, can you hear me?'

His eyes were closed and his breathing was ragged. Angus was deeply unconscious.

The horses stood close together, swishing at flies. Suddenly their heads went up and their ears forward, looking towards home. A figure came towards her and Jane looked up through tears to see Absalom standing over his boss's body.

Jane took a deep breath. 'Absalom, it's snake bite, as well as a blow on the head, he was knocked off the horse. Bring the trap here as fast as you can, we'll take him to Dr Robbie in Moe.'

'Yes, Mrs Jane...' the Ganai man nodded and didn't waste time with words. He picked up the reins of both horses and trotted off with them to the yard. In a very short time he was back with the vehicle and a fresh horse.

Together they managed to slide Angus into the trap, with the aid of a thin mattress normally used as a cushion on the seat. Jane took the reins and urged the horse to a fast pace, while Absalom held the unconscious Angus in his arms on the floor.

What had Angus done to deserve this?

## NINETEEN

The next two hours were a nightmare, a blur of swaying vehicle, dust and clattering hoofs. As they travelled, Absalom asked, 'Blackwood was burned?'

She told him what they had done and he beamed with relief for a moment, before he turned back to his stricken employer.

'Snake bite's very bad, Mrs Jane,' he muttered.

The late afternoon air was warm and full of the buzz of crickets when they reached the little town. The doctor was at home and with Absalom's help, moved Angus into the surgery on a stretcher, where they laid him on a bed. His head wound was still bleeding and the makeshift bandage was soaked.

The wound was carefully cleaned and treated with iodine. Perhaps the sting roused him; Angus moved and opened his eyes.

'What happened?' His face was white, in spite of the summer tan. 'I can't see!' He tried to sit up.

'Lie still, man,' Robbie said briefly. 'Just keep very still.' The doctor was intense, his whole being concentrated on his brother. 'I'm looking after you, right?'

Cold water compresses were applied to the arm, which was now swollen and bruised. In a hoarse voice Angus insisted, 'What happened?'

Jane moved to hold his other hand. 'I'm here, Angus. You had an accident.'

'Snake bit you, laddie,' Robbie told him quietly. 'We'll do the best we can.'

Isabel came in and led Jane away into their sitting room, where Robbie joined them after a few minutes.

'I've sent a drink out to your man with the horse.' He looked at Jane and she felt he must be worried about the baby. 'You've had a hard time of it, lassie. How did you manage last night? We could see the fire from here, of course.'

They drank tea. Jane told them about the fire and then had to ask the question burning on her mind. 'Can you do anything for snake bite?' Isabel reached for her hand.

'That's what worries me,' Robbie confessed, his dark eyes sombre. 'The head wound will heal. Angus is young and fit, but the poison ... we just don't know. I will give him a sedative, to keep him still.' He clearly couldn't do anything for snakebite.

'One day, I hope it's soon, somebody will discover an antidote for snake poison. Trouble is, different snakes probably have different chemicals to knock out their prey.' He looked at his watch, as if to time the progress of the poison. 'If Condy's crystals have any value, at least you treated him promptly with them, Jane. You've done the best you could.'

'What do you think will happen?' Jane wanted to go back to Angus, never to leave him.

'It's hard to say. It looks as though his blood won't clot, the head wound is still bleeding. That's what the poison does, but we don't know how poisonous that particular snake was. The kidneys may be affected. There may be paralysis.' Robbie was obviously struggling with emotion himself, trying to be objective. 'We'll have to keep him here, Jane, for some time. He needs to be watched carefully and kept cool.'

'On top of your other work...' Jane began, but Isabel interrupted.

'I'm a nurse, remember? I can help to look after Angus.' She gave Jane a heart-warming smile. 'If anybody can save him, we will.'

If... Just as she'd begun to appreciate Angus, he could be taken from her!

'You'd better stay here for a few days, Jane,' Isabel suggested after she'd given them an account of the fire at Blackwood. 'You must be exhausted.'

It was tempting; she could look after Angus herself, if she stayed.

'Thank you, that's kind. I will stay tonight and perhaps Absalom could go to see his cousins in the town. But tomorrow I must go home, we planned to move sheep and check the cattle, and the ones from Blackwood will have to be moved ... there's a lot to do.'

Isabel stared at her. 'You've become a farmer, Jane! Who would have thought it?'

Robbie grinned at her. 'Jane can do anything she sets her mind to.'

After a restless night, Jane crept along in the dawn to where Angus lay in the bedroom to which he'd been moved. He was still alive, still breathing; the poison had not killed him yet. She sat beside him.

'Jane...' he mumbled, his speech not clear. He did not seem to be conscious.

'Angus...' Jane took his hand and held it, choking back tears. In case he could hear her, she made an effort to sound normal. 'Robbie says you're young and fit, everything is on your side, Angus. Now, I will go back to Home Farm and do what needs to be done. Absalom can ride over to tell your mother, she'll want to see you.' *Or she might need to say goodbye.*

Life and death were always the business of the farm and Jane had become accustomed to it. She'd wept over the loss of small lambs and old dogs. But this was a tragedy. There were young widows in Gippsland, and young men who'd lost a beloved wife in childbirth. Life was fragile for all the settlers living on the edge of civilisation. If Angus recovered, she would never let him out of her sight!

Her being there when the accident happened had not prevented it, but at least he got help quickly. If he'd been riding in one of the far paddocks on his own, he could have died before anyone found him.

It hurt to leave Angus behind, gaunt and still against the white sheets. But it had to be done. Jane kissed his cheek and went out quickly without looking back, praying he would still be alive when she returned.

'I have to make a call in Moe before we go home,' Jane said as they moved off. Absalom had spent an evening with his cousins, slept on their floor and was ready to go. 'Drive to the bank, please, Absalom.'

'Yes, Mrs Jane.' He deftly turned the vehicle and they trotted up Lloyd Street to the bank. The air was fresh and clear after the storm; Jane felt a little more optimistic and she was totally unprepared for another blow.

At the bank she intended to find out their true financial position, so that she could tell Angus how many cattle and sheep he would need to sell. If he was ill for some time, she thought, she would have to do the selling with the help of Tom. She refused to think what she would do if he didn't come home.

In the bank manager's office, things took a turn for the worse. Mr Harding gave her a seat and then sat down behind his desk.

'I hear that your husband has met with an accident? There is an urgent matter to deal with – do you think that I could go to see him?'

'News travels fast in the bush,' Jane said tartly. 'I'm afraid my husband will not be able to do business for some time.' She explained what had happened and the manager looked even more serious. 'But I'm here to ask you–'

Mr Harding interrupted, 'In that case, I'm sorry, but you must deal with it yourself, Mrs Duncan. Our head office in Melbourne is calling in loans and yours is one of them, I'm afraid. We can give you no more credit. Your loan must be repaid by the end of the month.'

Jane was numb with shock. She knew that money had been borrowed. She knew that the farms were now worth very little, because of the drought and the fact that the fire would have taken most of the fences at Blackwood.

'But surely, you understand farming? Money comes in when stock and crops are sold. We've had years of drought and a fire only two nights ago...'

The man looked uncomfortable. 'Mrs Duncan, I understand that this will be difficult for you.' He must be used to dealing with widows and women at the end of their tether. 'But farmers, however much they complain about prices or the weather, always have assets to sell. And this is what you must do. You are not alone, there are many in your situation at present.'

'Our only assets are the breeding stock, our future!' Jane glared at him; the man was not a farmer.

Mr Harding sighed. 'And your land. Talk to Mr Duncan's mother, she is a sensible old lady. But tell her that I insist the money must be here by the end of the month. If the bank has to take possession, turn you out and sell your assets, it will be much worse for you.'

'How much do we owe?' Jane whispered. If Angus died, nothing else would matter. But if he lived ... she needed to keep the farm together for him.

'Two thousand pounds, Mrs Duncan.'

Riding home with Absalom, Jane wondered if things could be any worse. The man's dark face had a worried frown. 'Will Mr Angus be home soon?'

'Not soon, Absalom. His brother wants to look after him for a while. We will just have to manage the farm, you and I and Dolly.'

If they sold Blackwood now, supposing a buyer could be found, which was doubtful, the place would go for a fraction of its value. There were few fences, no feed and even if the rains came soon, it would be months before it would be productive again. The property would need to be advertised properly and sold by one of the auctioneers.

They passed the spot where Angus had fallen only yesterday and Jane shuddered. She couldn't talk to him about the loan. Even if he recovered quickly and was fully conscious, she couldn't tell him what was happening. His mother was old and tired, and the news of her son's accident was enough for her to bear for the present. Jane was on her own with the problem.

What about Garth? She'd suggested him before and Angus had rejected the idea. Garth had bought land and a house, as well as an expensive horse. He was unlikely to have much money left. Jane knew that the Ashbys' bank account was in her name as well, but that was no help if it were empty. Garth had looked after himself.

At the Home Farm, Dolly had kept the place spotless. Jane changed into her riding dress and rode out to move cattle and sheep; Angus had told her where he planned to put them next. The cattle from Blackwood she turned out into the bush, at a spot where there was plenty of water from a little creek. There was a gate in one of their boundary fences that had been used before for the same purpose. Absalom had gone to Blackwood with a letter from Jane that would tell Mrs Duncan what had happened to Angus.

For two days, Jane worked on the farm, her mind with Angus. She heard nothing from Moe. The problem of money went round and round in her head and at last she decided that Elspeth Duncan would have to be asked for advice; it was only right.

Even Angus could be told about the problem, if he was on the way to recovery. It was their farm and their money; she had little experience of business. She would go to see Angus in the morning and if Mrs Duncan was not there, go to Blackwood.

Jane drove herself to Moe in the trap the next day. Walking into the doctor's house she found his mother and Robbie in the kitchen with grave faces. Isabel was outside with the children.

'Bad news. I'm sorry, Jane. Angus is deeply unconscious. He's ... possibly beyond help. I don't know what else I can do, except keep him cool.' Robbie's voice was despairing.

Elspeth Duncan, the true pioneer's wife, was not weeping. She turned to Jane, full of concern. 'We must think of the bairn. Look after yourself, Jane, try to eat and sleep properly. These things happen, they can't be helped and tears will change nothing.' The older woman looked frail, but she was quite composed.

Jane sat beside Angus for an hour, but there was nothing she could do. His mother had decided to stay until the end, although the end was not mentioned. The only thing left for Jane was action; to go about her duties at Home Farm and wait for news.

'Could Angus – recover, do you think?' she asked the doctor, but he was unwilling to answer directly.

'We should never give up hope.'

Angus's wife set out for home with a heavy heart that the beautiful evening could not dispel.

Utterly weary, Jane was unyoking the horse in the stable at Home Farm when she heard a light clopping of hoofs in the yard. She went out, squinting against the evening sun and found a strange group outside the stable door.

A small donkey had pulled in a cart piled with goods, upon which sat a woman with a pipe in her mouth. A young man stood at the donkey's head.

'Mrs Jane.' It was Michael Dooley again, red faced and sheepish. 'We want to see you.'

Jane's patience snapped. 'Michael Dooley, I have had a difficult time and I do not want to see you!' She stamped her foot.

Ma Dooley clambered stiffly down from the cart. 'Don't get into a temper, now. We'se as badly off as youse, only worse. The shanty got burnt out in the fire, same as your paddocks at Blackwood Park. I knew it was coming and moved everything out ... we're off to start again, somewhere else.'

'I'm sorry to hear it, but not sorry you're leaving. You Dooleys caused me plenty of trouble.' Jane was surprised how bitter she felt.

'Ay, that's what we're here about.' Michael shook his head. 'You heard our Roy died, of the bone? He knew that's what killed him.' He looked round as if for Absalom, fearful of the man who had pointed the bone at his brother. 'And he told me that I would be next.'

Ma Dooley broke in, 'I've lost Liam and now Roy, on account of the bad gold, Raven's gold. Michael's me only boy left. So Roy said we was to give yourself back what's yours. To save the young boy, see. And Michael, he agrees.'

A wild hope surged over Jane, followed by

disappointment as she realized the implications. 'I can't take stolen gold. That would make me as bad as you. I'm not a thief!'

Michael dived under the load on the cart and came up with a heavy calico bag.

'We gave your brother some of what he lost. We can't get back your Dad's share, it's gone, the actual gold. But Raven said this here bag of money was fairly won at cards ... he played for high stakes, did Raven.'

'Do you believe it's not stolen?'

Ma Dooley lit her pipe. 'I do surely. Raven was a hard man, but he always told the truth. Himself told young Michael to give you this, as compensation for the trouble he caused you.' She cackled. 'Well, boys will be larrikins and Michael kept it, he wasn't going to hand it over to rich Duncans. But just before he died, Roy said to give it up, to give it to you. On pain of being cursed, just like he was. Here, 'tis not Raven's gold as such. It's Raven's cash. We reckoned that after the fire and all, you'll be needing all the money you can get.' She grinned. 'Where's your old man? Is he here at all?'

'He's in Moe.' Jane was going to tell them nothing. Michael put the bag down at her feet and Jane looked at it in disbelief. Could she take it? Would it be the answer to her problem?

The yard seemed to tilt and revolve, and Jane slowly crumpled into a heap. The world went black. The Dooleys were a bad dream, chasing her with hideous grins...

She had to get away from them, but her legs would not move. When she opened her eyes, she was lying in the yard and Dolly was bending over her. She looked round fearfully, but there was no-one else in the yard.

'Where are they? Where are those people?' Jane gasped.

'What people? I seen nobody. You are working too much, Mrs Jane. Come inside now and lie down.' Dolly helped Jane to her feet and underneath her skirt she found the calico bag. So the Dooley's visit had not been a delirious dream.

'Lock the gate, Dolly,' Jane said faintly. She staggered into the house, wondering if this was the beginning of the end for her unborn child. The poor little thing had been through so much already. Other women had told her that an expectant mother should look at beautiful things and think calm, pleasant thoughts in order to have a happy and beautiful baby. Perhaps settlers' babies were different, she thought now. They would have to face a harsh world from the start.

What if Angus died, leaving the poor child without a father? That was the hardest thought to bear. That evening, she ate supper and then opened the bag. It would be hard to estimate how much the gold was worth ... but what spilled out was not Raven's Gold. It was money, in bank notes and coins as Ma Dooley had said.

Jane counted it out and found that the bag held more than two thousand pounds; nearer three, in fact. This would see them through the drought and enable them to stock the farms again when the rains came.

'Thank you, Raven!' she whispered, weak with relief. She would have to take his word that the money was his to give, not raven's gold.

Some time later, Jane willed herself to go to bed. It was hard to sleep in the big empty bed, with no Angus to comfort her. But sleep came in the end and as far as she could tell, the baby slept too. She was beginning to think of him as a little human being.

Absalom was back by the next morning and said he would check the cattle and sheep. Jane climbed wearily into the trap once more and made her way down to Moe. Angus was still unconscious, his mother still by his bed. She was knitting, of course, passing the time usefully as she always did. Jane wished she could be as calm; it was hard not to cry when she saw how Angus seemed to look worse every day. Surely he couldn't fight the poison much longer?

'He's lasted longer than most people with a tiger-snake bite,' Robbie told them. 'They are extremely venomous.' He would say no more; Jane realized that he didn't want to raise false hopes. They were trickling drips of water into his mouth, to prevent his body from drying out, but that was risky. It might get into his lungs.

Next, she drove to the bank and handed over two thousand pounds to the astonished manager.

'I would like a receipt, of course. And the deeds returned to me.'

Mr Harding seemed almost disappointed that the Duncans were not going to be sold up, after all. He fussed about giving the legal documents into her keeping,

'If you insist, I will have to go into the vaults to find your papers.'

'I do insist, Mr Harding. It is at the request of my family, who I am here to represent.' He need not know that the other Duncans, as yet, knew nothing of the transaction.

The manager obviously wondered where the money had come from, but Jane ignored his hints. She was not going to tell him anything.

While he was out of the room, a young clerk came in and asked sympathetically how Angus was faring. The news of his accident had gone round and it seemed that the whole town was willing him to live; Jane felt comforted by the thought. In the middle of this wilderness, they were not alone. The people of Moe had good hearts and quiet Mr Duncan was well liked.

The young lad wished her well and as he was going out, he whispered, 'I think Mr Harding won't be happy. He was planning to buy your farm.'

Jane was angry, but she realized that someone would have bought it, if not Harding, and made a good profit when land prices improved again.

Jane went back to the doctor's; there was no change. She gave the title deeds of Blackwood Park to Robbie for safe keeping. He didn't ask why she had them, but she managed to imply that it was a fire precaution.

'I believe you have a fireproof safe,' she said. 'They will be much safer with you than at the farm.'

No change: just a deep unconsciousness from which Angus would probably not wake. There were things to face, Jane knew; a funeral, for one. The amiable vicar who had married them would now have to bury Angus. Mrs Duncan sat beside her son like stone, her calmness now a mask of misery.

# TWENTY

Isabel persuaded Jane to stay for the afternoon and she sat in their pleasant garden under a tree, thinking of a bleak future.

The scene with the bank manager was a foretaste of what was to come. She and Angus's mother would have to be tough business people, up against unscrupulous men.

*Oh Angus, come back to us...* She concentrated as Robbie had done, centring her thoughts on the still figure in the bed.

Something shifted; a slight breeze in the garden moved the branches. Gradually Jane relaxed the tension, and she let go. This was not something she could fight; she would have to accept the truth. For the sake of Angus's child, she must keep going. As she sat there, she accepted the inevitable.

It must be time to say goodbye. In a strange state of calm, she walked into Angus's room and knelt by the bed. She kissed his cheek and was turning away when the dark eyelashes fluttered.

'Jane...' his voice was hoarse, but now his eyes were open. 'Can you get me a drink?' She picked up a glass of water at his bedside. Jane supported him with her arm and let him take small sips. He looked into her face. 'I can see you!'

'Angus ... my love,' she was just as tongue-tied as he was. Was this the end? Surely not!

For some minutes, Jane gave Angus sips of water at intervals as his mind gradually reasserted itself over his wasted body; in a few days, the poison had reduced him to a shadow.

A few moments more and the patient smiled with cracked lips.

'That was a close call.' So he knew how ill he was. He tried to lift a hand, but the muscles were too weak. After a few minutes he made another effort. 'You're going to have ... to put up with me for a while yet.' He, at least, felt he had turned the corner.

Jane kissed him, then gently withdrew her arm and went to find Robbie, hardly daring to hope that Angus might be right. Robbie was out on a call, but Isabel came in and her bright eyes gave Jane more hope.

'Well done, Angus! I'll get your mother.'

Jane stayed in Moe that night; she could not bear to leave Angus. The Duncans all had a wary kind of hope on their faces; Robbie thought the worst was over, but in his cautious way he said, 'The laddie's not out of the wood just yet, the kidneys... But give him time. A Scot and a Duncan should be able to fight his way up from here.'

Fight was what Angus did, as he willed

himself to function again. But it was weeks more before Robbie would allow him to go home, weeks of invalid food, small walks with the aid of a stick and hours of sleep. One of the effects of the bite and the in-activity had been to weaken his muscles and they had to be slowly built up again. Robbie said he needed plenty of water to flush out those damaged kidneys.

Feeling as if their lives were suspended in time, Jane kept the Home Farm running and Mrs Duncan saw to Blackwood. As the weather cooled, more rain fell and the punished earth began to look green again.

As soon as she could, Jane told her mother-in-law about the bank and what she had been able to do about it. Winter was approaching and the autumn days were short. Jane had to explain that they could buy hay and grain to keep the livestock fed over winter, that they did not have to sell any more of them. The older woman was shocked.

'Why did you not tell me this before?'

'Because we were both far too worried about Angus to think of anything else,' Jane said gently.

'The money you were given may have been stolen. This is a bushranger you're talking about, Jane. And why would this Dooley give money to you?'

'It was supposed to be my share of the gold,

they said.' Jane smiled. 'Absalom should take the credit, he convinced them that they were cursed.' She explained about the curse, and the fact that the superstitious Irish had decided it was the only way to get rid of it. 'Absalom had a hand in this because he pointed the bone at Roy Dooley,' Jane told her. 'That's how it started.' She remembered Roy's cold eyes and hard hands, pushing her about when she was abducted. 'He died of marsh fever, I believe. But they thought it was the curse.'

'Why you, Jane?' Elspeth Duncan persisted.

'They treated me badly, I was lucky to escape from them. They thought the wrong had to be put right.' She sighed. 'They stole gold from our cottage, when it was burned down. Garth got some of it back, thanks to Absalom, but not all. I suppose they thought the rest was mine, but it had gone. So they sent money instead. They said it was honest money, not raven's gold. I was thankful for that, so I didn't argue. It saved the day for us, didn't it?' Jane shifted her bulk on the chair. Baby was growing; it would be wonderful to have Angus home, a new baby and the three of them together.

'You really think it's right to take it? Not to hand it in to the police?'

Jane thought of Raven's keen, dark face. 'The leader had a kind of honesty, I believe. Raven has gone back to England, he's Lord

Raven now. The bushranging was a kind of youthful prank and it's over.'

'He sounds like an evil man to me. But beggars can't be choosers, so I shall say no more. I suppose you did the right thing, Jane. You certainly had our interests at heart.'

This proved to be a good time to hand over Mrs Duncan's pistol, the one that Raven had given back to Jane. It was accepted without comment. So far, so good. The only hurdle remaining was Angus.

'You can leave me to talk to Angus about it, if you don't mind,' Jane said firmly.

On the happy winter day when Angus came home, he was not thinking about money. Jane drove him round the farm and he was pleased with the condition of the stock. The autumn rains had greened the paddocks and although the grass was short, things looked much better than they had in the summer.

'What a good little wife I have!' he said, smiling at her in the old way.

Jane had left the gate open, where the Blackwood cattle had been turned into the bush and all except one had come back into the paddock once the grass had grown again. Jane and Absalom had searched for the missing cow, but without success.

Angus seemed to have aged a little; he moved more slowly than before. He also seemed to be quite impatient at times, less tolerant, but Jane supposed he would in time be restored to full health. People died every year from snake bite in Victoria and now she knew what suffering it caused. Baby would have to be protected from snakes from birth.

Jane talked to Angus about the baby, due in a few weeks. Together they planned a nursery and Angus hired a carpenter to make the necessary alterations.

One day at the end of winter, Angus asked to see the bank records. 'It's time I sorted out the financial side of things,' he said glumly. He was always happier out of doors than in the office. 'I daren't think about it before now, but it's got to be faced.'

Jane found the documents he needed and then sat down.

'Angus, there is something I must tell you, before you look at these,' she began.

'Money's short, I suppose. I know it was so, that's why I sold the extra land. A pity, that. But after all we've been through ... money doesn't matter much. It's health that's important, Jane. You've been through the mill and Mother as well, lately.' He ran a weary hand through his short hair.

The next hurdle would be childbirth, but Jane didn't remind him of the dangers that would face her when baby was born; Robbie had promised to be there and she would be like Mrs Duncan and keep calm. She took a deep breath. 'What I have to tell you didn't please your mother very much, I'm afraid. While you were sick, it was when you were unconscious, Angus, the bank called in the loan. I didn't tell your mother at the time, she was worried enough. I've told her since.'

Angus sat up in his chair. 'And I was no help at all. You poor lassie, what did you do?'

'Harding at the bank said that if the money was not available, the bank would sell Black-wood. Imagine the heartbreak that would have caused.'

'Jane ... this is terrible.' Angus seemed lost for words.

'Then – it seemed like a miracle, something happened. Just at that time, the Dooleys returned some money to me. So I paid off the loan. That's all.' It sounded quite simple, put like that. Need she say more? 'Robbie has the title deeds in his safe.'

Angus jumped up as though he'd been shot, his dark eyes blazing with fury. 'You did what? Paid off our loan with Raven's gold? I can't believe it.' He thumped the table with his fist; Jane had never seen him angry like this before. 'How could you do such a thing, woman?' He was shouting and she suddenly felt afraid. 'Why did they give you money? Garth had got his gold back, he told us so.'

Jane dissolved into sobs; this was the worst she had ever felt. The room was swinging round and she felt faint.

Angus shouted, 'Tell me the truth. What was there between Raven and you? Marcia said something about you spending a lot of time with him ... when they locked you up. Drinking wine together, she said. I didn't take any notice at the time, Marcia invented stories at times. But now...' he stood up and came over to where she sat. 'Now I see it all,' he said bitterly.

'What would you have done? Please, Angus, I–'

'Don't try to make excuses!' he roared. He dragged her to her feet and shook her hard. 'You were his lover, I suppose. You little ... and all the time I thought...' he raised his hand, then dropped it and went out, banging the door behind him.

Some time later, the trap whirled out of the yard in a flurry of dust and Absalom knocked on the door apologetically.

'Boss's gone to Blackwood, Miss Jane. He's not happy.'

Jane was not happy, either; she doubted whether she would ever be happy again. Their life together was in ruins, all trust had gone. In a way she could see how it looked to Angus, but could he not have let her explain, as she had to his mother?

The worst thing of all was not his anger, but that he thought she'd been unfaithful to him. She'd only accepted the money to save Blackwood.

That night Jane did not sleep. There was nothing she could do now except await events. If Angus rejected her, she thought wearily, she would join her father in Melbourne.

The next day, Jane's pains started and she knew this was going to be her greatest test. Angus had not returned. She sent Absalom to fetch Robbie and she and Dolly made the preparations that Mrs Duncan had advised, months ago. Jane felt dead, numb with grief. She had lost Angus, after all their troubles. Even the baby was not so important compared with the loss of Angus. He would never forgive her, they would never be together again.

She had been attracted to Raven, just a little. But she'd never even thought of being unfaithful to Angus.

Robbie arrived as night fell, by when Jane was in great pain. It was going to be a difficult birth. The night was a long one, a haze of pain and unhappiness.

'Where's Angus? He should be here!' Robbie demanded.

'Gone to Blackwood,' Jane said faintly. He would know the truth soon enough. Angus could not bear the sight of his wife, he might not even believe that the baby was his. She was in such pain she didn't care any longer, about anything.

At some point, Robbie administered ether

and Jane dropped into oblivion.

The baby was a boy, as they had all hoped. Jane could do nothing but weep for him. What future would he have? She was too weak and miserable to take an interest; she fed him mechanically, feeling no love. He was washed and dressed by a nurse from Willow Grove and Robbie left, saying he would send a message to Blackwood to give them the news.

Dolly brought Jane a late rose from the garden. 'Sometimes people get sad after baby born,' she said. 'You will be better soon.'

Angus tore down the road until he realized that the harness might break; this was no way for a responsible farmer to behave. His anger kept bubbling, fed by his imagination. How could Jane have taken money from those villains? They were outlaws. What did she see in that evil Raven, the byword in Gippsland for stolen gold? He wanted to smash the man's head in.

By the time he got to Blackwood, anger had given way to bleak despair. They could never be happy again. Angus had never discussed Jane with his mother, but now he would have to tell her why their marriage was over.

Elspeth Duncan was surprised to see her son. 'I thought you would have stayed with Jane, now her time is near,' she said placidly.

'But it's good to see you, Angus.' Then she saw his expression. 'What is wrong, dear?'

Angus could find no words to tell her what was wrong. After a while he got it out, 'Everything. Jane and I ... it's over.'

There was silence after that. Mrs Duncan waited and waited, until at last Angus sat down with a big sigh.

'She took money from that bushranger. I can't ... forgive her. They must...' he was still trying to control the impulse to hit out, to break, to smash. 'They were too friendly – why would he give her money?'

Another silence followed, during which his mother brought out a jug of lemonade.

Time went by.

'There I was, lying helpless all those weeks, while ... all this was going on. Mother, I've just realized he visited her ... at the Home Farm. Absalom said the other day he saw a man on a big chestnut riding through our paddocks ... I believe it was Raven. Hell! She's too beautiful for me, obviously. And deceitful, too.'

Looking into the dear dark face, Elspeth Duncan wondered whether she could make him see the thing as she saw it. He was impetuous. His integrity was such that the whole episode would be distasteful to him. But she had thought it over and eventually accepted that Jane had been through a very difficult time and had done just what she ought, taking bushrangers' money included.

'Jane told me all about it,' Elspeth said mildly, and let that sink in.

He looked up. 'She did? And what did you say?'

'I could see how it happened, Angus. Absalom had convinced the Dooleys that they were cursed. He'd got them to give up Garth's gold, but then they had to do more. Ask Absalom. Raven had little to do with it, as far as I can see. Did she tell you the whole story?' His mother looked at him sternly.

'I didn't give her a chance. I ... shook her, I shouldn't have done that.'

'I agreed with Jane that since she was assured the money was legally obtained, she did right to accept it. That's the only reason we still have Blackwood, Angus. She did it for us, for you.'

Angus had his face in his hands, 'For me.'

Elspeth put a hand on his shoulder. 'Let's drive over to Home Farm, first thing in the morning. Go to bed now, Angus. You've had enough for one day.'

Angus was reluctant, but Elspeth Duncan insisted and she took the reins when the trap rolled out of the stable yard next day. She was anxious about the baby, but she also thought that if Jane had a chance to explain how the money had come to her, he might be prepared to forgive her. He was ominously quiet after the outbursts of the day before and he looked as though he had not slept at all.

As they drove along, Elspeth told him quietly about Absalom pointing the bone at Roy Dooley and the events that had followed. She wasn't a superstitious woman, but she wondered at the back of her mind what dark spirits may have been summoned.

Angus listened and said nothing, as was usual.

Talking about the bushrangers, Elspeth reminded him what hardships Jane had suffered and how she escaped twice, where another woman would have waited meekly for the ransom to be paid.

'In Jane you have a very determined wife, an independent woman. She has learned the work of the farm because she made up her mind to be a good wife.'

'So you don't ... blame her?' Angus stared straight ahead.

'Angus, while you were ill, Jane drove the trap up and down to Moe, yoked and unyoked, groomed the horses and checked the stock! On top of all that, she had to deal with the bank. It was a heroic effort, you know, from a woman who was bred in the city. You know her character, but now you find she has acted independently – for our good – and you can't forgive her. Think again, Angus. It's not too late to put things right.'

Angus shifted wearily on the hard bench as the trap jogged onwards. 'What about Raven?'

'The Dooleys gave her the money, not Raven. Young Michael and his dreadful mother came to the Home Farm.' Elspeth looked at the road ahead, between the horse's ears. 'Jane is honest and true. One day, you can ask her about Raven, but not yet. Take her on trust, Angus, for your own sake as well as hers ... and your baby.'

Baby Duncan had been fed and he slept on his mother's breast. Weary and faint from loss of blood, Jane slept too, dropping down and down into darkness. When she woke, the sun was streaming through the bedroom curtains. Remembering Angus, she felt a physical sensation as if her heart was a lump of lead. Angus had gone. He did not trust her.

Jane kept her eyes shut, unwilling to begin a day of misery. She moved slightly and found that her head was resting on a shoulder. An arm encircled both her and the baby. On the pillow beside her, Angus slept the sleep of exhaustion, dark rings under his eyes.

Turning her head on the pillow, Jane looked at the dark face beside her. In a few minutes he woke. 'Jane ... can you forgive me?'

That was all he needed to say, obviously all he could manage. Angus was back and the world was settling into place again. Some time in the future, they could talk over the misunderstanding, but not now. There was hard work ahead, possibly even hardship, but they would be together, three of them, for the future.

The new mother smiled and kissed him gently. The baby woke too, gazing at Angus with unfocussed eyes. 'What shall we call him?' she whispered. 'That's the important thing, just now.'

The publishers hope that this book has given you enjoyable reading. Large Print Books are especially designed to be as easy to see and hold as possible. If you wish a complete list of our books please ask at your local library or write directly to:

**Magna Large Print Books**
Magna House, Long Preston,
Skipton, North Yorkshire.
BD23 4ND

This Large Print Book, for people
who cannot read normal print,
is published under the auspices of

## THE ULVERSCROFT FOUNDATION

... we hope you have enjoyed this book.
Please think for a moment about those
who have worse eyesight than you ...
and are unable to even read or enjoy
Large Print without great difficulty.

You can help them by sending a
donation, large or small, to:

**The Ulverscroft Foundation,
1, The Green, Bradgate Road,
Anstey, Leicestershire, LE7 7FU,
England.**
or request a copy of our brochure for
more details.

The Foundation will use all donations
to assist those people who are visually
impaired and need special attention
with medical research, diagnosis
and treatment.

Thank you very much for your help.